THE E   HE ROMAN BATHS

KATE HARDY

Storm
PUBLISHING

Ebook ISBN: 978-1-80508-753-3
Paperback ISBN: 978-1-80508-754-0

Cover design by: Lisa Brewster
Cover images by: Shutterstock

Published by Storm Publishing.
For further information, visit:
www.stormpublishing.co

ALSO BY KATE HARDY

A Georgina Drake Mystery

The Body at Rookery Barn

The Body in the Ice House

The Body Under the Stage

The Body in the Lighthouse

For Gerard, Chris and Chloë – thank you for always indulging the Roman Britain stuff!

ONE

'It's really good of you to take the photographs of the mosaic for us, Georgie,' Bernard said warmly.

Georgina smiled from her seat at the wrought-iron table on the terrace looking over the herbaceous borders, which were starting to come beautifully into bloom. 'Apart from the fact that Sybbie's one of my best friends so of course I'd help, wild horses wouldn't keep me away from this. A Roman bath house with a mosaic floor that hasn't been seen in more than a hundred and fifty years is pretty special.' She knew her friend Rowena Langham, the county's finds liaison officer, would love to see this, too. Once Georgina had been introduced to the archaeologists who were investigating what they hoped would turn out to be Roman ruins at Little Wenborough Hall, she planned to ask them if Rowena could visit the site.

'We had absolutely no idea that anything was even under the paddock until we got the letter from the archaeology team last year, saying that they thought there were Roman ruins,' Sybbie said.

'We know there's the buried footings of a priory some-where near the house – the stone from the building was taken after the Dissolution and used elsewhere – but we've never thought about trying to find the priory. Maybe we should look for that, too, when this excavation is over,' Bernard said, his brown eyes alight with excitement. 'We didn't know there had been some archaeological research done here around the middle of the nineteenth century. When Trish – she's one of the archaeologists,' he added for Georgina's benefit, 'showed us the maps and a sketch of the mosaic in the bath house that was made back then, it gave me goose bumps. And then the first test pit brought up some tesserae, an oil flask and an intaglio from a ring – proving that we really had found the bath house.'

'He was as excited as I'd be if I ever found a letter or a diary entry to prove that Repton had a hand in our garden,' Sybbie said, looking fondly at her husband.

'There's a hypocaust underneath the bath house, too – the underfloor heating system. Trish can tell you all about it. She says the fact there was a place big enough to have a three-room bath house shows there was some kind of settlement here. Possibly a *mansio*, which was a kind of staging post, or a villa – I'm not quite sure which it is, but Trish says they've definitely found more of the building. Though we're the opposite side of Norwich from Venta Icenorum, and I would've expected a villa to be near a big settlement or on one of the major roads connected to it,' Bernard mused. 'Some Roman burials were found just outside Bawburgh, and apparently there are crop marks that might indicate a Roman road there, too, but nothing was found to support that during excavations. And at Crownthorpe—'

Sybbie glanced at her watch and put her hand on his arm. 'Darling, I'm so sorry to interrupt, but we need to meet Simon and Trish at the dig in twenty minutes. Would you be an angel and make us some more coffee?'

'Of course.' Bernard put his hand over hers briefly, then

picked up the empty cafetière and disappeared through the French doors into the kitchen.

'I really don't mind him talking about Roman history and geography,' Georgina said quietly. 'You didn't have to stop him on my account.'

'Dear girl,' Sybbie said affectionately. 'Bernard could rabbit about this stuff for England, bless him. But it's not that. I really wanted to ask your advice about something before we had breakfast, but Bernard came out to the terrace with us instead of sneaking into the study to pore over his maps – which rather scuppered my plans.'

'Advice? I'll do my best,' Georgina said, concerned. Sybbie was the most capable woman she knew. If she wanted advice, something was definitely a bit off-kilter. 'What's worrying you?'

'Cesca,' Sybbie said. 'Bernard says I'm fussing, but she's working much too hard, and I can't persuade her to ease up.'

Francesca, Sybbie's daughter-in-law, ran the farm shop café in the village Georgina had moved to three years ago, and made the most amazing food. 'Cesca only has one speed, and that's full pelt,' Georgina reminded her. 'And she's young. She's not even thirty. She'll be fine.'

Sybbie grimaced. 'I know, I know. But...' She huffed out a sigh. 'This is top secret, so please don't let on to her that you know – but she's pregnant. Eight weeks.'

'Oh, that's wonderful news,' Georgina said. Sybbie would make a fantastic grandmother.

'It's fabulous, but she needs to slow down,' Sybbie said, looking worried.

'Apart from the fact that Cesca would hate being constrained,' Georgina said, 'if she does slow down, people will notice that she's not her usual self, and they'll start asking questions and speculating. Rumours will be flying all round the village, and someone will ask her outright before she and Giles are ready to tell everyone their news.'

'That's true,' Sybbie admitted. 'But I still worry about her.'

'She's sensible, and she won't do anything that puts the baby at risk,' Georgina said. It wasn't like her friend to be a worrier. Why would Sybbie be fretting? The only things Georgina could think of was that Francesca had lost a baby in the past or there was a complication with the pregnancy, though it felt too intrusive to ask outright. She might have to wait until Sybbie confided more before she could reassure her friend.

'I would ask you to have a word with her, because she seems to listen to you more than she does to anyone else,' Sybbie said, turning her empty mug round in her hands and looking unexpectedly anxious. 'But then she'd know I'd told you, and I promised her I'd keep it quiet.'

'Maybe,' Georgina said, 'you could spin it that *you* need to slow down and you hate it; you'd be grateful if she kept you company, just sitting and relaxing and chatting.'

Sybbie shook her head. 'If I sit down and chat, then everyone's going to wor— Oh.' She rolled her eyes. 'The penny's just dropped. You made a good point, Georgie. If she does slow down, people will notice and start asking awkward questions.'

'Trust her,' Georgina said. 'If she does need to take it easier, she'll find a way of doing it.' She smiled. 'Eight weeks. That means a baby at the Manor just before Christmas. How *lovely*.'

'I'm going to learn to knit. I can't wait to be a grannie,' Sybbie said.

'I can't imagine you swapping your secateurs for knitting needles,' Georgina said, laughing. 'But I'd love to make a cross-stitch birth sampler for the baby. Perhaps we can choose a pattern together.' She took her phone from her pocket. 'In fact, why don't we...?'

Ten seconds later, they were looking at cross-stitch patterns and knitting patterns, noting down potentials.

'Coffee,' Bernard said, coming back with a fresh cafetière

and refilling their mugs. 'And you both look rather conspiratorial, hunched over the table like that.'

'No conspiracies. We're just looking at cross-stitch and knitting patterns,' Georgina said casually.

'To the best of my knowledge, neither of you knit,' Bernard said, looking straight at his wife. 'It sounds to me as if you've just broken a confidence, Syb.'

'Only a *tiny* bit. And only because you keep telling me I'm fussing too much and I needed to talk to someone who could reassure me properly, instead of brushing my worries aside.' Sybbie wrinkled her nose. 'Georgie won't tell.'

'Well, that goes without saying,' Bernard said, before Georgina could chip in and say that of course she'd keep the secret, and she was warmed by his confidence in her. 'But I think you've just put yourself in a tight spot, my best beloved.'

'A tight spot?' Sybbie asked.

He gave a cheerful smile. 'Let's just say that if any more Staffordshire dogs appear in this house within the next month, I might just have to tell Cesca my suspicions that you've been a tiny bit loose-lipped.'

'That's blackmail,' Sybbie countered. 'Perhaps we should ask Inspector Bradshaw to remind us what the legal penalty for blackmail is.'

'You can try, but Colin will be diplomatic and stay out of this,' Georgina said with a grin, knowing that her partner was fond of both Bernard and Sybbie and wouldn't take sides, either. All of Sybbie's friends knew about her out-of-control collection of Staffordshire china dogs, and her inability to pass an antique shop – particularly in Holt, the pretty Georgian market town a few miles away.

'Hard luck, Syb. No Staffordshire dogs for you, this month,' Bernard said, rubbing his hands gleefully.

'How did the archaeologists know to come and do the test

pits in your paddock?' Georgina asked, changing the subject to something less controversial.

'It all started last summer, actually,' Bernard told her. 'When Trish wrote to me, we'd had a very dry spell, which is apparently good for crop marks. She has letters, sketches and a couple of maps relating to the original dig, in the mid-1800s, and she hoped that we might be able to spot some evidence that the original team had found something significant. One of my friends is a keen pilot and he flew Trish and me over the paddocks so she could have a look at the site. She took a few photographs and said the crop marks looked very promising, so we agreed to let her team come with their machines and do a geophys survey. And obviously I have maps of how the estate looked in the mid-1800s, which she found quite helpful.' Bernard brightened. 'Have I shown you the maps, Georgie?'

'You can't do that now, darling, or we'll be late,' Sybbie said.

'I suppose.' Bernard looked disappointed. 'Giles and I have been volunteering on the dig since they dug the first test pit, and I found a tessera – one of the mosaic tiles.' He pulled a small bag from his pocket and handed it to Georgina. The bag was neatly labelled and contained a square piece of whitish stone about the size of her thumbnail. 'Obviously I'll give it back at the end of the dig,' he said. 'But Trish said I could hang on to it for now. Finding this, and knowing it's part of the floor in the bath house... it's unbelievably exciting to have a connection to someone who lived in exactly the same place as I do, maybe two thousand years ago.'

'I completely get that,' Georgina said. 'And I'd love to see your maps, later on,' she added, meaning it.

'Be prepared to stay in his man cave for ages,' Sybbie warned with an indulgent smile. She glanced at her watch again. 'We really had better get going. Max, Jet, on your beds, because I don't want you getting in the way of Old Tom' – her head gardener – 'while he's working,' she directed, and the two black Labradors trotted obediently indoors to curl up in their wicker basket by the Aga. 'It's a shame you didn't bring Bert to come and play with them, Georgie,' she said.

Georgina's liver-and-white springer spaniel, adopted the previous summer when his owner moved to sheltered accommodation and couldn't take him with her, usually accompanied her everywhere, including when she was working. But today she'd thought it might be too busy for him, with all the students. 'I'm sure he'd rather come and play when they can all romp round your garden,' Georgina said. 'He's fine having a nap back at home.'

They headed round the back of the house to the paddock. Instead of being the grassy space Georgina was used to, it now contained several large straight-sided trenches, marked into squares by lines of string, and with thick walls in various places, made from flints and narrow tiles. Figures in hoodies and jeans – students, Georgina guessed – were kneeling on mats, carefully scraping away at the earth with trowels; some were wielding clipboards and marking findspots on gridded paper; and others were sifting through the spoil heap. One of the areas had a tarpaulin cover over it, which Georgina assumed was the mosaic floor she'd promised to photograph; a woman who looked to be in her late thirties was standing next to the cover, holding a phone to her ear and looking concerned.

'That's Trish – Dr Melton,' Bernard said. 'She's the second-in-command. Simon Butterfield's the lead archaeologist; he should be meeting us, too.'

As they walked over to Trish, the woman slid her phone into her pocket. 'Hello, Bernard. Sybbie. Good to see you both,' she said, and turned to Georgina. 'And you must be Mrs Drake, the photographer? Lovely to meet you.'

'And you,' Georgina said politely. 'And do call me Georgie, Dr Melton.'

'I'm Trish,' the archaeologist responded, shaking Georgina's hand warmly. 'I'm sorry, I don't have a clue where Simon is. Nobody's seen him this morning, and I've been trying his phone for ages, but it just goes straight to voicemail,' she added, looking exasperated. 'It's not like him to miss a photo opportunity.' Then she winced. 'Sorry. That didn't come out right.' She flushed, looking awkward.

So the lead archaeologist loved publicity? Clearly there was a bit of tension between the two of them, Georgina thought.

'Don't worry. It won't go any further than us,' Bernard assured her.

'Thank you.' Trish frowned. 'It's not fair to leave you all waiting for him to turn up. I'll take you through the rest of the site first, Georgie, and show you what we've got here. Then perhaps we can get started on the photographs, and maybe do a group photo with Simon at the end, if he's turned up by then?'

'That works for me,' Georgina said.

'What we've got here is the bath house, though there's more to the building complex, which we think stretches out at right angles to the bath house and moves out of the paddock,' Trish said. 'We're still not sure whether it was a private villa or a *mansio* – a staging post – but hopefully we can work on it more in the future, with Bernard and Sybbie's permission, and find out.' She led them to the furthest end of the complex. 'It was a brilliant system they had. You'd start here in the changing rooms, the *apodyterium*. You'd strip and leave your clothes here in little wooden cupboards, then use the latrines. Then you'd go to the *tepidarium* – the warm room – here, which was filled with steam, and just relax a bit.'

'So Roman baths were pretty much like a modern spa?' Georgina asked, fascinated.

'Without a jacuzzi, but you'd get the steam room and a plunge pool,' Trish said. 'When you were ready, you'd go to the *caldarium* – the hot room – which was heated by boilers. That's the one we've got covered at the moment, because of the mosaic floor. That was also a steam room, but hotter. The steam went under the floor through the hypocaust, between the stacks of square tiles which supported the floor, and up through ducts in the walls. The ceilings would've been vaulted, to reduce all the condensation.'

'It's amazing to think all this was built nearly two thousand years ago – and we use similar principles now,' Georgina said.

'Maybe we should remodel our bathroom,' Sybbie suggested, giving Bernard a wicked grin. 'Mosaic floor, steam room...'

'In your dreams, Syb,' he teased back.

'I remember going to the fort at Hadrian's Wall, years ago, when my kids were small,' Georgina said. 'Didn't the Romans used to cover themselves in oil before bathing? I always thought the baths might be a bit gungy.'

Trish smiled. 'They'd scrape all the oil off before they got in a bath. They didn't have soap, so a slave would rub them with oil to loosen the dirt on their skin, then scrape it off with a strigil. They might spend a while in a hot bath, then have a dip in the cold pool in the *frigidarium* to close their pores before drying off and getting dressed again. And we know that some fairly high-status people used the bath, because of the intaglio we found in the drain.'

'Trish was telling me that gemstones were stuck into rings with a vegetable glue that tended to melt in the steam room, so they'd just fall off the ring and the owner wouldn't notice until later,' Bernard said.

'Wouldn't it have been more sensible to leave the ring in the changing room?' Georgina asked.

'Then it might get stolen. Bit of a lose-lose situation, I suppose – but it's good for us, because when the baths were cleaned out, the gemstones would fall into the drain... where we found them,' Trish said.

'And the steam room's the one with the amazing floor,' Bernard added.

Which Georgina couldn't wait to see; Sybbie had described the peacock to her, and it sounded amazing. She could see why Bernard's attention had been so caught by the dig; she was finding the tour of the dig fascinating, too, especially learning about the little bits of everyday life that had so many echoes from the past with the way things were done now. Those connections made the past feel so much closer.

'Didn't the steam affect the mosaic?' Georgina asked.

'No. There was a concrete floor above the hypocaust, and the tesserae were set into a layer of mortar above that,' Trish explained. 'There would be furnaces just outside the baths, with a stoke hole, and they'd put lead boilers above the furnaces to heat the water for the baths and the steam room.'

'Where did the water come from?' Georgina asked.

'We think they might've taken it from the river, which isn't that far from here, or there might have been some hot springs nearby that have vanished over the years,' Trish said. 'Though we haven't come across any sulphur deposits, so I think it's more likely that they sent slaves with buckets to the river.'

Finally, they left the trenches where the students had been working and reached an area that had been covered over by a lumpy tarpaulin, and Georgina guessed this was the star of the show: the mosaic floor. 'I can't wait to see the peacock,' she said.

Trish glanced at her watch and tried Simon's phone again. 'Nothing. It's still going to voicemail after ringing out. Maybe his phone's on silent and he doesn't realise it. Well, I'm not going to make you wait for him any longer.'

'Do you want me to help you with the tarpaulin?' Bernard asked.

'Thanks. That'd be good,' Trish said gratefully.

They stood at opposite ends of the tarpaulin. 'Let's start at this end and pull the tarp across to the back,' she directed.

'Then we can fold it up and get it out of the way for the photographs.'

Except, as Trish and Bernard hauled the tarpaulin out of the way, Georgina could see that something was very badly wrong. There was no way the mosaic floor was going to be photographed today.

Lying in the middle of the mosaic, his head turned slightly to the side so they could see his face, was a man. A dark substance – presumably blood – had seeped around his head onto the pale tesserae, and Georgina was pretty sure he wasn't breathing.

It wasn't the first time she'd seen a dead body, but even so it was a shock. This was someone's son. Maybe someone's partner, or someone's father. All the love, all the possibilities, snuffed out in a few minutes.

Just like it had been when she'd lost her husband: she'd come home from a photography shoot to find Stephen had died from a heart attack while she'd been at work.

'Oh, my God! Simon!' Trish said, her voice hoarse and whispery with shock.

The words were enough to make Georgina pull herself together. This might be an accident, but it didn't look like that to her. It was more likely to be a crime scene, and they needed to keep the surroundings as free from contamination as possible. Trish was moving forward, as if to climb into the trench. Before Trish could contaminate the crime scene, Georgina called, 'Wait!'

Trish frowned. 'But we have to check if he's breathing. We might need to give him CPR until an ambulance gets here. Can someone phone an ambulance?'

'My partner's a detective,' Georgina said. 'I've learned from him that the police like to preserve the area around a body. I'm sorry, but judging from the blood round his head, I'd say it's a bit too late for CPR.'

'But what if it isn't?' Trish asked.

Sybbie gave them both an assessing look. As her friend had been there when a dead body was found at Hartington Hall, Georgina was pretty sure that Sybbie had picked up the rudiments of how an investigation worked. Hopefully she'd find a tactful way of telling Trish that she'd be on the suspect list, as one of the last people likely to have seen Simon alive.

'Georgie's very familiar with procedures,' Sybbie said calmly. 'I think she's the best one to check if he's still breathing. I'll call nine-nine-nine. Trish, can you make sure nobody comes over to this area? We need to keep things clear for the police.'

Aware of the importance of not contaminating a potential crime scene with footprints, Georgie rummaged in her coat pocket for the dog-poo bags she usually kept there and tied them over her shoes before climbing into the trench and picking her way over to the centre of the mosaic floor. She noted a couple of muddy footprints that might be useful to the scene of crimes team.

Close up, she could see that Simon had been hit over the head and she'd been right to think that the dark substance around him was blood; she could smell the coppery scent, and there was a deep cut on the back of his head. Grimly, she slid a dog-poo bag onto her hand to avoid contaminating evidence and checked his forehead – which was ice-cold – and then felt for the pulse at his wrist. Nonexistent, as she'd expected. Simon had obviously been dead for a while; she knew from Colin that bodies took a while to be cold to the touch, so the body must've lain here overnight and the tarpaulin hadn't protected him from the coldness of the night air. She waved to get Sybbie's attention, then shook her head to signal that nothing could be done for him; Sybbie nodded acknowledgement and continued talking on her phone, presumably to the emergency services controller.

Georgina walked carefully back to the side of the trench and accepted Bernard's help to pull her out.

'They're sending paramedics to confirm the death and the police are on their way,' Sybbie said, when she ended her call. 'Hopefully it'll be Colin and his team.'

'Hopefully.' Georgina shivered.

And then a familiar voice sounded in her ear – Doris, the young woman who'd died at the house where Georgina lived now, and had somehow managed to make contact with Georgina through her hearing aids. Over the past year, Doris had helped Georgina solve several cold cases. 'Georgie, we need to talk...'

TWO

'I need a moment on my own,' Georgina said to Sybbie, 'if you don't mind.' Although she'd become close to Sybbie since moving to Little Wenborough, Georgina hadn't told her friend about Doris. The only people who knew that Georgina could hear Doris's ghost were Jack, Doris's younger brother, and his wife, Tracey, and they'd been incredibly sceptical when Georgina had first broached the subject. Georgina had learned that it was easier to find somewhere quiet where she could murmur to Doris, maybe pretending to be on the phone if someone asked who she was talking to.

The students were all still working; some of them had head-phones in, and some were really focused. Clearly they hadn't realised that a dead body had just been found, only a few metres away from them.

'Do you know anything about the body, Doris?' Georgina asked quietly.

'The archaeologist who was found dead on the mosaic floor? Sorry, I'm afraid I don't,' Doris said.

'Did you want to talk to me about someone else?' From

previous experience, Georgina was pretty sure it would be someone from the past.

'Yes. Timothy Marsden. He was one of the archaeologists who uncovered the bath house and the mosaic floor, back in 1865,' Doris said. 'He was a friend of the family. He was thrilled to be part of the excavation team. And he remembers it being a kind of golden summer, doing the work he loved most and being with his closest friend... and he'd fallen in love.'

'What happened? Can he remember where he died? Where he's buried?' Georgina asked.

'It's a bit of a tricky one,' Doris said.

'We've worked with tricky situations before,' Georgina said. 'Obviously you can see I left Bert at home – though, even if he had been here, we really can't direct him to dig in the middle of an excavation site.'

'Actually, we can't direct him to dig *anywhere*,' Doris said. 'Because I don't actually know where Timothy's body is.'

That was the last thing Georgina had expected her to say. In all the cold cases where they'd worked together, Doris had known exactly where the body was buried and had encouraged Bert to help Georgina find it. 'But you've spoken to him, and he wants us to investigate his death? How can we do that, without a body as evidence?' she asked.

'I have absolutely no idea,' Doris said. 'We'll have to find another way in.'

'Documents, maybe,' Georgina said. Her daughter, Beatrice, worked for a probate genealogy company when she wasn't acting, and had taught Georgina how to research people in historical records. And hadn't Bernard said something about letters, maps and sketches dating from the Victorian excavation? Perhaps there would be a mention of Timothy Marsden among them. 'Is there anything you can tell me? You said he was working as part of the excavation team and he'd fallen in love.'

'Timothy found the mosaic floor and the hypocaust underneath it,' Doris said. 'He remembers that, and he remembers falling in love. Not much else, though, at the moment: just the sound of an explosion, a terrific pain in his back and then darkness.'

This was similar to how previous cold cases had gone, and how Doris's own case had started: the murder victim had only been able to remember sketchy details, but as Georgina investigated and discovered documents and facts, they sparked off more memories, helping her to solve the case.

'From that description, it sounds as if maybe he was shot in the back,' Georgina said thoughtfully.

'That's what it sounds like to me, too,' Doris agreed.

'But who would have shot him, and why? Was it some kind of fight? Who did he fall in love with, and what happened to them? Maybe there are answers there?' Georgina asked, thinking out loud.

'We need to find something that will trigger some memories for him,' Doris said.

'If he was here on the original excavation, and he was a family friend, maybe there's some information about him in the house's archives,' Georgina said. 'Apparently one of the archaeologists has some letters from someone involved with the original dig. Maybe there's a mention of Timothy.'

'Maybe,' Doris said. 'Colin will be here soon – and everyone's going to notice if you're still here talking to me. You'd better go.'

'All right. We'll talk later,' Georgina said.

She walked back to join the others, her mind whirling.

'Are you all right, Georgie?' Bernard checked.

She nodded. 'It's not the first dead body I've seen.' She blew out a breath. 'Though I have to admit I don't think I'll ever get used to them. I couldn't do Colin's job.'

'Can I get you some hot, sweet tea?' he asked.

'That's very kind of you to offer, Bernard, but no, thanks. I'm fine,' she reassured him.

Colin eased his car up the driveway of Little Wenborough Manor, his sergeant, Mo Tesfaye, sitting beside him and his constable, Larissa Foulkes, in the back. The manor house was a gorgeous Tudor pile, built of red brick in the shape of an E; the gables had stepped ends and the windows had stone mullions. There were two groups of four tall, barley-sugar twist chimneys on each end of the house, and wisteria grew round the doorway of the porch.

The very first time Colin had come here, it had been in his professional capacity, to ask Lady Wyatt about oleander. Over the last year, because of his relationship with Georgina, he'd become friends with Sybbie and Bernard. He hated to think that they were going to be caught up in a potential murder enquiry. Georgina, too, because she'd come here to photograph the archaeology team's findings at the dig – and instead had discovered a dead body.

He parked near the paddock, then he and Mo made their way over to the group standing by the trench.

'Georgie, Sybbie, Bernard,' he said, nodding at them. As always, his heart gave that tiny little leap when he looked at Georgina. Her kindness and warmth would be very much needed by the people around the dig today, he thought.

Sybbie quickly introduced them to the one person he didn't know by the trench. 'Trish, this is Detective Inspector Colin Bradshaw – Georgie's partner; Detective Sergeant Mo Tesfaye; and Detective Constable Larissa Foulkes. Colin, Mo, Larissa: this is Dr Trish Melton from St Edmund's College, London. Now that Simon's dead, I guess you must be in charge, Trish?'

'Yes,' Trish said, though her voice sounded hollow and her face was pale with shock.

Dr Trish Melton definitely looked like Colin's idea of an archaeologist: wearing faded jeans, sturdy boots, an olive-coloured sweater and a sunhat that made him think of Indiana Jones – as well as the TV archaeologist he had a slight crush on, which he hadn't admitted to Georgina. Trish looked to be in her late thirties, he judged, and she had the same no-nonsense air about her that Sybbie did.

'It's pretty clear from what the call handler told me that the death is unlikely to be from natural causes,' Colin said, looking at the blood that had pooled over the mosaic floor around Simon's head. 'Obviously I need to check the body for myself, so I'll do that and call the scene of crimes team, and I need to take statements from those of you who found the body, as well as from everyone who was in the area last night and this morn-ing. Dr Melton, could you please gather your students? I'm afraid we'll have to ask them not to talk to each other until after they've given their statements – Mo will look after them.'

'They can't just keep going with their work while you're waiting to interview them?' Trish asked.

'I'm afraid not,' Colin said. 'When the scene of crimes team get here, I'll also need them to check the tools before they can be used again. Though the students will be free to go back to work as soon as they've checked and signed their statements.'

'I'll organise some hot drinks,' Sybbie said.

'*After* I've interviewed you, Sybbie, if you don't mind,' Colin said. 'I know you called it in, but who found the body?'

'Me, Sybbie, Bernard and Trish,' Georgina said. 'I'll help Sybbie with the drinks after you've interviewed me.'

'All right,' Colin said. 'Is there somewhere quiet here we can use for interviews?'

'There's the finds tent,' Trish said, gesturing to the white marquee-like tent at the side of the dig. 'There are a couple of tables and chairs in there.'

'Thank you, Dr Melton.'

'In the circumstances, you'd better call me Trish,' she said. 'I'll go and round up the students. I assume I can at least explain to them that Simon's dead and they need to make a statement?'

'Don't worry – Mo will do that and answer any questions,' Colin said gently. 'Take him with you.'

Trish nodded, and went with Mo to talk to the students.

'I'll check the body and be with you in a couple of minutes,' Colin said, taking shoe-covers and gloves from his pocket.

'I used Bert's poo bags over my shoes when I went over to check, and when I touched Simon's forehead and checked for a pulse,' Georgina said.

'Good thinking,' Colin said, smiling at her. 'I'm not doubting your judgement.'

'But I'm a member of the public and you're doing your job properly,' Georgina said, clearly understanding his position.

He climbed into the trench and went to check the body. Cold, no pulse; there was a pool of blood around the head, an obvious wound and the hair was matted. He took a couple of initial photographs on his phone, made notes, called the scene of crimes team and the medical examiner, then returned to the little group at the side of the trench. 'Larissa, can you secure the scene and guard it until the SOCO arrives, please?'

'Sure, guv,' Larissa said.

'Georgie, before we start – are you all right?' Colin asked, taking her hand briefly and squeezing it to let her know she had his support. Finding a dead body was never easy, and he knew it would also bring back bad memories of coming back from work to find her late husband, Stephen, dead from a heart attack.

'I'm fine,' she said, her green eyes clear. 'Obviously it was a shock when Bernard and Trish pulled back the tarpaulin and we saw the body, because I was expecting to take photographs, and that poor man...' She grimaced. 'But you're here, so every-thing's going to be sorted out properly.'

Even though he'd been doing this job for a long time, her

confidence in him made Colin feel warm all over. 'Are you ready to give me your witness statement, or would you like a bit of time, first?'

'I'm fine to give the statement,' she said. 'At least then I'll feel I'm doing something.'

He appreciated that, too. 'OK. But if you need a break at any point, just say.'

'Thank you.' She smiled. 'It feels a bit odd, being here with you in your professional role.'

'And you in yours,' he said. 'I prefer my working life separate from my private life, too.' He narrowed his eyes. 'And it worries me when you're involved in something like this.'

'I'm not really involved. I was just there when the body was discovered,' she said.

'Bernard, Sybbie – would you mind waiting here with Larissa, please?' Colin asked.

'Of course.' Bernard answered for both of them.

Colin and Georgina made their way over to the tent. It was a small marquee, draped with a heavy white fabric, with a clear zipped panel to act as the doorway. Inside, as Trish had mentioned, there were a couple of large folding tables with collapsible chairs set at both of them; there were clear storage boxes at the side of the tables, obviously for keeping the finds in, as well as files with sheets to catalogue the finds, clear bags and pens. Thankfully there was enough clear space at one of the tables so he could use it without having to disturb the files and archaeological finds already set out there.

Colin offered Georgina a chair at the table he wanted to use, then moved another chair next to hers so he could sit opposite her. Once he had a notebook and pen in front of him, he said, 'In your own words, Georgie, could you please tell me what happened?'

'I was supposed to be photographing the mosaic, this morning,' she said. 'Simon Butterfield – the lead archaeologist –

wasn't here, and Trish said he wasn't answering his phone. She was a bit annoyed that he was keeping us all waiting, so she talked us through the site. Bernard was helping Trish pull the tarpaulin back to uncover the mosaic floor when we all saw the body. Trish confirmed it was Simon. Sybbie called nine-nine-nine and I covered my shoes with poo bags before I went to check whether he was still alive, so hopefully I haven't contaminated any evidence.'

The resourcefulness was typical Georgina. He'd used some of Bert's empty poo bags over his shoes at a crime scene, too, before now.

'I did notice a couple of muddy footprints,' she continued, 'but I have no idea whether that's important. I avoided them, just in case. Simon wasn't breathing and didn't have a pulse, his body was cold and it was very clear that he was dead. It looks to me as if he was hit over the head with something because there's a pool of blood round his head and his hair's matted' – exactly what Colin had seen for himself – 'but obviously forensics and pathology will be able to tell you more than I can on that front.'

'Anything you'd like to add?' he asked, knowing how shrewd Georgina was – and that, as a photographer, she often noticed things other people missed.

'I feel a bit guilty saying this, but I think there might've been some tension between Trish and Simon. She said it wasn't like him to miss the chance of a photo opportunity,' Georgina said. 'It wasn't so much what she said as the way she said it – as if she were thoroughly fed up with him. Though that *doesn't* mean that she was the one who bashed him over the head.'

'Agreed. But if they didn't get on, and he was the sort who liked everyone to know he was in charge, he might not have got on with other people at the dig, either,' Colin said. 'That's useful to know – and something to check. Thank you. How did Trish seem when the body was found?'

'She looked and sounded shocked,' Georgina said. 'She

wanted to go and see if he was breathing – I had to ask her not to, because of possibly contaminating the evidence.'

Colin was pretty sure that Georgina had also worked out that Trish would be a suspect, and the last thing he needed was a suspect blundering around a crime scene and confusing any traces.

'To me, she came across as a genuinely concerned colleague who didn't like him very much, but who would do the right thing in a difficult situation.'

Colin trusted Georgina's judgement – and he liked how concise her thoughts were. He made a note. 'What happened then?'

'I went to check the body,' she said. 'Sybbie rang the emergency services. The rest, you know.'

'OK,' he said. Though there was a significant absence he'd noticed. 'Is Bert not with you today?'

When Georgina shook her head, he said, 'So no digging up of ancient skeletons to complicate things?'

'Not today,' she said lightly.

Something about her tone and the fact she wasn't meeting his eyes made him wonder: was there something she wasn't telling him? But what? He hoped there wasn't anything wrong with Bert; he knew how much she adored her spaniel. Though now wasn't the time to ask her.

'Thank you. That's all helpful.' He wrote a couple more notes and turned over the page. 'Sorry – I do have one more question.' Which might lead to a couple more, depending on her answer. 'Had you met anyone from the dig before today?'

'No,' she said. 'Though obviously, with the dig taking place in their paddock, Sybbie and Bernard have had dealings with everyone on the team. They might be able to give you more information. Sybbie hasn't really talked to me about it – only that Bernard's really excited and driving her a bit mad with ancient estate maps.'

'It's a man thing,' Colin said. 'I think I'd be the same.'

She grinned. 'I think you and Bernard could both be very nerdy about this, if we let you. Though I rather like the idea of you dressing up in a toga.'

'So we're moving away from Mr Darcy' – the role played by an actor who had only the faintest resemblance to him, in Colin's opinion, but every female he met over the age of forty seemed to think otherwise – 'towards what? Mark Antony?'

'Works for me. *I dreamt there was an emperor Antony,*' she quoted.

'*Age cannot wither her, nor custom stale /Her infinite variety,*' he quoted back, liking the fact that she went slightly pink. He knew she'd know the rest of the quote; not only had her degree been in English, but her husband, Stephen, had been a renowned theatre actor and director, and she was very well-versed in Shakespeare.

'Well, Inspector. I don't think that should be part of the statement,' she said, mock-primly.

'You started it,' he said with a grin. He finished writing up her statement. 'Seriously, though, can you read this through and sign it? And obviously tell me to correct anything I might have misunderstood or missed.'

'Of course.' She read the statement and signed it. 'Do you want to talk to Sybbie, next? Then we'll send coffee in with Bernard or Trish.'

'Thank you,' he said.

She stood up, leaned over and kissed him lightly. 'I'm sorry you've been dragged into all of this.'

'It's my job,' he reminded her. 'And it's easier for me to deal with it because I'm not emotionally involved with anyone connected to the case.'

'I guess,' she said. 'Look, I know your schedule's going to be all over the place now. I'll cook something for dinner that I can reheat quickly.'

'You're right about my schedule, and I appreciate the offer,' he said, 'though don't feel you have to wait for me.'

'We'll play it by ear.' She kissed him again. 'I hope the rest of your day isn't too hideous.'

'Or yours,' he said, 'because you definitely can't take pictures of the mosaic until at least tomorrow, if not later.'

'I know.' She smiled at him, and went to send in the next interviewee.

Sybbie's account of finding the body matched Georgina's, and so did Bernard's.

'Obviously you and Sybbie have had contact with the archaeology team before today. What were your impressions of Simon Butterfield?' Colin asked Bernard.

'I don't feel comfortable speaking ill of the dead,' Bernard said.

'Put it this way: I could do with some background,' Colin said, 'from someone who's neutral – who definitely doesn't have a professional axe to grind. Not that I'm accusing Dr Melton of anything, of course.'

'Ah,' Bernard said. 'In that case, I thought he was rather keen on the sound of his own voice, and not particularly fond of listening. Dismissive of the students rather than drawing them out – Trish comes across as a much better teacher. She gets the students to think.'

Colin had asked Sybbie the same questions; she hadn't warmed to Simon Butterfield either, he thought. 'Thank you. That's helpful,' he said.

Once Bernard had checked and signed his statement and left the tent, Trish came in, bearing coffee.

'Thank you,' Colin said gratefully.

Her account of finding the body also matched that of the other people who'd been there.

'I'd like some background, if you don't mind,' Colin said.

'Can you tell me about the dig and how your involvement came about?'

'My four-times-great-uncle, Timothy Marsden, was involved in a dig here back in 1865,' Trish said. 'Some tesserae were found here back then, during ploughing. Frederick Walters – Bernard's three-times-great-uncle – was at university with Timothy and asked him to come and help with the excavation. They found the bath house and the hypocaust with the mosaic floor. I don't know exactly what happened next, but I'm pretty sure the remains were covered up again to protect them. I've got sketches and letters that Timothy sent to his older sister, Clara, my three-times-great-gran. I contacted Bernard last year to ask what he knew about the mosaic floor. He said he'd never heard of it, so I asked if I could do some preliminary work here at Little Wenborough. One of his friends flew us over the estate and I took photos – the crop marks of the villa here were quite clear. I asked Bernard for permission to do some geophys and then make a few test trenches to see if we could find the mosaic floor. Last week, we found it, along with the hypocaust.'

'And Simon was your boss?' Colin asked.

'Simon works – *worked*,' she corrected herself, 'in the same department as me. He's not my line manager, but he's senior to me.' She paused. 'He wanted to be involved in the project.'

Remembering what Georgina had told him, Colin thought it sounded as if Trish hadn't wanted Simon there and resented him muscling in on the project she'd clearly set up. 'How did you get on with him?' he asked, keeping his voice neutral.

She wrinkled her nose. 'You're going to find out anyway, so I might as well tell you myself. He isn't – *wasn't* – just a colleague. He was also my brother-in-law. He was married to my little sister, Joanna.' Her voice was carefully expressionless when she added, 'I introduced them.' Her expression was at odds with her tone, and told Colin that she very much regretted that act.

'How did you get on with Simon?' he asked.

'We had... differences of opinion, let's say,' she said.

He let the silence spin out, and eventually she sighed. 'All right. Professionally, we didn't get on. But I didn't kill him.'

Of course she'd say that. But it was his job to find out who *had* killed Simon Butterfield. He wished Georgina was still here. She had a knack for getting people to open up to her. 'How did you get on with him personally?' he asked. 'As your brother-in-law?'

'Not great,' she said, and sighed again. 'All right. I'll be honest. I didn't know him that well when I introduced him to Joanna, but the more I got to know him, the less I liked him.'

'It must've been difficult, with him being married to your sister,' he said, and waited again.

But she seemed prepared for the question, because she shrugged. 'Most people I know have at least one difficult in-law they have to make an effort with, to keep the peace. I got round it by meeting my sister for lunch during the week rather than seeing her at weekends, and at family dos I'd make sure I was in the kitchen. It's easy enough to avoid rows if you avoid the people who cause them,' she said.

Colin understood exactly what she was telling him without saying so explicitly: Simon was the sort of guest who expected to be waited on and wouldn't clear tables, let alone offer to help with the washing up. OK. He'd try a different direction to see if Trish would open up a bit more. 'How long have you been working on the dig?'

'We started here two weeks ago,' she said. 'We've got another week left until term starts – and we need to cover everything back over and fill in the trenches before then.'

Which explained why she'd sounded so anxious to continue the work. 'And Simon was the lead archaeologist?'

Was he imagining it, or was there a flash of anger in her eyes? 'Yes.'

He'd explore that later. 'When did you last see him?'

'Last night. We all walked down to the Red Lion for dinner. We probably got there about seven. I stayed until about half past eight, and came back here because I wanted to take advantage of the peace and quiet to do some admin work. I don't share a tent with anyone, so I'm afraid I don't know what time everyone else got back.'

'How did Simon get on with the students?' Colin asked.

'He liked lecturing,' Trish said.

Which was pretty much what Bernard had told him. 'What about teaching?'

'As I said, he liked lecturing,' Trish repeated.

Which wasn't quite the same thing. 'I know people don't like speaking ill of the dead,' he said, 'but this is a murder investigation. I'm looking for facts.'

She winced. 'This feels more like my personal opinion. But, OK, I'll tell you. He's not that popular in the department. He wants his name on every discovery, whether it's his or not. And he's not great with the students. He sees them in terms of grades that reflect on his teaching, not as people who might be struggling with things outside their studies and could do with a bit of support and kindness.'

Which tied in with what Bernard had said, too.

'How did he get involved with your dig?' Colin asked.

'I admit, that's a sore point,' Trish said. 'I wanted to lead it, because it's linked to my family history. I did all the groundwork in contacting Bernard and arranging things here. It's *my* project. But Simon pretty much bulldozed his way in. A long-lost Roman mosaic floor, particularly in an area of the country that's not known for many examples of mosaics, was too much for him to resist.' She gritted her teeth. 'Sorry. I know that sounds territorial. Normally, I don't mind sharing resources with anyone else. I believe in teamwork and everyone getting credit where it's due. But when Simon just swanned in and made it all about himself, I resented it. Which I know makes it sound as if I had a motive to kill him, but I didn't.'

'Was there anyone in particular he clashed with here?' Colin asked.

'Besides me? None of the students would've killed him, either, if that's what you're asking. They all grumbled about him never returning their essays on time, and never being available for help if they're stuck. But they love being on a dig – bringing something lost to light and being the first person to see or touch that artefact in centuries. That gets you through anything else you might be feeling.'

Colin intended to ask them himself, but if Trish was telling the truth, the killer was unlikely to be a student. And if Trish was the killer, surely she'd be quick to cast suspicion on someone else to take the heat off herself, rather than admitting to disliking him? Unless, of course, that was a double bluff.

'Have there been any problems with anyone local, since you've been working here?'

Trish shook her head. 'We've held a couple of open mornings and the students have loved taking people round and telling them about the site. We've been made very welcome at the Red Lion and the farm shop café. Nobody's been looking daggers at us or muttering in corners about how we shouldn't be here, interfering in things. Actually, people have brought us things they've dug up in their own gardens, in case it's connected to the site – and I have to admit I love it when that happens. I've always got time to talk to people about archaeology. It's so important to stay connected to the past.'

'Thank you, Trish. I think that's it, for now,' Colin said. 'I might have more questions, later. Could you read through your statement and let me know if anything needs changing, and then sign it?'

Once she'd done that, he smiled at her. 'If you can send the next person in, that'd be great.'

'Of course,' Trish said. She paused. 'Can I ring Joanna – my sister – and tell her what's happened? Because she needs to know Simon's dead, and I think it might be kinder coming from me.'

'I think,' Colin said gently, 'it might be an idea to wait a little, until we know more about how he died. And then we'll help you break the news to her.'

'All right,' she said. 'But my sister's a bit...' She paused, as if searching for the right word. 'Fragile. Plus she's hours away, in London. If you want me to identify him, to spare her having to see any of this – well, I'd like to do that for her, if I can.'

'That,' Colin said, 'would be useful. Thank you.'

All the students corroborated what Trish had said. There were various comments about Simon being the first to have his photo taken or talk to a reporter, and the last to hand back essays; they all seemed to prefer Trish.

But two of the students added extra information.

'I feel a bit guilty saying this,' Adam said, 'but Trish didn't get on with him very well. She thought she should've been the lead archaeologist here, because she's the one who found the site and organised everything. But I guess he's the senior lecturer, so he pulled rank and took over.'

Colin already knew that, but he thanked Adam for the information.

'What sort of time did you get back from the Red Lion, last night?' he asked.

'About eleven, I think. We walked back when the pub closed,' Adam said.

'Was Simon with you?'

'No. He'd left earlier. I don't know when – I didn't really notice. It was after Trish left, though. They didn't go together.'

'Did you see him over breakfast?'

'I didn't see anyone over breakfast,' Adam said. 'I overdid it with the beer.'

'Got it,' Colin said.

But Helena, the last of the students he interviewed, told him something Trish really should've mentioned. 'We had a visit from the nighthawks at the beginning of last week,' she said. 'It was the day Dilip found a gold ring in the drain of the bath house.'

'Nighthawks?' Colin asked.

'Metal detectorists,' Helena said. 'Not the normal ones – they're always good about noting down exactly what they found and where, and they're happy to work with us. I mean the sort who don't report their finds. They're not interested in the history, just the money. They come at night, dig where they think they might find something they can sell on the black market, and the first we know about it is the next morning, when we come on site and there are all these random holes everywhere.'

'Do you have any idea what was taken?'

'No,' Helena said with a sigh. 'We found an intaglio in the drain – that's a gemstone with carving on it, the sort people used on a seal – and little bits of personal stuff. There were a couple of coins, plus Dilip's gold ring. The nighthawks dug around there, so they could've taken anything that fell down a drain in a bath house.' She shrugged. 'It could've been coins, a strigil, tweezers or jewellery – anything from earrings to a bracelet or a pendant.'

'Did you report their visit?' Colin asked.

'Simon said there wasn't any point. And I guess he was right. It would've been a waste of police time. None of us heard or saw anything, so there weren't any leads, and as I just told you, we don't have a clue what was taken,' she said. 'How can you report a crime, let alone solve it, when you've got nothing to go on?'

'That's true,' Colin agreed. 'Do nighthawks turn up at every dig?'

'If the location's been reported in the press,' Helena said. 'They always seem to happen on Simon's digs, but maybe that's because he always leaks things to reporters.'

Which would then give Simon a photo opportunity – and that fitted with what Colin had already heard about him. Colin had another word with Trish, who confirmed the nighthawks' visit. 'Why didn't you report it?' he asked, wondering if her response would be different from Helena's.

'I wanted to,' she said, 'but Simon said we had no evidence of what was taken, so it was pointless wasting police time. We set up temporary security lights, instead. They seemed to do the trick, because we haven't been bothered by nighthawks since.'

'Do nighthawks raid every dig?' he asked, waiting to see if she'd expand on what Helena had told him.

'It depends on what's been reported in the press. Which is why we don't tend to talk about finding gold and silver, because we don't want people trampling all over the site and digging wherever they like,' Trish said. 'Obviously not all metal detectorists are nighthawks. A detectorist found the hoard near the Romano-British temple at Crownthorpe, just the other side of Norwich, and reported it properly – there was a Roman-style bronze drinking set with cups, and they're really special because the drinking cups had little Celtic swimming ducks on the handles.' She gave him a wry smile. 'A part of me was hoping we'd find something like that. Or, given we know there was a bath house here, at least a copper cosmetic pestle with a decorative handle.'

'Could Simon have had a run-in with nighthawks last night?' he asked.

'I don't know,' Trish said. 'Like I said, we hadn't had a problem with them since we put the security lights up, apart from the students moaning when the lights were set off –

presumably by wildlife.' She frowned. 'Actually, thinking about it, I don't know whether the security lights came on last night. They didn't wake me, and nobody moaned about it this morning.' She bit her lip. 'What if the nighthawks had been waiting for us all to go to the pub last night, and interfered with the lights? And then if Simon decided to do a last-minute look round the site after the students turned in, suppose he caught someone digging?'

It was a theory. Colin wondered where she'd take it. 'And then there was a fight?' That was where the theory fell down. 'Surely someone would have heard the noise?'

'Didn't someone bash him on the back of the head?' Trish asked. 'And if they were behind him and hit him before he could yell for help, we wouldn't have known anything was wrong.' Her eyes were wide with horror. 'And then they left him under that tarpaulin...'

THREE

'Can I ask you what you know about the original dig that found the mosaic floor, Bernard?' Georgina asked.

'Pretty much what Trish told me when she asked me for permission to dig,' Bernard said. 'The field was being ploughed when some tesserae came to light. My great-great-great-uncle Frederick was a bit of an antiquarian, and he obviously recognised the tesserae as being part of a Roman mosaic. He was at Cambridge with Trish's relative, Timothy Marsden – they were both Trinity men. Frederick knew Timothy shared his interest in Roman Britain, so he asked him to come and help excavate the field.'

The name sent a shiver down Georgina's spine. If Bernard had heard of Timothy Marsden, it meant there had to be some kind of documentation – either through Trish, or in the archives at Little Wenborough Manor.

'Trish has letters that Timothy sent to his sister – that's her great-whatever-grandmother,' Bernard continued. 'And I told you earlier about the sketches and the maps. I'm sure she'll show them to you, if you ask.'

'Good idea,' Georgina said. 'Do you have any information in your archives?'

'We still have all Frederick's papers. At the very least there will be some correspondence, and maybe a diary. He was the heir to the estate, you see,' Bernard said. 'But his wife died in childbirth, along with the baby, and he couldn't bear to remarry. Terribly sad. He died ten years later – we think probably of a broken heart. His younger brother, my great-great-grandfather Robert, inherited the title and the estate.'

'I see,' Georgina said.

'And the lady of the house usually kept a commonplace book; you might find something in one of them. Sybbie's already pored through them, trying to find a Repton reference, though so far with no luck. She might remember if she's seen something about the dig. You're most welcome to take a look.' He smiled. 'I know you'll be careful with the documents and won't muddle things up between boxes.'

'Thank you, Bernard,' Georgina said. 'I'd really like that.'

'Just tell Sybbie and she'll show you where everything is,' Bernard said. 'But perhaps I can show you the estate maps I was telling you about earlier?'

'That would be lovely,' Georgina said, meaning it. 'I mentioned them to Colin, and he sounded interested, too – nothing to do with the case,' she said quickly.

'He's a man after my own heart,' Bernard said. 'I'll have a chat with him later.'

'How are you doing?' Georgina asked, an hour or so later, once Bernard had finished showing her the maps, coming over to where Trish was working at the dig.

'I'll get there,' Trish said. 'It's rough on the students. I mean, if Simon had been taken ill, or been killed in an accident, it would be one thing. But for someone to bash him over the head,

leave him to die and then cover him over with the tarpaulin...'
She shivered. 'I admit, he often rubbed me up the wrong way,
but I wouldn't wish that on my worst enemy.'

'I realise you have a million and one things to do,' Georgina
said, 'but you've had a horrible morning and you're looking a bit
frazzled. How about I take you for a coffee in the farm shop café
and a slice of the best lemon cake known to the universe? I guar-
antee just a tiny break – and Cesca's cake – will make you feel
better able to cope with everything.'

Trish looked torn. 'You're probably right. I could do with a
change of scenery for a few minutes,' she said. 'But I've got the
students to think about.'

'Are any of them postgrads who could supervise the
younger ones?' Georgina asked.

'They're all second and third years. They pretty much
know what they're doing and I don't have to supervise them
every second,' Trish said thoughtfully. 'I'll let Helena know
where I'm going, so they can get me quickly if they need me.
She's the brightest of the bunch; I'm really hoping she'll stay on
to do her master's and then her doctorate.'

'That sounds good,' Georgina said with a smile. 'And maybe
we can ignore the present for a few minutes to give you some
breathing space and talk about what your uncle discovered here,
instead. Bernard said you'd got some letters and sketches.'

Trish nodded. 'I've got photocopies in my tent. I'll go and
get them and have a quick word with Helena.'

A few minutes later, they were sitting at a quiet table in the
farm shop café, with coffee and lemon cake.

Trish closed her eyes in bliss after the first mouthful. 'That's
got to be the best lemon cake ever,' she said.

'Agreed. The recipe's top secret,' Georgina said, 'but it's
irresistible.'

'I'm definitely going to take some home to my partner,' Trish
said. 'Drew loves lemon cake.'

'My partner does, too,' Georgina said with a smile.

'I haven't told Drew about any of this, yet. Or my daughter. Or my sister.' Trish bit her lip. 'How am I going to tell her that her husband's dead?'

'Simon's your brother-in-law?' Georgina asked.

Trish nodded. 'And Jojo – my sister – is a bit... well, for want of a better word, fragile.'

'I'm not going to pry. And you don't have to tell her all on your own,' Georgina said gently. 'Colin will help you.'

Trish frowned. 'How? My sister's in London.'

'He'll find a way,' Georgina said. 'But we're here so you can get a couple of minutes to breathe, and not have to think about all the difficult stuff.'

'The past feels a lot less complicated than the present, right now,' Trish said wryly. 'And you said you wanted to know a bit more about the original dig.' She put an A4-sized box file on the table. 'The sketches and letters are in here,' she said. 'Timothy Marsden was my great-great-great-great-uncle,' she explained, counting on her fingers. 'My great-great-great-gran Clara was his oldest sister. He was very close to her, and from the letters it seemed that she was as much of an antiquarian as he was. He went to stay with the Walters family to help his friend Frederick with the excavation. They'd been at Cambridge together and they were both fascinated by Roman history. Timothy and Frederick pored over books and old maps, and together they worked out where the site was.'

'Can you imagine how exciting that must've been?' Georgina asked. 'Being the first person to see that floor in nearly two thousand years.' Granted, there had been a dead body on the floor when Georgina had seen it, but she'd still been able to appreciate the design – and the peacock was *stunning*.

Trish nodded. 'Even for us, it was a thrill – it's more than a hundred and fifty years since Frederick and Timothy worked on the site. Plus we've found things that they might not have been able to find back then. Anyway, Timothy wrote to Clara every week about the dig and drew her sketches of the progress. She kept all his letters, and the family papers eventually came down to me. When I found the sketch of the floor and read through the letters, I realised that the dig must've been covered over again when they'd finished excavating and then been forgotten about. Nobody seemed to have heard of a possible villa or mosaic floor at Little Wenborough, and there weren't any finds recorded in the heritage archives. I wondered if it might still be there, exactly as Timothy and Frederick had left it, so I got in touch with Bernard. The crop marks made me pretty sure that the paddock was the spot Timothy had worked on. Bernard's estate maps suggested it, too. And actually finding the floor – the floor that Timothy sketched all those years ago, with that incredible peacock...' She blinked back the tears.

'It must've felt very special,' Georgina said quietly.

'It did,' Trish said. 'We've brought his discovery back into the public eye.' She took a deep breath. 'But the saddest thing is that he vanished after the dig, just like the mosaic.'

'Vanished? How do you mean?' Georgina asked.

'His letters to Clara simply stopped. It wasn't like him, so she wondered if maybe he'd been taken ill. She wrote to the Walters family to find out if her brother was all right. But she had a rather cold and curt reply from Frederick's father, saying that Timothy was no longer staying with them and he presumed Timothy had returned to his family in London.'

'That's strange. Timothy was good friends with Frederick, wasn't he?' Georgina asked. 'Something must've happened for him to leave here – and for Frederick's father to cut Clara off like that. Some kind of misunderstanding, maybe?'

'I don't know. But Timothy certainly didn't return to his family in London,' Trish said. 'He never came back at all.'

Because he'd been shot in the back while he was still in Norfolk, Georgina thought. And she really, really hoped that the person who'd shot him didn't turn out to be Frederick. She couldn't imagine anyone related to Bernard being dishonourable, but weren't there black sheep in any family? Then again, hadn't Bernard said that Frederick died of a broken heart? And hadn't Doris said that Timothy remembered being really happy and falling in love?

Something didn't quite add up, here.

She was going to have to be very careful indeed about her research. The last thing she wanted to do was to uncover something that would hurt Sybbie or her family. She also needed to be careful what she said to Trish. 'I wonder what happened? Maybe he did go somewhere else and there was an accident before he could update Clara,' she said. Though if Timothy had been murdered and the killer had got away with it, there wouldn't be any records at all.

'It's a mystery,' Trish said. 'He must've gone *somewhere* from here. People can't just disappear.'

'Maybe he got an offer to work on something else?' Georgina suggested.

'There were all the excavations in Pompeii,' Trish mused. 'Maybe he went there. But surely they would've known here if he was going to Italy, or even Egypt? And surely he would've at least told Clara he was going abroad?'

'Bernard's given me permission to look through the family papers,' Georgina said. 'If I find any clues about where Timothy went, I'll let you know.'

'Thank you,' Trish said.

'Can you find out some names?' Doris asked quietly. 'Then I can put them to Timothy.'

Georgina was a little startled, not realising that Doris had come to the café with her, but nodded once in acknowledgement, knowing that Doris would realise what she was saying but she wouldn't look odd to anyone else. 'My daughter, Beatrice, works as a genealogist, when she isn't acting. She's taught me how to look up things in the records,' she said. 'Now so many of the civil records and parish records have been digitised, it's a lot easier to find things. You might be able to find out something about Timothy on one of the genealogy websites.'

'I wondered that. I even started doing our family tree, though I haven't been able to find out very much about Timothy.' Trish took out her phone and opened a genealogy app. 'This is all I've got. Timothy Robert Marsden, born 20 January 1837, fourth child of Robert Isaac Marsden and Alicia Marsden, née Thompson. I couldn't find a death record anywhere. Timothy was in the 1851 and 1861 census, but I couldn't find him in 1871 or 1881. His older brothers were Robert and Charles, and his sister was Clara.'

'Do you want me to see if I can find anything?' Georgina said. 'I can't promise I'll definitely find you an answer, but I've helped a couple of people solve family mysteries.' With a lot of help from Doris, though she could hardly explain that to a virtual stranger.

'That'd be really kind,' Trish said.

'If you don't mind, I'll take some notes about your family tree to help me,' Georgina said, 'and maybe I could photograph the letters and sketches?'

'They're photocopies rather than the originals, so I can lend them to you, if that helps you find out what happened,' Trish said. 'If you give me your email address, I'll send you the family tree stuff.'

'Thank you,' Georgina said. 'I'll take good care of the box. And would you mind me taking copies of the photocopies, so I can use them for working drafts?'

'That's fine,' Trish said. 'I ought to let Bernard and Sybbie have a copy of the sketch and the relevant letters afterwards, too, considering it's part of the history of their house and their family.'

'I'm sure they'd really appreciate that,' Georgina said.

. . .

Later that afternoon, Trish formally identified Simon's body. Colin had arranged for a colleague in London to visit Joanna at work, to break the news that Simon was dead; mindful of Trish's comment that her sister was fragile, Colin had also asked them to video call him as soon as they'd broken the news, so Trish could talk to her sister and he could support Trish.

'But – how did he die?' Joanna asked plaintively, her eyes red and her cheeks streaked with tears. 'When?'

'We're investigating that,' Colin said. 'As soon as I know more, I'll call you and let you know, and I'll keep your sister in the loop.'

'Dead,' Joanna repeated. 'He *can't* be.'

'I'm sorry, Jojo. I was one of the people who found his body,' Trish said gently. 'And I've identified him, so you don't have to come all the way down here to do it.'

'I...' Joanna shook her head. 'I don't know what to do now.'

Colin had had to break bad news many times over his career, and it never got easier. 'It's a shock, so try to be kind to yourself,' he said. 'We can organise a family liaison officer to help you. Once the pathologist has done her report, when you feel you're ready to see Simon's body, we can arrange to bring you here. Or his body can be brought back to London.'

'And I'll be there,' Trish said. 'It's going to be OK, Jojo. You still have me and Laura. We'll look after you. I'll talk to you soon.'

Joanna nodded, and the screen went blank.

'Who's Laura?' Colin asked.

'My daughter,' Trish said. 'She's the most sensible eighteen-year-old I've ever met. And she's close to her aunt. She'll be there for Joanna.' She glanced at her watch. 'Laura said she had a shift this morning at the bakery where she has a Saturday job, but she should be home by now. I'll give her a ring and tell her what happened, and ask her to call in at Jojo's this evening.'

Now probably wasn't the right time to ask, but Colin wondered. Trish had been candid about the fact she hadn't got on with her brother-in-law and tended to avoid him. Joanna must've been aware of the tension between them. Had it made things awkward between the sisters? And was there more to the difficulties between Simon and Trish than simply professional rivalry or a personality clash?

FOUR

Colin had already messaged Georgina to say that he was going to be late and suggested she should eat dinner without him. Georgina reheated her portion of the risotto she'd made earlier, took the papers out of Trish's box and read Timothy's letters in order as she ate.

'He was obviously very close to Clara,' Doris remarked.

'Yes. It's clear from his letters that he liked the Walters family very much and Frederick was his best friend,' Georgina said. 'I wonder what happened to make Frederick's father so frosty when Clara asked about him?'

'I don't know,' Doris said. 'Timothy remembers Clara, but not his older brothers. He remembers being very good friends with Frederick.'

'Could that be why Frederick's father changed his attitude?' Georgina asked. 'Were Timothy and Frederick more than just very good friends? Was Frederick the one Timothy fell in love with?'

'I'll ask him and see what he says,' Doris said. 'Why else might Frederick's father disapprove of him?'

'Perhaps we're making the wrong assumption that Timothy

might have been romantically involved with Frederick. Did Frederick have a sister, perhaps, or was there a cousin staying with the family, or did Timothy fall for a servant or someone his family wouldn't accept as his partner because they were the wrong class? Did he seduce her and then walk away when it got complicated?' Georgina wrinkled her nose. 'No. The man who wrote these letters doesn't seem like a rake. I don't think he was the type who would've seduced a woman and abandoned her. Plus if Frederick did have a sister or a cousin and Timothy fell in love with her, surely Frederick would've been happy for her to marry his best friend – someone he was close to and trusted?'

'Unless she was already promised to someone else,' Doris suggested. 'And you know what it was like in Victorian times. I know Timothy became friends with Frederick at Cambridge, but if he wasn't the oldest son or his family wasn't actually titled, would Frederick's father have refused him as a potential match for Frederick's sister?' Doris said. 'Perhaps you could ask Bernard if he has a bit more information about his family.'

'I'd rather wait until we've got a better idea of what happened to Timothy. If this becomes messy, I don't want to hurt Bernard or Sybbie,' Georgina said.

'All right. I'll ask Timothy,' Doris said.

'And I'll make a start on the genealogy research,' Georgina said.

Bert sat up, his ears lifting, and his tail began to wag.

'Colin's back,' Doris said. 'I'd better go. See you later.'

Georgina bit her lip. She was going to have to tell Colin about Doris, at some point. She'd learned over the past few months that secrets could fester, and lead to much more damage when they finally came out. Though she was worried about how he was going to react. What would he think when she told him that she could hear a ghost – that she talked to a ghost and had become friends with her? Colin could be a bit stuffy, but Georgina reminded herself that he was a reasonable man and he

knew she wasn't flaky. So would he accept what she told him as
the truth? Or would he react as badly as Jack and Tracey
Beauchamp had, when she'd first told them she could hear the
voice of Jack's sister?

Her musing was interrupted by Colin walking into the
kitchen and giving her a hug. He looked tired, she thought, as he
took off his coat and sat down at the table.

'Tough day?' she asked, putting a bowl of risotto in the
microwave to reheat.

'A bit,' Colin said. 'The body you found is with the pathologist, and I'm pretty sure the death wasn't from natural causes –
but until I get the report, I won't know for sure that the head
wound was the thing that killed him, or what made the wound.
I think it's likely to be some kind of tool used at the dig, but the
archaeologists' tools have all been checked – spades, shovels,
rakes, mallets – and there isn't a trace of blood on them. As the
archaeologists all use gloves when they're working, there aren't
any fingerprints around the site either.' He grimaced. 'Nobody
seemed to like Simon Butterfield very much, but nobody
seemed to hate him enough to want to kill him. Right now, I
have no suspects. Plus I have very sketchy details of an unre-
ported theft from the site by nighthawks that might be
connected to the death. Though it's horrendously vague,
because nobody seems to have any idea what might have been
taken, or who the nighthawks are.' He shook his head. 'At the
moment, I have precisely nowhere to go.'

'That must be so frustrating,' she said.

'It is,' Colin agreed ruefully.

'Maybe forensics will come up with something you can use
to make a start on the case,' she said. 'Or pathology.'

'I hope so. Otherwise I'm going to have to take a closer look
at his colleagues, family and friends.' He accepted the bowl of
risotto gratefully. 'Thank you for dinner. You have no idea how
much I appreciate this.'

Georgina let him eat in peace. He refused a second helping, or the offer of fruit for pudding, but smiled at her when she suggested a mug of tea. 'That would be wonderful. Thanks. Sorry, I should've asked you earlier. How has the rest of your day been?' he asked. 'Obviously finding Simon's body meant you couldn't photograph the mosaic.'

'Hopefully we can try again later in the week,' she said. After the archaeologists had been allowed to clean up the blood – and provided said blood hadn't stained the mosaic. There was no way she could take a picture of a floor with clear signs of a recent death on it.

'You're looking a bit antsy,' he said.

There was a kind of studied neutrality in his tone. As if he was trying very hard not to look at her from a policeman's point of view, but he'd picked up that something wasn't quite right. That there was something she wasn't telling him.

'I'm fine,' she fibbed, feeling guilty for lying to him – but was now the right time to tell him about Doris? Then again, when *would* be the right time?

Colin made a fuss of Bert and took a sip of his tea. 'It's just as well you weren't there today, Bert. If you'd dug a hole in the middle of the dig, you could've been in serious trouble. Digging on historical sites without a permit is a heritage crime, you know.'

Bert wagged his tail and leaned happily against Colin's legs.

'Plus we really don't need a second dead body to complicate things,' he finished, scratching behind Bert's ears.

Georgina winced. 'Um. Funny you should say that.'

His eyes widened with surprise. 'Don't tell me you've found another body?'

'Not an actual body,' she said. 'But there *is* a mystery attached to the original excavation. Trish was saying that her ancestor Timothy – who worked on the dig back in 1865 – disappeared. Nobody had any idea where he went or what happened to him. Timothy used to write to his sister every week from Little Wenborough Manor, where he was staying with Frederick Walters; Trish still has the letters, and she's lent me the photocopies of them. Anyway, Timothy suddenly stopped writing. His sister thought maybe he'd fallen ill, so she wrote to Frederick's family, asking about him. She got a really frosty reply from Frederick's father, saying that Timothy had left the Manor and they presumed he'd returned to his family in London.'

'I agree: that does sound a bit strange. Maybe he went somewhere else on the way back to London,' Colin suggested, 'but he was taken ill and died before he could tell his family where he was.'

Georgina wrinkled her nose. 'Perhaps. But there's no death record for him, and he doesn't show up in any of the census returns, either. He simply vanished.'

'He was an archaeologist. Could he have gone abroad?' Colin asked. 'Egypt and Pompeii were both being excavated, weren't they, back then?'

'If he'd gone abroad, there would still be a paper trail, because a lot of records have been digitised,' she said.

He looked at her. 'Are you all right, Georgie? You seem a bit... I don't know. Out of sorts. I thought that earlier, too, when I took your witness statement. Something's bothering you.'

What was bothering her was the fact that she'd been keeping a secret from him. Doris. For months now she'd wanted to tell him, but she was worried about whether he'd believe her. Colin was grounded. Practical. Like Doris's brother, Jack – who'd flown off the handle when Georgina had told him the truth about his sister. She had absolutely no idea what Colin was going to say when – if? – she told him.

On the other hand, how could she keep this relationship going when she was hiding such a huge secret from him? If she was going to ask him to move in, then she didn't want any secrets between them. He'd told her about the case in his past that had broken him and fractured his marriage; she owed him similar honesty.

'Talk to me,' he said.

Now, when he was tired and busy, was the wrong time to broach the subject. 'It'll keep. You're busy,' she said awkwardly.

'I'm never too busy for you,' he said, his voice gentle. 'Besides, it'll give me something to think about instead of brooding about the fact I'm stuck on my case and getting grumpy about it.'

'It's a weird question, but I was wondering. If you knew that someone had been killed in a particular spot, but the body wasn't there,' she asked carefully, 'what might have happened to it?'

'The most likely thing is that the body was moved and buried elsewhere,' Colin said. 'Though if the killer was panicking and in a rush, they might still have left some evidence behind.' He frowned. 'And you said "knew". How would you know about someone being killed at a particular spot?'

Georgina took a deep breath. Perhaps this was her chance to tell him, after all. 'Because I think Timothy Marsden was killed during the dig, back in 1865.'

Colin blinked. 'That's a bit of a leap, Georgie. What makes you say that?'

'This is going to sound a bit off-the-wall,' she warned, 'but please hear me out. I don't just think Timothy was killed, I *know* he was killed. Just as I knew before I started researching that Anne Lusher was buried under the Great Oak at Hartington Hall, that Friedrich Schmidt was buried under the stage at the theatre and that Ryan Everett was buried at the lighthouse.'

Colin's frown deepened. 'I don't understand. How could you have known any of that before you looked them up in the records?'

'Through Doris Beauchamp,' Georgina said.

'Doris Beauchamp?'

'The girl who died at the bottom of the stairs in this house, on the day I was born,' she reminded him.

'I remember you researching her case.' Colin leaned his elbows on the table and steepled his fingers. 'Georgie, are you trying to tell me you think you're her reincarnation, or something?'

'No, of course not. But it *is* a personal link between us. I think it might be the reason why I can hear her.'

'You can *hear* her?' He frowned. 'What do you mean? How can you hear her?'

'Through my hearing aids. Nobody else can hear her voice – we've tried, and all they hear is static.'

He looked taken aback. 'Who's tried?'

'Well, Jack and Tracey Beauchamp,' she said. 'Doris's younger brother and his wife. You met them last year.'

'Hang on. I'm still trying to get my head round this. Are you saying that you talk to ghosts?'

'No. *A* ghost. Singular.' Georgina felt her face heat, because it wasn't strictly true. She'd also heard her late husband, Stephen, speaking to her in the theatre after their daughter had performed in *Macbeth*. But she had the feeling that Colin would react even less well to that particular nugget of information. 'Over the last few months, Doris has become my friend.'

Colin couldn't quite believe he was hearing this.

Georgina seriously believed that she was friends with a *ghost*?

'We've had this conversation before,' he said, a memory surfacing through the bewilderment in his mind. 'You asked me once, what if the dead could ask questions? And I told you that the dead can't talk. In my experience, there's no such thing as a ghost. Memories, regrets and guilty consciences, yes, and they can sometimes make people *think* they see things. And yes, there's physical evidence we can't see with our eyes, but a pathologist or a forensic expert can find in a lab. But ghosts...' He shook his head. 'No. They don't exist.'

He thought about it. Georgina had mentioned the subject of ghosts again after that conversation, a couple of times. She'd asked him what he thought about people reporting time slips; he'd told her someone might believe they'd had an experience, but there was always a rational explanation for it.

'Georgie. Tell me you don't really believe this,' he said, unable to get his head around what she was claiming.

'Don't dismiss it out of hand, Colin,' she urged. 'There are more things in heaven and earth.'

'Don't try to Shakespeare me out of this,' he said. Normally, he loved it when she quoted at him – like the way she'd teased him earlier about being like Antony if he wore a toga. Right now, it annoyed him. He'd hit brick wall after brick wall in his investigation today, and now she was trying to tell him that a *ghost* could help to solve things? It was the last straw in a seriously frustrating day. Georgina was always so sensible and logical. What had happened to make her believe in all this stuff? Or was it that she was still missing Stephen very badly, and she'd fallen victim to some con artist who was pretending they could contact him for her?

'People who claim to be mediums are really good at cold reading,' he began, trying to keep his tone gentle and not show his irritation. 'They start off with a vague statement that hooks people in, and then they try some high-probability guesses. They pick up on their subject's body language and facial expressions to see if their guesses are in the right direction. If they're right, they reinforce what they've said; if they're not, they move on quickly and try a different guess. Eventually their target believes they're hearing a message from a dear departed one.'

'I haven't been talking to a medium, Colin,' she said quietly. 'I'm saying that, for nearly a year now, I've been able to hear and speak to Doris Beauchamp. Her death wasn't an accident. You *know* that. I uncovered the truth of what happened to her.'

He didn't have an answer for that, but he knew she couldn't possibly have heard the answer from a ghost. Not when ghosts didn't exist.

'And she's helped me solve the cold cases. We're not entirely sure how it works, but victims whose deaths also weren't accidents seem to be able to get in touch with her when we're near the spot where they died or were buried, and then Doris and I work together to find out what really happened to them.'

Was this some kind of elaborate joke, one she was taking a bit too far? Colin wondered. Or did Georgina really believe what she was saying? 'There isn't a shred of scientific proof that ghosts exist,' he reminded her. 'The photographs of "ghosts" have all been debunked. You're a photographer; surely you know that?'

'Of course I do,' she said, a sharp edge of annoyance in her voice. 'Orbs on a photograph are usually caused by insects, dust or lens flare. As for the faces or figures, a lot of them are double exposures, either accidental or deliberate; or they're pareidolia, like the face on the Cydonia region of Mars.'

If she could see the logic in that, why couldn't she see how ghosts could be explained away, too? he wondered.

'Though Doris and I did spend an afternoon taking photos, just in case.' She shrugged. 'Nothing showed on any of them, whether they were digital or analogue. I can't see her or touch her, just hear her. And there isn't any rattling of chains or anything like that. It's just like having a normal conversation with someone on my phone. Though obviously I don't want people realising I'm talking to someone invisible, in case they ask awkward questions, so half the time I pretend I'm on my phone or just a middle-aged woman muttering to myself.'

But wasn't that precisely what she was doing – talking to herself? Letting herself believe something that wasn't true? Or was this her way of trying to tease him out of his scratchy mood? If it was that, it definitely wasn't working. 'If this is some sort of joke, Georgie, it's gone a bit too far and it's not funny.'

'It's not a joke,' she said. 'I proved it to Jack and Tracey Beauchamp.'

He narrowed his eyes at her. 'How?'

'I told them where there was once a loose slab around the fireplace, where his dad found a coin and a musket ball,' Georgina said.

Colin shook his head in disbelief. 'Given how old this house is, of course anyone who lives here would find forgotten items from the past when they were doing repairs or renovating the house. You've just mentioned two of the most common things people find under floorboards. It's a coincidence.'

She folded her arms, looking frustrated. 'No, Colin, it's more than that. Look at the cold cases I've worked on.'

'You solved them with documentary evidence,' Colin said. 'Letters, diaries, records. The probate genealogy work Bea does means that she's learned how to use records to unravel a trail. She's taught you how to do it – and you're good at it, too.'

'Has it ever occurred to you to ask where I found the names of the people in the first place? Before I started looking?' she asked.

'Doris was in the local newspaper archives.' He went through them systematically. 'Anne's name was in the Hartington archives. Friedrich's name was in the theatre programmes. Ryan was on the missing person's list.'

A muscle twitched in Georgina's jaw. 'I found their names there, yes. But I knew about them before I started looking for them. I knew who I was looking for, which saved me a lot of time.' She folded her arms and glared at him. 'Clearly you don't believe me.'

'I'm not saying you're a liar, Georgie,' he said, not wanting to get into a ridiculous argument with her – one that neither of them could win, because there wasn't a compromise. You couldn't half believe something. 'I just don't believe in ghosts.'

'All right,' she said, her temper getting the better of her. 'I'm telling you now that Timothy Marsden was shot in the back, in 1865. Doris says he remembers hearing an explosion and then there was a terrific pain in his back. I don't know who killed him, or why, or whether it was deliberate or an accident, but I'm going to find out and give his spirit some closure. I think he died at Little Wenborough Manor, probably somewhere near the dig site, and that's why he disappeared. But this time there isn't a body, so we can't direct Bert to dig anywhere and unearth part of the skeleton. I'm going to solve the puzzle, Colin, and find the evidence – and then you'll know I'm telling the truth.'

Maybe Georgina had the kind of realistic dreams that made you think something had happened, even when it hadn't, Colin thought. But he wasn't going to say that. 'I don't want to fight with you, Georgie.'

'I don't want to fight with you, either,' she said. 'Tell you what – let's try something else. You want proof? I'll stand here in the kitchen, with my face to the dresser and my back to you. Write something down in your notebook, or draw something, turn the notebook face-down on the table, and Doris will tell me what you did. The fact there's no way I can see what you're doing – or your reflection – should prove to you that I'm telling the truth.'

She went and stood with her face to the dresser. 'I'll count to ten. Then I'll turn round and tell you.'

Georgina could be unbelievably stubborn, Colin thought. 'So are you saying Doris is with you now?'

'Yes.'

'And was this her suggestion?'

'No. It's mine. If you must know, Doris says this is risky because your opinions are set and you won't change them, and she doesn't want me to end up having a massive row with you.'

Which was the sort of thing a friend would say – but there was nobody there in the room apart from the two of them and Bert. Was Georgina hearing voices that weren't there? She'd been close to death on several occasions recently. Was the shock only coming out now? Should he ring Bea and Will, her children, and let them know he was worried about her?

With her back towards him, Georgina counted out loud to ten.

Colin put his notebook face-down on the table.

She turned to face him again. 'You didn't write or draw anything,' she said.

'That doesn't prove a thing. In terms of probability, that was fifty-fifty,' Colin said. 'Either I wrote something, or I wrote nothing. But you made an educated guess and picked the more likely option; you already know I don't believe in ghosts, so it follows that I wasn't likely to write anything.'

'You can be really pompous and stuffy, sometimes.' She glared at him.

'And you're resorting to insults because you know I'm right,' he said, stung that she thought that of him. 'Have you told Will or Bea that you talk to ghosts?'

'No,' she said.

'No, because you know they'd start worrying about you.' He sighed. '*I'm* worried about you, Georgie.'

'Don't be. I'm perfectly sane. And I'm telling you now because we're together and I don't want to keep any secrets from you.' She looked furiously at him. 'Bert knows when Doris is around. She's directed him to dig in a certain spot – that's how he found the remains. For pity's sake, you were *there* when he uncovered the body by the lighthouse, a couple of months ago. You were the one holding his lead at the time!'

Bert whined softly, and left Colin to sit in a spot not *quite* at Georgina's feet, but in a space near her, as if he was sitting in front of 'Doris' – a ghost Colin knew couldn't possibly exist.

Georgina had a point about the body by the lighthouse. Then again, so did he. Dogs had a much better sense of smell than humans did, but that didn't necessarily mean a dog would be able to sniff out a skeleton; Colin thought that suggesting it would only annoy Georgina. 'What about Sybbie?' he asked. 'Or Cesca, or Jodie?' Her 'Three Musketeers' friends, the ones she was closest to in Little Wenborough. 'Have you mentioned Doris to them?'

'No,' Georgina said.

'Because you know they'll say the same as me and they'll worry about you, too. Maybe—'

'Don't you *dare*,' Georgina cut in, 'suggest that I need to go and see Dr Fairley. Or ask Sally Forrester' – the part-time GP from the next village, who also ran the Feathers, the pub where Colin and Georgina often ate – 'if she can recommend someone I could talk to.'

Colin flinched, feeling guilty colour wash into his face. He *had* been about to suggest talking to Sally. 'You're building this up into something it isn't.'

She folded her arms and glared at him again. 'The bottom line is, you don't believe me and you think I'm having some kind of mental breakdown.'

'I believe you think you hear something,' he said carefully.

'I'm as sane as you are, Colin,' she said, pulling out a chair and sitting down.

Sometimes he didn't feel all that sane. He'd definitely had dark nights of the soul. But he'd still never believed he could talk to the dead – or, rather, that they could talk back to him.

'The first time I heard Doris talk, I thought I'd accidentally switched my phone to a radio station broadcasting a play – you know, like when you accidentally pocket-dial someone,' Georgina said. 'She told me not to go into Rookery Barn. Except I did, and I found Roland Garnett's dead body in the bedroom. And then she kept talking to me. I was worried that maybe she was the person who'd killed him and she was hiding somewhere, talking to me.'

'Why didn't you say anything to one of the officers who came here?' he asked.

'And what would they have thought?' She rolled her eyes. 'Oh, look, here's a middle-aged woman who lives on her own and has a very vivid imagination?'

At the age of fifty-three, Georgina *was* a middle-aged woman, and she had a creative job that went well with that vivid imagination; but Colin decided not to say that. Though she didn't live quite on her own; she had her spaniel for company, and Colin stayed over most nights, nowadays. 'They would have at least checked for evidence of someone being here.'

'But that's my point, Colin. There *isn't* any evidence, because Doris is a ghost and she doesn't leave any physical traces. I didn't believe in her at first, either. Until she got me to look her up in the civil records.'

'She lived in your house, half a century ago. She died tragically young, and you found out what really happened to her. I understand all that,' Colin said. 'But I'm sorry, Georgie. I can't – I just *can't* believe that you hear her voice.'

'I don't understand it, either.' Her face looked pinched. 'But it's real, Colin. I'm not lying.'

'Of course you're not lying.'

'And I'm not deluded or having some kind of breakdown, either.' She shook her head in frustration. 'This has been going on for months and months. Doris and I talk about Shakespeare and poetry – she was going to be an English teacher. We watch dramas together. We listen to audiobooks together. We've become *friends*.'

But it just wasn't possible. Ghosts didn't exist. It was obvious that Georgina believed in this ghost, but he couldn't. He had no idea what to do or how to react, so he simply stared at her.

She drummed her fingers on the table, clearly impatient with his refusal to believe her. 'All right. Think about Sherlock Holmes – and yes, I'm perfectly aware that he's a fictional character. But that whole thing about eliminating the impossible, and what's left has to be the truth, however improbable... that's true, isn't it?'

'Except,' Colin said, 'ghosts *are* impossible, Georgie. And I know what *Hamlet* says, too, apart from the fact you've already quoted that particular speech at me.' He huffed out a breath. 'That's the whole point about fiction, Georgie. It isn't true. Sherlock Holmes, Miss Marple, Inspector Morse – none of them existed in real life.'

'But fiction contains truths, dressed up as drama,' she countered. 'It gives people the space to think about issues.'

'I don't want to argue with you,' he said again. 'But I don't believe in ghosts, and nothing you do or say is going to convince me.' He couldn't handle any more of this conversation, and he didn't want to say something he'd come to regret later. Better to put some space between them, for now. 'I think,' he said, 'it might be a good idea if I went back to my place in Norwich. Thank you for dinner. And I'm sorry...'

He was sorry for a lot of things.

Including walking out on her right now.

But it was the only way he could think of to stop the argument turning into the kind of row there was no coming back from.

FIVE

'Oh, Georgie. I'm so sorry,' Doris said, when Colin had closed the kitchen door quietly behind him. 'The last thing I wanted to do was to come between you and Colin.'

'I thought he was better than that,' Georgina said. 'I thought he'd at least listen to what I had to say and think rationally about it. I'm so disappointed in him. Stubborn, stuffy, *blinkered* man!' She banged her fist on the table in frustration.

Bert whined and nudged her knee, and Georgina bent to make a fuss of him.

'He'll calm down,' Doris said, sounding hopeful.

'I don't know about *him* calming down – as far as I'm concerned, he needs to apologise to both of us before he sets foot in this house again,' Georgina said crossly. 'It's insulting. You exist, all right. And I don't need help from a psychiatrist.'

She was still feeling hurt and angry, the next morning, when she called in to the farm shop to pick up some supplies.

'A ready meal for one and no cake?' Francesca frowned. 'Is everything all right, Georgie?'

'Yes. Why wouldn't it be?' Georgina snapped.

The younger woman's eyes widened. 'Ouch. Sorry for asking.'

Georgina grimaced, realising how unfair she was being. 'Sorry, Cesca. I shouldn't take it out on you.'

'What's happened? Actually, no, we can't talk here. I'll get Rachel to take over from me. Go into my office, take a seat and I'll bring you a coffee,' Francesca said.

Georgina went into the office at the far end of the farm shop, taking the visitor's chair in Francesca's very tidy, very modern office. The only things on her friend's desk were a spider plant, a laptop and a coaster for a mug; everything else was tucked neatly away in a filing cabinet or the bookcase next to her desk. There was a year planner on the pinboard, as well as a several charts.

A couple of minutes later, Francesca came in with a tray containing a mug of coffee for Georgina, a red berry tea for herself and two pieces of lemon cake.

'Eat the cake and do a couple of breathing exercises,' she directed.

The lemon cake helped.

But should she tell Francesca what was wrong? Or would her friend side with Colin and think that Georgina had completely lost it? Then again, she didn't have a choice now. If she didn't tell her friends about Doris, it meant there was some truth in what Colin had said yesterday. And Francesca *had* asked.

'OK. The sugar should be kicking in by now. Talk to me,' Francesca said.

'This could ruin our friendship,' Georgina warned. 'In fact, it could ruin my friendships with everyone.'

'You'd have to do something fairly extreme for that to happen,' Francesca said mildly. 'Tell me what's upset you.'

'I had a fight with Colin last night,' Georgina confessed. 'He went back to his place, and I don't know when or if he's coming back.'

'That sounds a bit dramatic for you – or Colin,' Francesca said, raising her eyebrows.

'It was,' Georgina admitted. 'Tell me, Cesca – what's your opinion of ghosts?'

Francesca looked surprised. 'Haven't we talked about that before, when you first found out about that poor girl who died in your house?'

'Mmm,' Georgina said.

'I always thought it was just, you know, an entertaining story. Like the one Sybbie tells about the bit of the garden where if you throw a tennis ball and it lands there, the dogs will just circle it, refusing to set foot inside and you have to fetch it for them,' Francesca said. 'I love the way she acts that one out. But then...' She paused. 'Something a bit odd happened, the week before last.'

'What?' Georgina asked.

'I'd gone to fetch the Scrabble board from the drawing room – Sybbie and I were challenging Bernard and Giles to a game after dinner.'

Georgina remembered Sybbie once telling her about the Grey Lady of Little Wenborough Manor, who sometimes appeared in the drawing room. Was Francesca about to tell her she'd seen a ghost?

'The curtains were closed, and the overhead light in there has been playing up for ages – I think Bernard needs to get the dimmer switch looked at,' Francesca continued. 'Anyway, I saw this woman. She was a bit younger than me, by the look of her. Her dark hair was worn in a slightly old-fashioned style – in a bun, with rolls at the side. And maybe it was the light, but she looked...' She wrinkled her nose. 'The best way I can describe it is like a photograph on your phone, when you're playing about with colours and you take the saturation right down.'

'Grey and pale?' Georgina suggested.

Francesca nodded. 'I wasn't scared. Something about her told me she was kind. Gentle. She smiled at me. Then I blinked, and she was gone.'

'Did you tell Sybbie?' Georgina asked.

'No. I tried to convince myself it was just my imagination. But I've seen her a couple more times in the Manor, now. Every time, she smiles. It's almost as if she's keeping an eye on me.'

'Sybbie told me there's a family story about when women see the Grey Lady,' Georgina said quietly.

'Ah. *That* story. I've kind of outed myself, then,' Francesca said.

'Yes, you have. Congratulations. And don't worry – I won't tell anyone,' Georgina promised. 'But maybe you should talk to Sybbie? I know she's worried that you're working too hard.'

'She's already told you about the baby, hasn't she?' Francesca asked wryly.

'Um.' Georgina winced. 'I didn't mean to drop her in it. Cesca, she didn't tell me just to pass on a juicy bit of gossip. She adores you. She's worried about you, and Bernard was doing the "middle-aged man brushing everything emotional to one side" thing. She wanted someone to talk to, and she knew she could trust me to keep it confidential.'

'Is that why you asked me about ghosts?' Francesca asked. 'To get me to tell you about the baby, and then you could persuade me to talk to Sybbie?'

'Actually, no.' Georgina gave her a crooked smile. 'I asked about ghosts because that's why I had a fight with Colin.'

'You had a fight with him about ghosts?' Francesca sounded surprised.

'About a particular ghost,' Georgina said. 'Doris, the girl who died in my house on the day I was born.'

'I think all the hairs have just gone up on my arms,' Francesca said, rubbing her arms.

'Don't worry. She's not an M.R. James-type vengeful spirit. She's not in the slightest bit scary. But Colin thinks I'm barking mad. According to him, there's no such thing as a ghost. There's no scientific proof, therefore I must be imagining things.' Georgina shook her head. 'But I'm not. I hear her voice in my hearing aids.'

'What, as if you're listening to an audiobook or a play?' Francesca asked, looking intrigued.

'Exactly like that,' Georgina said, relieved that Francesca seemed to be so understanding – or at least was listening to her without dismissing it out of hand. 'Nobody else can hear her. Her brother tried listening to my hearing aids, when I told him about her, but all he could hear was static. He had to wait for Doris to tell me the answers to his questions.'

'That's quite...' Francesca blinked. 'Does Sybbie know about this?'

'No. Apart from telling Doris's brother and sister-in-law, I haven't said anything to anyone. Not until my row with Colin, last night.'

'You can talk to ghosts.' Francesca looked thoughtful. 'I wonder if you can talk to the Grey Lady at the Manor?'

'I doubt it,' Georgina said. 'I couldn't hear Anne at Hartington Hall.'

'The woman whose remains you found buried under the oak tree,' Francesca remembered.

'Anne told her story to Doris – as much as she could remember; Doris told me, and we pieced the rest of it together through documents in the archives,' Georgina said.

'I really think you should talk to Sybbie,' Francesca said. 'For what it's worth, Georgie, I believe you. Maybe a couple of weeks ago, I would've suggested that seeing a ghost was a trick of the light – or, in your case, that there was some setting on your hearing aids that meant you were picking up sounds from something else without realising it – but now I've seen the Grey Lady for myself. And there are things we know now that wouldn't have made sense to anyone two hundred years ago. I mean, back then, what would people have thought about mobile phones and video calls? Maybe ghosts are like that for us now, and at some time in the future we'll understand them.'

It was funny how that made Georgina feel so much better. 'Thank you, Cesca,' she said. 'I think *you* should talk to Sybbie, too.'

Francesca looked at her watch. 'She'll be in the greenhouse right now. Let's take our drinks over – and I'll take her tea and a brownie.'

Sybbie was indeed in the large old-fashioned greenhouse, pricking out seedlings.

'What's this, a delegation?' she asked.

'Simply tea and cake, dearest ma-in-law,' Francesca said with a smile, nodding at the tray Georgina had insisted on carrying.

'Though we both wanted a chat with you,' Georgina said.

'That sounds faintly ominous,' Sybbie said, taking the tray and putting it on the greenhouse staging, and gesturing to Francesca to take the chair. 'Thank you. Is the brownie to sweeten me up for something?'

'No, it's because it's time you had a break and a sit-down. Even though you've just given me your chair,' Francesca said. 'I told Georgie about the baby, by the way. Not that she needed me to.'

Sybbie's cheeks went pink. 'I'm sorry, Cesca. I know you told me in confidence, and I honestly haven't said a word to anyone else.'

'You had my best interests at heart,' Francesca said, 'and I would pick Georgie any day as someone you can trust to keep things quiet. And stop worrying about me. I'll rest properly when I need to. I'm sitting down now, am I not?'

'For about three seconds,' Sybbie said, rolling her eyes. 'What did you want to talk to me about, Georgie?'

'This is all going to sound a bit weird.' Georgina took a deep breath. 'We've talked about ghosts before. You told me about the dogs avoiding that area in the garden, and we both know what it means if you smell lavender really strongly at Hartington Hall.'

'Ye-es,' Sybbie said.

'Plus you told me about the Grey Lady here,' Georgina added.

'And I saw her, the other week,' Francesca piped in, as if it was the most ordinary thing in the world to see a ghost.

'Did you?' Sybbie looked surprised. 'When?'

'The night Giles and I thrashed you and Bernard at Scrabble. She was in the drawing room, and she smiled at me,' Francesca explained. 'I've seen her a couple of times since then, too. Just a little glimpse, as if she's checking in on me.'

'You must be having a girl,' Sybbie said, looking wistful.

'A girl?' Francesca looked shocked. 'How do you know that?'

'The Grey Lady only appears when you're having a girl. Bernard's grandmother saw her when she was pregnant with his aunt. Bernard's mother never saw her.' Sybbie shrugged. 'I didn't see her when I was pregnant with Giles.'

'You need to ask Sybbie about when *she did* see the Grey Lady – whose name is Lizzie, by the way,' Doris murmured. 'But not in front of Cesca.'

Georgina gave a very slight nod to make sure Doris knew she'd got the message.

'So are you here for moral support, Georgie, while my daughter-in-law worries that I'm going to think she's gone crackers?' Sybbie asked.

'No. Cesca's here for moral support for me, because maybe

you're going to think that *I've* gone crackers,' Georgina said. 'There's a ghost at Rookery Farm, too. Doris.'

'The girl who died. I remember. You researched her story,' Sybbie said. 'Have you seen her?' She sounded intrigued rather than judgemental, which made Georgina relax.

'No. I, um, hear her,' Georgina said, and explained about the hearing aids, how she'd started communicating with Doris and how Doris had helped her solve the cold cases.

'Well, then,' Sybbie said, patting her arm. 'Not everything can be explained. And I have to admit, I was starting to wonder how you always know just where to look for documents and the like. I wasn't sure whether it's that you're terribly clever and see connections that the rest of us aren't quite bright enough to spot, or whether you have more than your fair share of luck and we ought to ask you to pick our numbers for the lottery. But now I know the real reason.'

Her friends had accepted what she said without arguing with her – and it felt as if a weight had just fallen off Georgina's shoulders. 'So you don't think I've completely lost my marbles and need to have a word with Dr Fairley or Sally Forrester?' she checked.

'No, dear girl,' Sybbie said. 'You're perfectly sane. Who said you've gone mad?'

Georgina winced. 'I had a row about it with Colin, last night.'

'Hmm,' Sybbie said. 'When we're young, we like to think we'll handle things better than our parents did. We like to think we're more enlightened and that we'll stay that way. But unfortunately time has a habit of making us more rigid, not more flexible. Colin's a good man, but he can be a tiny bit stuffy at times.' She raised her eyebrows. 'If we didn't tease him about his resemblance to a certain actor in a certain period drama to loosen him up a bit, I think there's a danger he could become quite uptight.' She grinned. 'You missed a chance, there, you know. You should've told him he was as proud and prejudiced as Mr Darcy.'

Georgina couldn't help smiling at the good-natured teasing, even though she was miserable. 'I think telling him about Doris was a step too far. He left.'

Sybbie rolled her eyes. '*Men*. Why they have to be difficult instead of being sensible and talking things through...' She shook her head. 'But why on earth did you tell him in the first place?'

'Because,' Georgina said, 'I wanted his advice.'

Francesca raised her eyebrows. 'I think my dearest ma-in-law might be a much better bet when it comes to that particular subject, Georgie.'

'What did you need advice about?' Sybbie asked.

'The dig,' Georgina said.

'There's another skeleton?' Sybbie asked, clearly thinking back to what had happened at Hartington Hall. 'Do you need us to run interference while Bert escapes and finds the spot where it's buried, then digs where he's not supposed to – oh, and please tell me it's not in the middle of that gorgeous peacock mosaic?'

'Thank you for the offer, but no, and the peacock's quite safe,' Georgina said. 'This time, there isn't a body.'

'How,' Francesca asked, 'do you know that?'

'Doris,' Georgina said. 'I would have confided in you earlier, Sybbie, but this might have something to do with Bernard's family, and it's...' She bit her lip. 'Well, awkward.'

'Dear girl, I know you'd never do anything to deliberately hurt Bernard or me,' Sybbie said. 'And he's already given you permission to look in the family archives. He won't go back on his word. So whose is the body, and what's the issue?'

'It's Timothy Marsden – Trish's great-uncle who was involved with the first dig,' Georgina said. 'Doris says he was working at the dig – he was very happy – and he fell in love with someone. Then the next thing he can remember is an explosion and a terrific pain in his back. We think someone shot him in the back.'

'That would fit with an explosion and a pain in the back,' Sybbie said. 'But who killed him?' Then her eyes widened. 'You don't think one of Bernard's family...?'

'I hope not,' Georgina said. 'Timothy was best friends with Bernard's ancestor, Frederick.'

'The one who died from a broken heart, after his wife died,' Sybbie mused.

Georgina nodded. 'But suddenly Timothy stopped writing letters to his older sister, Clara. When she wrote to the Manor, asking about her brother, Frederick's father wrote back and said Timothy had left, presumably returning to his family in London.'

'Except he never arrived, from the sound of it,' Francesca said. 'Because he was killed. Here in Little Wenborough?'

'I think,' Sybbie said, 'we have a mystery to solve. But you're right, Georgie. Maybe we shouldn't involve Bernard just yet. Not until we know a bit more.'

'Much as I would love to help you both – and Doris – investigate,' Francesca said, 'I have a business to run. Before you ask, Sybbie, yes, I'll make sure I rest properly. I'm going to learn to delegate.'

'And you can start with this,' Sybbie said, gesturing to the tray. 'We'll bring it back in a bit.'

'All right,' Francesca said, and left the greenhouse with a smile.

Georgina waited until Francesca had closed the greenhouse door and was well out of earshot. 'So when did you see the Grey Lady, Sybbie?' she asked quietly.

Sybbie blew out a breath. 'Did you work that out for yourself, or did Doris tell you to ask?'

'Doris,' Georgina said.

'Well, if I had any doubts before, you've definitely convinced me now. I haven't told a soul about seeing the Grey Lady. Not even Bernard.' Sybbie took a sip of tea to compose herself. 'Obviously I won't breathe a word about it to Cesca, but I miscarried at eight weeks, about six months before I fell pregnant with Giles. Obviously it was too early to tell if the baby was a girl or a boy, but I was convinced it was a girl. I was going to call her Sarah.'

Now Georgina understood Doris's warning, and also why Sybbie was worrying so much about Francesca, because her daughter-in-law was eight weeks pregnant right now.

'I was in bits,' Sybbie continued. 'So was Bernard, but his way of coping was to throw himself into his work. I suppose I did the same; at least physical work in the garden tired me out enough so I could get some rest at night. Anyway, I'd gone to bed early one night, and I was halfway to crying myself to sleep when I became suddenly aware of... a presence, let's say. I looked up, and the Grey Lady was sitting on the end of my bed. She wasn't frightening – she felt comforting,' Sybbie said. 'She told me that she was sorry I'd had such a heartbreaking loss, but next time it would be all right. I mean, I know the family story is that you see her when you're having a girl and I didn't see her when I was pregnant, I saw her after I'd lost the baby, but I...' She shook her head. 'Well, she could hardly appear to me and tell me I was going to lose the baby, could she? It felt as if she was trying to comfort me, at a time when I really needed that.'

'I get that,' Georgina said gently.

'When I fell pregnant with Giles,' Sybbie continued, 'I was so paranoid for the first few weeks, terrified that I'd lose this baby, too. The day I was eight weeks pregnant with him, I couldn't settle all day. The slightest twinge made me feel sick with worry. But we got past it. I got to twelve weeks. Day by day I grew more confident. And – well, I have my lovely boy.' She gave a wry smile. 'I had to wait for him to marry Cesca before I finally got a daughter, mind. But I'm so grateful for them both.'

'Oh, Sybbie.' Georgina hugged her hard. 'I'm so sorry you lost your baby.'

'*Don't* tell Cesca,' Sybbie said.

'Of course I won't. And that's why Doris told me not to ask you in front of her,' Georgina said.

'I often wonder, did our Grey Lady lose a baby?' Sybbie asked. 'A girl, perhaps, and that's why she keeps an eye on any woman in the Manor who's pregnant with a girl?'

'Maybe,' Georgina said. 'Her name's Lizzie, according to Doris.'

'Lizzie. That's a nice name. Sometimes,' Sybbie said, 'you can't explain something in rational terms. And it's my belief that love is too strong to just vanish when someone dies. I think that's why our Grey Lady – our Lizzie – stays around. Because she cares about this family. It's love and reassurance keeping her here.'

Georgina had to blink away the tears. 'That's a lovely way of looking at it.'

Sybbie looked at her. 'What are you going to do about Colin?'

'I don't know,' Georgina said honestly. 'I'm not going to deny what I know is true, just to make him feel better. But he can't deal with what I told him. Maybe we need a few days apart to think things over.'

'Don't do or say anything rash,' Sybbie advised. 'I know how lonely you've been since you lost Stephen. Colin's made you smile again, and I think you're good for each other. Besides, nobody's perfect.'

'That's true. I'm certainly not, and I don't expect anyone else to be,' Georgina said. 'I was going to suggest we made it a bit more official between us and he moves in with me. That's why I told him about Doris – I didn't want to have such a huge secret between us. And it looks as if I was right to tell him. It would've been far worse if he'd moved in, found out about Doris and then walked out on me.' She shook her head. 'I don't know if I can be with someone who doesn't believe me, though.' She wrinkled her nose. 'I can't do anything about it right now, so it's pointless running over and over it in my head. I'd rather keep myself busy. Can I start digging in your archives?'

'Dear girl, of course you can.' Sybbie smiled at her. 'And I would be delighted to help you.' She glanced at the paper carrier bag emblazoned with the farm shop's name. 'Does that need to go in the fridge?'

'Yes, please,' Georgina said gratefully.

SIX

Colin sat at his desk and stared at the text that had just popped up on his phone screen.

> I think we could do with a few days apart.
> Georgina

It didn't even sound like the sort of text she usually sent. There was none of the warmth he was used to in her messages. She'd used her full first name, instead of her initial. And, most tellingly, there was no kiss at the end. This felt even more stilted and formal than the very first texts they'd exchanged after he'd initially met her, last year.

She was clearly still angry with him after their row last night.

He felt sick. Was she breaking up with him? Did she expect him to apologise?

Of course he'd apologise for upsetting her. He *loved* her, for pity's sake, even if he wasn't very good at telling her so. But how could she expect him to believe in something that he knew in his bones simply didn't exist? It wasn't reasonable – or fair.

It didn't help that he'd slept so badly, the night before. He'd spent so many nights at Georgie's that he wasn't used to sleeping in his own bed anymore. And his bed had definitely felt too wide, without her in his arms. Waking up alone had made the morning feel leaden and lumpy even before he'd dragged himself out of bed and into the police station.

He couldn't quite bring himself to answer her text.

He couldn't throw himself into work, either, because he was stuck. He needed the pathology report on the dead body, but Sammy Grainger had other cases she needed to deal with before she could conduct the post-mortem on Simon Butterfield. At the moment, Colin had no confirmation of the rough time of death or the cause of death. It looked to him as if Simon had been killed by someone striking his head with some kind of weapon – most probably a spade of some sort, if the theory that Simon had disturbed the nighthawks was correct – but was that really the case, or was the head injury taking Colin's attention away from what had really happened? Until he heard back from Sammy, he didn't really have enough information to pull together a proper list of suspects, let alone solve the crime. The footprints Georgina had seen turned out to be Simon's, and all the recent calls and messages on his phone had been from his wife. The only odd thing was that the body had been moved slightly, possibly from being on his front to on his back. By the person who'd hit him? Or by someone who'd found him and panicked?

Trish Melton had been Simon's second-in-command at the dig. Colin considered the facts. She was one of the last people who'd seen him alive, and was one of the people who'd found his corpse; plus she was Simon's sister-in-law, which blurred the lines between work and family. She'd disliked Simon and felt he'd bulldozed his way into her project as lead archaeologist – but was that enough of a motive for her to kill him? Was there something relevant in their family life?

She'd been open about not having an alibi for the night

Simon was killed, but was it a double bluff? Would she have had the strength to deal the killing blow? She was wiry, and if she was used to digging then she probably could have hefted the theoretical shovel at Simon's head quite easily. But there was a big difference between theory and practice; she might have been physically able to do it, but did she have the killer's mindset that would have allowed her to hit him over the head?

The students were each other's alibis, as they'd all shared a tent with another person. They all seemed to prefer Trish to Simon, too, but Colin hadn't got a sense of active loathing from any of them when he'd interviewed them about Simon. Unless his instincts were letting him down at work as badly as they were letting him down in his private life, he thought with a sigh.

Aside from the archaeology team, Bernard and Sybbie were each other's alibi. Neither of them had particularly warmed to Simon, but neither of them had a motive to kill him, either. He knew he needed to approach this without bias, because they were his friends; but the lack of motive pointed strongly to them not being the killers.

The nighthawks who'd raided the dig? If Simon had caught them digging up treasure, they would've wanted to silence him. That gave them the motive, the opportunity – and, if they'd used a spade or whatever to hit him over the head, the means

But. There was a huge problem: Colin didn't have a clue who these alleged nighthawks were. Could they be local, and perhaps known to the police already? Or had they come here from somewhere further afield, as part of a wider network?

He'd go through the files here, and then maybe he'd have a word with his old team in London. Someone there might know more about the nationwide operation to crack down on heritage crimes. Until then, without a lead, he had nowhere to go. For a moment, he found himself entertaining the idea that Georgina's ghostly friend might be able to tell him something... but then he shook himself. Utterly ridiculous. Supernatural beings didn't exist.

Though there was something that had been niggling at him since he'd interviewed the students. He checked his notes. Helena had told him about the nighthawks, and she'd said something that might just be significant: *They always seem to happen on Simon's digs.*

Was it true? If so, why? Was it as Trish had said, that Simon had reported things very early, to feed his vanity, and the nighthawks had spotted the opportunities? Or had Simon had a connection to the nighthawks? Could he have been part of the network, or passed on information? But if so, why? Surely, as an archaeologist, Simon would've wanted to preserve the history around the finds? And why would the nighthawks want to kill him, given that he was helping them?

Tired of questions without answers, Colin called his old team. He found himself patched through to Mei Zhang, the inspector who'd worked with him and Georgina when the actor playing Banquo had been murdered at the Regency Theatre in Islington.

'Good to speak to you again, Mei,' he said. 'It's Colin Bradshaw in Norwich.'

'What can I do for you, Colin?' she asked.

He ran her through the brief details of his case. 'One of the students said the site had been raided by nighthawks, a few days ago. The other archaeologist confirmed it, but said they didn't know what had been taken, or by whom. I'm guessing that there's a group of people involved in a national network of heritage thieves, and I was wondering if the Heritage Crimes team have a list of people known to work in this area. They're based near you, aren't they?'

'Yes.'

'I know you're probably up to your eyes,' Colin said, 'but can I ask a favour and see if you could get someone to check it for me? Because apparently this isn't the first time it's happened on one of Simon Butterfield's digs. I want to see if there's any kind of pattern to the nighthawks' raids. He works at St Edmund's College in London.'

'Butterfield,' Mei said. 'That name rings a bell, but not St Edmund's College. Hang on, and I'll have a look on the computer.' Colin could hear the sound of keys clicking in the background. 'Right. Yes, it seems we've got several reports from the university about nighthawks at digs, going back over the last five years, although they're in different parts of the country. Looking very quickly at them, it seems that several of the digs concerned were led by Simon Butterfield.'

So there was a potential link? Colin's hopes rose.

'But the evidence seems to consist mainly of holes in the ground, dug at random, and it's possible that some of those holes were caused by animals,' Mei continued. 'The archaeology team working on the digs never saw anyone digging, and during questioning it seemed they didn't have any idea what might have been taken, either.' She sighed. 'That's why most of the instances of nighthawks aren't reported well, and it's even harder to prosecute. It's categorised as theft, but when the details are this sketchy, we can't do much about it.'

'So quite a few of the reports were on Simon's digs? That does suggest they might be linked,' Colin said. 'But surely someone must've seen *something*. People can't actually appear silently and vanish again without a trace.' *Like a ghost.* He pushed the thought aside.

'These people use very sophisticated equipment. Including night-vision goggles, so they don't need to use any kind of lights – which means they're not drawing visual attention to themselves, and they're also not stumbling around in the dark, making a noise that might disturb anyone,' Mei said. 'Apparently sometimes they wander around at a dig during the day, scoping out the site – a clipboard and a hi-vis vest make them look like genuine volunteers on a dig. An ordinary-looking guy who doesn't stand out from anyone else in the team... Who's going to challenge him?' She paused. 'There is something else. I might be making an assumption, but last month one of my team was seconded to another department, looking at a museum where things have gone missing. Lots of little things that had been donated decades ago, so the cataloguing and records weren't like they are nowadays, and nobody noticed the items were missing until there was a recent audit. They're not quite sure what's gone because it was never recorded properly in the first place, but now they're aware of the problem, they're changing their processes.'

'Little things. The sort of items that nighthawks might sell to a private collector?' Colin asked.

'According to Fitz – my DC – it was mainly gems, but also some very small pieces of jewellery,' Mei confirmed. 'And what made me think of it just now is that one of the people at the museum is called Butterfield. I remember Fitz mentioning it. It's not a particularly common name. Let me check.' Colin heard a few more keys tapping. 'Yes. Joanna Butterfield.'

'Unless there's more than one Joanna Butterfield in London, that might well be Simon's wife,' Colin said. 'I don't know her occupation, though, only her address.'

'Does your Joanna Butterfield have an Islington address?' Mei asked.

'Yes. Does yours?' Colin checked.

'Yes. So I think it's pretty safe to assume they're the same person. Plus it would make sense that someone working in heritage would end up married to someone in the same line, just as coppers tend to marry coppers and medics tend to marry medics. Can you send me your notes?' Mei asked. 'And I'll send you mine.'

'Of course. Do you think she might be involved in the thefts at the museum?' Colin asked.

'Not necessarily. At least, it hasn't been flagged. But if she – or one of her colleagues – is responsible, they might have buyers lined up. Buyers that might also be happy to take small finds from an archaeology dig,' Mei said. 'That could be a link.'

'We don't have any proof that Simon was involved with the nighthawks,' Colin said. 'But it's a line of enquiry. Maybe he caught them in the middle of digging, and they hit him to shut him up – which would make it manslaughter rather than a planned murder.'

'Or maybe he was involved with them, and there was an argument over how the items were sold and how the money was divided up,' Mei said.

'I'll get my notes together for you now,' Colin said. 'If I find anything here that helps the case on your end, or you find anything there that helps mine, let's pass it on.'

'All right. Let's confer again later,' Mei said.

At least he had some leads he could throw himself into, now. But he knew he wouldn't settle until he'd answered Georgina's text.

She thought they needed some space. All his arguments sounded pathetic and needy when he tried typing them out. In the end, he simply typed OK and sent the message.

SEVEN

'Bernard's Aunt Anna was very keen on genealogy. She drew up the family tree, and I know Bernard updated it when Giles was born,' Sybbie said, ushering Georgina into the house.

Max and Jet pattered along behind them, following them into the library.

Sybbie tried a couple of drawers in the map cabinet, then smiled. 'Here we are. The Walters family.' She drew out a large sheet of paper and spread it on the desk next to the cabinet, weighing down the corners with a couple of books, then traced the line back. 'Giles, born 1994. Bernard, 1961. Thomas, Bernard's father, 1931. Grandpa Robert, 1901. Great-grandpa William, 1871. And here we are. Great-great-grandpa Robert, 1841. Robert's older brother, Frederick – the Frederick involved in the dig – was born in 1837. Sadly, it also seems there was a little girl born in 1839, but she only survived for a week, poor thing. And look here – Elizabeth Rutherford, 1843. Died 1866, Little Wenborough.' She raised her eyebrows and looked at Georgina. 'You said the Grey Lady was called Lizzie. I wonder whether Elizabeth Rutherford might be our Grey Lady, because her baby's death is recorded here, too – on the same day, see? A little girl.' She shivered. 'Sarah.'

The same name that Sybbie had planned to give the baby she'd lost. 'That's so sad,' Georgina said, looking at the family tree. 'But didn't Bernard say Frederick's wife, rather than his sister, died in childbirth?'

'Felicity,' Sybbie confirmed. 'Here. It says she married Frederick in 1868 and died in 1869 – along with their son, Thomas. So it looks as if both women died from the same cause.' She looked sad. 'Childbirth was so dangerous, back in those days. And so many babies didn't make it out of infancy.'

'That's very true,' Georgina said. 'So we know for definite that Frederick had a younger sister as well as a younger brother. In 1865, Elizabeth was twenty-two. She might have been fascinated by Timothy.'

'According to the family tree, Elizabeth married Edwin Rutherford of Great Wenborough Hall in October 1865 – the same year as the dig,' Sybbie said.

'Which is also fairly shortly after we think Timothy died,' Georgina said. 'Do you know anything about the Rutherfords, or Great Wenborough Hall?'

'Not a huge amount,' Sybbie admitted. 'The family died out in the late 1800s and the hall was left empty until the War Office commandeered it at the beginning of the First World War. It was used a place to train infantry, and it was demolished a few years later. The house was roughly in the middle of where the football and cricket pitches are now. There are probably some old photographs online, or Billy at the butcher's might have something in the local historical society's files.'

'We'll ask him.' Georgina jotted down a note. 'It's just struck me – isn't it a bit odd that Elizabeth died in Little Wenborough?'

'How do you mean?' Sybbie asked.

'If she was married to Edwin Rutherford and lived with him at Great Wenborough Hall, surely she would've been planning to give birth there?' Georgina said. 'Unless she was visiting her family; but that late into a pregnancy, wouldn't it have been easier for them to visit her?'

'Maybe.' Sybbie took another look at the dates. 'The baby looks to have been a honeymoon baby,' she said. 'Unless... do you think there's a possibility that it might be Timothy's baby? We know through Doris that he died, but maybe Lizzie only knew that he'd vanished and not returned, and perhaps the marriage with Edwin was – I don't know, expedient and rather quick?'

'That's a good point. If Frederick's father thought Timothy had made Lizzie pregnant and abandoned her, that would also explain why Trish's great-gran got such a frosty reception from him,' Georgina said.

'Can you ask Doris?' Sybbie asked. 'And... she managed to talk to Anne at Hartington – was that because Anne contacted her, or can Doris contact Lizzie?'

'I don't know. I'll ask,' Georgina said. 'And I think we need to talk to Bea. She might have some ideas about where we can look next in the records.'

She left Bea a message, not expecting it to be picked up until later, but her daughter rang back almost immediately. 'I know you were taking photos of that Roman mosaic floor this week. I was expecting you to send a few through, but you never did. Did you find another body underneath it, or something?' Bea asked.

'Not *quite*,' Georgina said, and explained about Simon's death and the mystery of Timothy's disappearance.

'That must be quite a shock for everyone,' Bea said. 'Mum, I've got a few days off before we start rehearsals. Give me a few minutes to pack, and I'll get the train back to Norfolk. Then I get to see you, and I can help you with your research if you'll test me on my lines.'

'Of course I will. It'd be so lovely to see you,' Georgina said. 'Let me know what time your train gets in, and I'll pick you up.'

'I think seeing her will do you good,' Sybbie said when Georgina ended the call.

'Very much so,' Georgina agreed.

'I'm afraid it's a bit difficult to pin down the exact time of death,' Sammy said, 'because it was quite cold last night, and the tarpaulin covering the trench wouldn't really have kept in that much heat.'

'What's your best guess?' Colin asked.

'Between midnight and two,' Sammy said. 'The cause of death was that blow to the back of his head; it fractured his skull and caused a haemorrhage. He was otherwise fit and well – no signs of any heart disease or anything that might have caused him to collapse. It might comfort his family if you tell them that he wouldn't have known much about it.'

'Thank you,' Colin said. 'Any idea what the weapon might have been?'

'There aren't any particular features. Something with a flat surface. Was any kind of weapon found at the scene?' Sammy asked.

'No, but I was wondering whether it could've been a spade or shovel – and whoever was using it might have taken it with them.'

'The flat of a spade is a definite possibility,' Sammy said. 'That could be helpful in profiling the killer. Whoever delivered the blow must've been tall enough to swing the weapon at the victim's head – and strong enough to make the blow count.'

Trish, at five feet three, might have been strong enough, but she wouldn't have been tall enough, Colin thought. 'Did anything else come up to make you think the cause of death might have been something else, and the blow to the head was done afterwards to cover it up?' he checked.

'No. I think you can safely say this was the head wound. The victim had his back turned, and there aren't any defensive wounds, so he obviously wasn't expecting it.'

'Surely he would've heard something? I mean, you can't exactly sneak up to someone if you're going to swing a spade at their head,' Colin said.

'True. But the contents of his stomach tell me Simon Butterfield had definitely been drinking that evening, and alcohol might've affected him enough for him not to have noticed any sounds,' Sammy said. 'He'd consumed beer and a couple of whisky chasers, along with a roast dinner.'

Which corroborated what the students and Trish had said about them all eating dinner at the Red Lion. 'So I'm looking for someone tall enough and strong enough to swing a spade at the head of a six-foot-tall man,' Colin said. 'Thank you, Sammy. That's useful.' To a degree.

It was looking more likely that one of the nighthawks had killed Simon, he thought as he ended the call. But where did he begin finding them?

'Mum!' Bea quickened her pace across the railway station concourse and hugged Georgina hard. 'It's so good to see you.'

'And you, darling.' Georgina hugged her back, and together they headed for the car park.

'I can't wait to see Bert.' Bea put her bag in the back of the car, then climbed into the passenger seat. 'Is Young Tom doing much in the garden?'

Georgina had thought for a while that Bea rather liked her

gardener – who'd been recommended to her by Sybbie – and it was very much mutual. 'He still comes on Mondays and Thursdays,' she said. 'The tulips he's planted in the pots are coming out now, and they look amazing.'

'That's good.'

Bea chattered happily about the theatre and London until they got back to Rookery Barn and she'd taken her things up to her room. She came down and made a fuss of Bert while Georgina made mugs of coffee.

'How about I treat us to dinner at the Feathers tonight?' she asked.

'You don't have t—' Georgina began.

'I know, but I *want* to,' Bea cut in. 'I assume Colin will join us?'

'No,' Georgina said quietly.

'Oh, of course – he'll be busy solving the question of who killed the poor man at the dig,' Bea said.

'Mmm,' Georgina prevaricated.

But clearly something of the truth showed in her face, because Bea said, 'Mum, what aren't you telling me?'

Georgina sighed. 'Colin and I are taking a bit of a break.'

'What? Why? What's happened?' Bea frowned. 'I mean – Will and I have been waiting for the announcement he was going to move in with you properly, not just stay here most nights.'

Georgina had thought things were heading that way, too. But not after their fight. And not after that cold little reply to her text. 'It's complicated,' she said.

'You're my mum, and I don't have any say in who you date,' Bea said quietly. 'But if Colin's done anything to upset you, then he'll be answering to me and Will.'

'It's complicated,' Georgina repeated.

'I don't understand,' Bea said.

Neither had Colin. Though Sybbie and Francesca had been

surprisingly open to what Georgina had told them. And, given that her daughter worked in a very superstitious industry, Georgina had a feeling that Bea might just listen to her, too. 'What's your view on ghosts?' she asked carefully.

'I've worked in places where odd things have happened – things I can't explain,' Bea said. 'Dad did, too. And since you and Bert found poor Friedrich's remains at the Regency, things there have been... well, there's a different energy about the place, I guess.'

Georgina only realised she'd been holding her breath when she started breathing again. 'So you wouldn't think I'm totally crazy if I told you that I'd had a ghostly encounter here?'

'Mum, this place is, what, four hundred years old, in parts? There's bound to be at least one spooky story.' Bea looked thoughtful. 'Like that poor girl who died here.'

'Doris. Yes. It's her, actually.'

Bea looked at her and blinked. 'You've seen her?'

'No,' Georgina said. 'I hear her.' She explained how she'd first heard Doris's voice, the previous summer, and how Doris had helped her with the previous cold cases.

'I don't quite know what to think,' Bea said. 'But you're not really the fanciful sort. If you tell me you've heard her speaking to you, I believe you. And it certainly explains why you were so obsessed with finding the truth about Doris's death.'

'You believe me,' Georgina said, and her knees felt weak with relief.

'Of course I believe you, Mum. Can anyone else hear her?' Bea asked. 'Could I hear her, if I held your hearing aids to my ears?'

'No. I tried that with Jack, her brother,' Georgina said. 'All he heard was static.'

'Is Doris here now?'

'No. She's not here all the time. Bert hears her, too,'

Georgina added. 'She's encouraged him to dig where the bodies are buried.'

'Hmm. Wasn't Colin holding his lead, the last time he did that?' Bea asked, with a smile. And then her smile faded. 'Hang on. One minute, you're getting on really well with Colin. Then you tell me you're on a break, and *then* you're talking to me about ghosts. Am I making too much of it, or is there a connection between those facts?'

Georgina winced. 'Colin doesn't believe in ghosts. He thinks it's to do with memories and guilty consciences, or people who are really good at cold reading taking advantage of people who are vulnerable.'

'Will and I were talking about ghosts, last time we were here,' Bea said, surprising her. 'I spend a lot of time in ancient buildings, and sometimes there's an atmosphere I can't explain. Will reckons there's a lot in the universe that we can't explain.'

'Cesca said something like that, earlier today – that if someone living two hundred years ago saw a video call on a smartphone, they'd think it was magic or a ghost, something they couldn't explain,' Georgina mused. 'And she thinks ghosts are probably like that for us.'

Bea blinked. 'You talked to Cesca about your ghost?'

'And Sybbie,' Georgina admitted. 'You and Will were next on my list.'

'I would've liked to be rather higher up that list. So would Will,' Bea said. 'And you told Colin first.' She looked and sounded hurt that her mother hadn't trusted her.

'I'm sorry, sweetheart,' Georgina said. 'It all sounds so flaky. I guess I know how much you and Will worry about me, and I didn't want to give you both yet another reason to fret.'

'That,' Bea said, 'worries me even more. You kept secrets from us and we didn't have a clue. How can we be sure you'll let us know if anything goes wrong in the future? And you're *hours* away from us, Mum. It takes Will at least four hours to drive here even if he doesn't pick me up on the way, and if I take the train, it's getting on for three hours door to door. What if...?' She choked off the rest of the sentence.

Georgina winced, having a good idea what Bea meant. She'd already lost one parent. What if Georgina became seriously ill, or even died? 'I'm sorry,' she said again. 'I really don't want you to worry about me. But I have a good network of friends here. They know how to get hold of you and Will in an emergency.' And there was Colin. Or was there? He'd walked out on her; she'd told him she thought they needed a break... and he'd agreed.

She didn't want Bea worrying about that, so she shelved it for now. 'As for telling Colin first – I kept it from him for months,' Georgina said. And she was so hurt that she'd opened her heart to him and he hadn't believed her. She forced herself to give him an excuse. 'Though he's having a hard time at work right now.'

'That doesn't give him the right to take it out on you. Or to disbelieve you,' Bea said crossly. She bit her lip. 'Mum, I know this is a horrible question – but... have you – has Doris – spoken to Dad?'

Bea had half expected Bea to ask that. 'Sort of. I often talk to him when I'm on my own,' Georgina said. 'Not that I ever expected an answer. But I swear I heard his voice on your opening night at the Regency. He watched the show. And he told me he was very, very proud of you and you were a fantastic Lady Macbeth.'

Tears filled Bea's eyes. 'I miss him, Mum.'

'So do I, darling.' Georgina hugged her. 'But remember that Larkin poem, "An Arundel Tomb". There are things for which I would cheerfully chuck the man's books off my shelf, but that last line... It's all about love, Bea. Love is something that never dies.'

'Shakespeare says that, too. *Love alters not with his brief hours and weeks, /But bears it out even to the edge of doom,'* Bea said. 'I wanted Dad to read that at my wedding.'

'*I'll* read it at your wedding,' Georgina promised, her voice cracking. 'And your dad will be right there next to me.'

Bea hugged her back. 'As for Colin – I reckon he'll come round when he's had time to think about it. But I hope you make him grovel a bit.'

EIGHT

'I have a few more questions, I'm afraid,' Colin said to Trish. 'If we could perhaps find a quiet space to talk?'

'I don't really want to kick everyone out of the finds tent and hold up all the cataloguing,' Trish said. 'Can we just go somewhere out of earshot to talk? Or the farm shop café?'

'I don't really want people overhearing,' Colin said. 'How about my car?'

'Sure.' Trish followed him to his car; he opened the passenger door for her, then climbed into his own seat.

'How's your sister doing?' he asked.

'Not great. She really loved Simon,' Trish said. The expression on her face finished the rest of the sentence for her: *God only knows why*. 'Do you have any idea yet when his body will be released?'

'No,' Colin said. 'This is a murder inquiry.'

Trish's eyes widened as if she suddenly realised the implication – that she might be one of the suspects. 'Hang on. Do I need a solicitor?'

'Not at the moment,' he said. 'Unless there's something you'd like to tell me?'

She shook her head. 'I've already told you I didn't get on that well with him, but I didn't kill him.'

'If you know of anyone who did have a motive to kill him, no matter how slender,' Colin said quietly, 'it would be very useful to know now.'

'No. As I said, most of the students grumbled about him, but I can't see any of them killing him. What was the cause of death? The head wound?'

'Yes,' Colin said. 'The scene of crimes team has already checked your tools. But could there have been any other implements that weren't in use yesterday and were put away in a store?'

'You think someone from the dig killed him?' Trish's eyes widened.

'At the moment,' Colin said, 'we can't rule anyone out. I need to talk to everyone again and recheck what they might have heard or seen during the night.'

'I honestly didn't hear a thing. I was tired and went to bed before Simon and the students came back from the pub,' Trish said. 'Though obviously I was alone, so I can't prove that.'

'It must take quite a bit of strength to dig out all the soil from the trenches,' he said.

'Some of that's done by a mechanical digger,' she said, 'in places where we know from the geophys that there's a lot of non-yielding topsoil, like here.'

'Non-yielding topsoil?' Colin asked.

'It means the soil's at the surface, and it contains very little of archaeological interest,' she said. 'So we can take the top layer off without ruining the archaeological record. But, yes, if the soil's really compacted, we might have to use a mattock to break it up, and that takes effort. We use the spades and shovels to clear bulk debris into a wheelbarrow, and we sieve the soil to check for any finds. Sieved soil goes into the spoil heap, and it'll be used to backfill the trenches. Once we've cleared the top bit,

we put a grid in to help with identification and recording –
that's where we use pegs and twine.'

'What kind of tools do you use for that?' he asked.

'Plumb lines, spirit levels, measuring tapes, and mallets to
bang in the pegs,' she said.

A mallet was another possibility for the murder weapon,
Colin thought. Or maybe not; Sammy had talked about a flat
surface, making a spade or shovel the more likely implement. A
mallet was small enough to leave the impression of its edges,
and the head wound hadn't been a square.

'Once the grid's in, we work with trowels and paintbrushes,'
Trish said. 'And there are a lot of black rubber buckets for the
finds.'

'Right.' Colin made some more notes.

'Are you going to want to see all of those, too?' she asked.

'Possibly,' he said. 'But what I need from you now is a bit
more background on each of the students.'

'I really don't think any of them would want to kill him,'
Trish said. 'As I said, they moan about him, but that's as far as
any of them would go.'

'The thing is,' Colin said, 'everyone is capable of murder,
given the right circumstances.' With a pang, he thought of
Georgina. She'd once told him that although she'd never
thought she could kill anyone, she'd changed her mind; when
someone had threatened Bea, she'd been shocked to realise that
she would've happily taken matters into her own hands and
killed that person. Just as he would want to protect his own
daughter, Cathy.

He'd wanted to introduce Georgina to Cathy. He'd even
been planning a weekend in London where they could perhaps
meet on neutral territory and get to know each other a little. But
now, after his row on Monday night with Georgina, he didn't
think it was a good idea.

He shook himself. Not now. He needed to focus on work,

not the mess of his private life. 'Tell me about the students, Trish,' he invited.

'Isn't it against data protection rules, discussing personal information?' Trish asked.

'This is a murder investigation,' he reminded her. 'Which means there's a lawful reason for you to give me the information.'

Trish still didn't look happy about it, but she agreed. Nothing she said stood out, until she got to the last two students.

'Helena's my best student,' she said. 'She's got a special interest in Roman Britain, so I'm hoping I can persuade her to stay with us and do some more work on this site, if Bernard's happy for us to come back and work on where we think more of the villa remains are.'

Helena was the one who'd told Colin about the nighthawks. She'd struck him as an earnest young woman, clearly well-read and passionate about her subject.

'But she's been going off the boil a bit, recently,' Trish continued, surprising him.

'Any particular reason?' Colin asked.

'My guess is boyfriend trouble,' Trish said. 'I think he's turning out not to be the good guy she thought he was, and it's distracting her. She was late with her last essay, and it wasn't up to her usual standard. I did sit down with her and ask if I could help with anything, but she wouldn't open up to me.'

Colin made a note to check out the boyfriend. Could there be a link with the nighthawks? And if Helena had unwittingly given him the information about the dig which he'd passed on to the nighthawks – or, worse still, he was one of them – then maybe Simon had recognised him, and the boyfriend had tried to cover it up by bashing Simon over the head. Definitely a possible motive.

'And then there's Adam,' Trish said, rolling her eyes. 'He's not a bad lad, exactly, but he's lazy. Always late with his assignments, always full of excuses, always complaining. I try to be impartial, but honestly, I feel he's wasting a place that could've been taken by someone who's really interested in the subject and would put the work in. But Simon seems to rate him. Seemed,' she corrected herself. 'At least, he's always been happy for Adam to be on any fieldwork trips.'

Adam: the student who'd been hungover. And surely if one tutor had noticed that a student was underperforming, the others would notice, too? And Trish had said before that Simon saw students in terms of grades. Why would he have been happy for a student who got low grades to be on his fieldwork trips?

But talking to the students again got Colin no further forward with the case. Helena didn't meet his eye very often, giving him the distinct feeling that she was hiding something, though whether that was relevant to Simon Butterfield wasn't clear. Adam was a bit on the cocky side – almost like someone who'd got away with something. Or maybe that was just his personality and Colin was reading too much into it.

Yet again he thought of Georgina. She always managed to get people to open up to her, with her warmth and kindness. And she'd helped him in previous investigations by persuading people to talk…

He pushed the thought away. She'd said she wanted some space between them. And, until he'd worked out how they were going to compromise over this ghost business, he rather thought she was right. He'd have to be careful not to bump into her on the site, given that she was a close friend of Sybbie and would be taking photographs of the dig, once the forensics team had finished and the blood had been cleaned from the mosaic.

Life, he thought, could be ridiculously complicated…

NINE

Later on Tuesday afternoon, Georgie and Bea headed over to see Sybbie, to continue their research into Timothy.

'Let's go to the muniments room, where all the house documents are kept,' Sybbie said, leading them into a room in the middle of the ground floor. Wooden shelving lined the walls, and wooden bookcases jutted out in rows across the room. Some of the shelves held large leather-bound books; others contained box files; and still more contained archival boxes. At one end of the room there was a small table and an office chair.

'So if we're looking at 1865, we need to start with this box,' Sybbie said, going to one of the shelves with the archive boxes. She lifted up a box marked *1861–1865* and set it on the table. 'Everything is tied up in bundles – either by date or by person. What are we looking for?'

'Letters,' Georgina said. 'Plus anything written by Frederick, Lizzie and perhaps Lizzie's mum.'

'Her name was Amelia,' Sybbie said.

'As well as diaries, there might be a commonplace book,' Bea added. 'Which is pretty much an early version of scrapbooking crossed with a bullet journal – it might have sketches, newspaper cuttings and even photographs, if we're lucky. If we divide the bundles between us, we can work through until we find any mentions of Timothy or the dig. And we can check records as we go – you brought your laptop, didn't you, Mum?'

'It's in my satchel,' Georgina confirmed.

'Good. Let's use the dining room table,' Sybbie said, wrinkling her nose at the small table in front of them. 'There are three of us, and we need a bit more room to spread out.'

Bea scooped up the box, and she and Georgina followed Sybbie to the dining room, which was painted a deep red and had rich brocade curtains.

The polished oak dining table was big enough to sit sixteen people; the fireplace next to it was an ornate stone affair, with a cast-iron grating, firedogs and companion set. On top of the mantelpiece sat several pairs of Sybbie's beloved Staffordshire dogs and an ormolu clock; various landscapes and portraits in gilt frames hung on the walls.

'Seeing all this,' Bea said, 'is when I realise how posh you really are, Sybbie.'

Sybbie chuckled. 'Not *that* posh. Bernard and I tend to eat in the kitchen, unless we have people over for dinner – and even then, unless there's a huge gathering, we'll only use one end of the table. There's nothing worse than bellowing at each other from opposite ends of this beast.' She patted the table. 'Though I suppose two hundred years ago you would've needed this kind of space, for house parties and the like. Terribly Jane Austen.' She rolled her eyes. 'Imagine the kind of bores you would've had to put up with, for days and days and days on end.'

'You would've made your excuses and escaped to the garden with your pruning shears,' Georgina said with a grin.

'I certainly would,' Sybbie agreed. 'Which would strictly have been the territory of the head gardener. I suppose the other thing about being Lady Wyatt is that I could do what I liked and people would just have to put up with my eccentricities.'

'I can just see you as a modern-day Violet Crawley, when you get older,' Georgina teased.

'I should jolly well hope so,' Sybbie said with a twinkle in her eye. She looked at Bea. 'The box will be fine on the rug. We can take the bundles out one by one. Georgie, do we know the dates of the dig?'

'They started work beginning of June 1865, according to the letters Timothy wrote to Clara,' Georgina said. 'I photocopied the papers Trish lent me. The letter from Frederick's father saying that Timothy had left was written in September.'

'So shall we start with June?' Sybbie suggested.

'Maybe a bit earlier,' Georgina said. 'Frederick wrote to Timothy, I believe, asking him to come and help excavate, so Timothy's reply should be somewhere here. And it all started after ploughing.'

'When are the fields ploughed, Sybbie?' Bea asked.

'For spring barley and wheat, usually February to March, and they sow in March,' Sybbie said.

'Then I think we should start looking from the beginning of the year,' Bea said. 'Obviously the letters will all be *to* Frederick, Lizzie and Amelia, rather than from them. So we'll have to read between the lines a bit to work out what they might have said to whoever was replying.'

'And it looks as if they were all good correspondents,' Sybbie said as she took out the first few bundles. 'That's useful; it looks as if they're bundled by person rather than by date. Shall I take Frederick, you take Lizzie, Bea, and you take Amelia, Georgie? And we'll put everything back in the order we found them.'

Georgina and Bea agreed.

'If we find anything useful, I'll take a photograph,' Georgina said. 'I'll make a separate table noting what the photographs are of, which bundle it came from and whereabouts it is in the bundle, so we can refer back to the originals if we need to.'

'That works for me,' Sybbie said. 'Georgie, is Doris with you? And can she hear me?'

'Yes and yes,' Georgina said.

'I can't hear you, Doris, and I'm sorry for that, but welcome to Little Wenborough Manor. And thank you for helping us find out the truth,' Sybbie said.

'That's so...' Doris's voice faded, and she gave an audible gulp. 'Please say thank you to her, Georgie, for – well, *accepting* me.'

Georgina relayed the message.

'You're part of the team, Doris. And any friend of my mum's is a friend of mine,' Bea added.

'I really, *really* like your daughter and Sybbie,' Doris said. Her voice sounded wobbly, as if she were close to tears.

Georgina felt tears prick her own eyes. She'd half expected her daughter and her friend to display the same level of scepticism as Colin had; yet they hadn't dismissed her words out of hand. They'd asked questions, but they'd accepted Doris's existence. 'OK, you two. Doris appreciates the support – we both do – but please stop making her cry. And we have a job to do,' Georgina said lightly.

'Yes, boss,' Sybbie teased. 'Doris, did Georgie ask you if you could talk to Lizzie?'

Georgina relayed the reply. 'Yes, but Lizzie only remembers her last couple of days before she died.'

'So is she reunited with Timothy, now?' Sybbie asked.

'No, they're still separate – I don't think they can be together until we find out what happened to him,' Doris said. 'This afterlife business isn't as clear-cut as you'd think it would be. I can talk to both of them, and relay messages, but a lot depends on what they remember.'

'Right,' Georgina said, and explained to Bea and Sybbie.

'By the way, you're right about why she looks out for people here,' Doris added.

'Looks out for people?' Bea asked, when Georgina repeated Doris's words.

Sybbie gave her a rundown of what they knew about the Grey Lady of Little Wenborough Manor. 'Doris, please can you thank her from me for being so kind when I needed hope so badly?' she added.

Georgina felt her eyes sting with unshed tears. Lizzie's ghost was definitely all about love.

They sat down with their bundles of correspondence and worked their way through the letters. The only sound was the rustling of paper.

'I've got something from Timothy to Frederick here,' Sybbie announced. 'March 1965. So that ties in with what we know already. The field had been ploughed to prepare for sowing the spring barley, and that's when the tesserae were found. Frederick obviously sent a couple of samples to London, and Timothy wrote back thanking him for the tesserae, agreeing that the site might be of great interest and saying he was going to look at some maps in the university library. He asked Frederick to look at the estate maps to see if there was any indication of a villa or a spring in the field names.'

'Maps which Bernard showed me yesterday,' Georgina said.

Sybbie nodded. 'And there's a follow-up letter from Timothy, with a sketch of a map showing the Roman roads around here. Look, there's the one at Bawburgh, and the one by Venta Icenorum at Caistor St Edmund.'

'Ooh – you can see the main Roman road to London more or less follows the A140 towards Ipswich,' Bea said, coming to join them. 'Amazing to think the route's hardly changed in all those years.'

Georgina photographed both letters and noted them in her table.

'Bernard will be delighted to see these,' Sybbie said.

A little later, she said, 'Here's another one. At the end of

April, Timothy says he's arranged to take leave from the university and they can start excavating next month. He's drawn up a plan of what he thinks they should do. And he says he would be delighted to accept the offer to stay at Little Wenborough Manor.'

There was very little in the following letters to Frederick until mid-May, where Timothy wrote with his travel plans. 'He says he's going to catch the eight o'clock train from Bishopsgate and take the Cambridge line to Norwich,' Sybbie said. 'And listen to this: *Bradshaw's says I will be at Norwich at one.*'

Georgina knew from a TV show that Bradshaw's had published railway timetables.

'I wonder if the publisher was any relation to Colin?' Sybbie asked idly.

Georgina was aware that both her daughter and her friend were regarding her with what felt like pity, and it grated. 'I doubt it,' she said, as coolly as she could. 'Anything more?'

'The next letter,' Sybbie said. '*Thank you for your kind offer to send the carriage to meet me, which I shall gladly accept.*'

'Timothy's coming from London to Norwich by train to help with the dig, and they're meeting him at the station to bring him to Little Wenborough – not much changes, does it?' Bea asked with a smile.

'No,' Georgina said.

'And he says here, *I look forward to seeing you again and renewing my acquaintance with your family.* They seem to be on good terms. So what happened to make Timothy fall out with them?' Sybbie asked.

'I still think it has to be forbidden love,' Georgina said. 'My guess is he fell for either Frederick or Lizzie. If it was Frederick, he'd know there could be no future in it because even if they'd gone to Italy, where they could've lived together, Frederick was the heir to the title and he would've felt the responsibility to get married and have an heir himself.'

'What about Lizzie? What would've been the barrier there?' Sybbie asked.

'Could she have been already betrothed to someone else?' Bea asked.

'We know she married Edwin Rutherford in 1866,' Sybbie said. 'So there's a possibility she was already betrothed to him before she met Timothy.'

'Just about the only power women had, back then, was that they could break an engagement without penalty,' Bea said. 'And a woman could sue a man for breach of promise if he was the one to break the engagement.'

'So far, I haven't found any mention of an engagement in Amelia's correspondence,' Georgina said.

'There's nothing in Lizzie's, either,' Bea admitted.

'Supposing she wasn't betrothed to Edwin – supposing he was a rebound?' Georgina said. 'If Lizzie fell in love with Timothy, what was to stop them being together?'

'Does Doris have any ideas?' Sybbie asked. 'Has Timothy told her any more than that he heard an explosion and felt a pain in his back, and he'd fallen in love with someone?'

'He remembers his sister, Clara, and that he was good friends with Frederick,' Georgina said. 'Doris?'

'He says he loved Frederick like a brother,' Doris said. 'I did ask if he felt anything else towards Frederick, and he was a bit awkward. He said he'd known a couple of men at Cambridge who were Uranians, but he'd never wanted to be anyone's companion himself.'

Georgina relayed the information to Bea and Sybbie.

'Uranians. That sounds like a Victorian man's way of telling you he wasn't gay,' Bea said. 'Was Timothy interested in Lizzie?'

'He says he would never have done anything to dishonour her. He was the youngest son in his family. Had he been the oldest, like Frederick, his prospects would surely have led her parents to agree to him being her suitor,' Doris said.

This time, after Georgina had repeated Doris's words, Sybbie frowned. 'The land and the bulk of the money used to go to the oldest son rather than being divided between several children, because otherwise, within a couple of generations, the plots of land wouldn't be enough to support the house and a family. And if you know the oldest son is going to be the heir, you can teach them what they need to know about running the estate from an early age.' Her frown deepened. 'But surely Timothy would've had some money of his own, even as the youngest son. He must've had some kind of inheritance from his grandmothers or maiden aunts. And didn't you say he worked for the university? That means he would've had a salary.'

'I'm sure I read something about university fellows not being allowed to get married,' Bea said. 'So in that case he would've had to choose between his job and Lizzie.'

'Or find another job that paid him well enough to let him support Lizzie,' Georgina said. 'By 1865, the nobility was a bit more sensible, wasn't it? Not so much of the nonsense the *ton* used to spout about gentlemen who didn't work, or bored young men gambling thousands on which raindrop would travel down a window the quickest.'

'Perhaps,' Sybbie said. 'But there was still a degree of snobbery – and I know, I know, coming from someone who has a title…' She grimaced. 'The thing is, as a younger son, Timothy wouldn't have had a title. If Lizzie's parents were set on her marrying someone with a title, they wouldn't have accepted him as a suitor.'

'Is that how it was, Doris?' Georgina asked.

'I'll see what Timothy or Lizzie says,' was the answer.

'We have to wait for a bit,' Georgina said. 'Let's carry on working through the correspondence.'

'So far, Lizzie's correspondence has more to do with

arrangements to visit the theatre in Norwich, and to attend several balls – some at the houses of local gentry, and one at the Assembly House,' Bea said.

'Amelia's is about invitations to house parties and distant cousins having babies, and plans for the London Season,' Georgina said. 'Strictly speaking, the family would have been in London between May and August. Then again, if Lizzie was the only daughter, and she was twenty-two in 1865 – I have remembered that accurately, Sybbie?'

'Yes,' Sybbie confirmed. 'She would've come out when she was eighteen – so that's 1861.'

'All the women in Bernard's family portraits are pretty,' Georgina mused. 'And she was from a good family. I'm guessing it's likely she had offers of marriage in her first Season, and if she'd refused them all, then definitely more in the second. If she wasn't betrothed, surely she would've been in London, attending balls and letting her mother make a match?'

'Or she'd found a reason to persuade her mother to stay at home rather than go to London,' Sybbie said. 'Maybe if her health was delicate? Or if there was some kind of epidemic going on in London that they wanted to avoid – cholera, perhaps?'

'Let me look it up,' Bea said. 'Mum, is your laptop's password still the same?'

'Yes,' Georgina confirmed.

A couple of minutes later, Bea shook her head. 'There was a bad outbreak of cholera in 1854, followed by the Great Stink in 1858 – when the smell of sewage in the Thames was so bad that they had to close Parliament. The new sewer network was opened in 1865, and the last bad outbreak in the areas of London not connected to the new sewer network was in 1866.' She shrugged. 'Perhaps she had a more personal reason for not being in London.'

'Back to the letters,' Sybbie said with a grin.

* * *

Colin was seriously considering ignoring his phone ringing, until he saw Mei Zhang's name on the screen.

'Mei? What can I do for you?' he asked.

'It's more what I can do for you,' she said. 'I've been talking to Shanese, the family liaison officer working with Joanna Butterfield. Shanese has a copper's hunch.'

'I'm listening,' Colin said.

'She's spent a fair bit of time with Joanna. Shanese is an experienced FLO, and she says something doesn't feel quite right. Yes, Joanna's upset that Simon's dead – but there's something else, too. Relief, Shanese thought.'

'He doesn't seem to have been popular with anyone I've spoken to here,' Colin said. 'I'd say he was a difficult colleague. Maybe he was a difficult husband, too.'

'I think we need to check the hospital records,' Mei said.

'Do you think she might have walked into a few too many doors, or fallen down a few too many stairs?' Colin asked.

'Possibly. Or he might have been more subtle than that,' Mei said. 'A bit of gaslighting, perhaps.'

'He didn't get on with her sister. Maybe Joanna was just relieved to know she wasn't going to have to be torn between them anymore. Will you keep me posted, please?' Colin asked.

'Of course,' Mei promised.

TEN

By the end of the afternoon, Georgina, Sybbie and Bea had found nothing more of interest in the correspondence around the time of the dig, though they all felt that September seemed unusually light on letters. That was when Timothy had disappeared; but even so they'd expected to see more correspondence. Had something else happened?

They agreed to meet back at Little Wenborough Manor in the morning, and Bea treated Georgina to dinner at the Feathers.

'Is Colin not with you tonight?' Sally asked.

'He's working on a case,' Bea said with a quick smile. 'So Mum and I get a nice girly dinner.'

'Thank you,' Georgina said after Sally had taken their order. 'I really didn't want to have to explain that things are tricky.'

'It's nobody else's business,' Bea said. 'And every relationship has its sticky patches. Everyone has a fight at some point.'

'I guess.' Georgina grimaced. 'Right now, I can't see a workable compromise to get us through this.'

Bea reached over and squeezed her hand. 'Because you're right in the middle of it. Maybe you're overthinking things,

Mum. Just let it go for a bit. Sometimes things work themselves out on their own.'

'When did you get so wise?' Georgina asked wryly.

The following day, when they arrived at Little Wenborough Manor, they discovered that Sybbie had already been working through a small leather journal.

'Sorry. I know we were doing this together and I should have waited for you,' she said, 'but Bernard and I had a look through the box last night, and we found a diary and this *amazing* commonplace book. He remembers his grandmother keeping one, and there are all sorts of things in here. Recipes, home remedies for all sorts of things, handwritten copies of poems Amelia liked, notes of exhibitions she wanted to see in London, clippings from the newspaper – and photographs. I can't wait to show you what we uncovered.' She smiled. 'I quite see why you're fascinated with old documents, Georgie. We were both completely swept up by it.'

'They're your documents,' Georgina said, smiling back. 'We're privileged that you're sharing them with us. What did you find?'

'This is where I feel almost like one of the experts on a TV genealogy programme, telling you about important moments,' Sybbie said. 'Most of them are related to Frederick, Timothy and Lizzie, but I found this newspaper clipping that's just perfect for Bea. It's from the *Norfolk Chronicle*, from March 16, 1863.' She opened the first page she'd marked. 'Professor J. H. Pepper lectured at Noverre's Rooms, Norwich, on "Optical Illusions", and for the first time exhibited in the city the now well-known illusion, "Pepper's Ghost".'

'Amazing,' Bea said with a smile. 'And we used that very same illusion at the Regency Theatre this year – more than a hundred and fifty years later. It still works perfectly.'

'What else did you find?' Georgina asked.

'You said there were photographs,' Bea added.

'This is the first one – a photograph of the Walters family in front of this house. 1861,' Sybbie said. She flipped the pages to the next market. 'Amelia, William, Frederick, Robert and Elizabeth.' She pointed them out. 'Amelia was forty-six, William was fifty, Frederick was twenty-four, Robert was twenty, and Lizzie was eighteen.'

Georgina and Bea looked at the photograph. 'How amazing to have photographs of your family from that long ago,' Georgina said. 'I assume it was taken by one of the travelling photographers? Or was someone in Bernard's family or one of their friends keen on new ideas and experimenting?'

'I'm not sure,' Sybbie said. 'But Bernard was rather thrilled to see a photograph of his great-great-grandfather *and* his great-great-great-grandfather. Obviously, you're both welcome to look through the book in more detail and see if I've missed anything, but I wanted to save us all a little bit of time.' She turned to the next marked page. 'London, 1862, obviously during the Season because there are a few theatre playbills pasted in, and look at this!'

'Receipt for Blister'd Feet,' Georgina read aloud, deciphering the handwriting. '*Prick the bladders and let the water out* – oh, no! That's the quickest way to start an infection. *Take in your hand a few drops of Gin...*'

'That's going to sting,' Bea said.

'It gets worse,' Georgina said. '*Drop into it a few drops of tallow, with the above rub the blister'd places well.*'

'I,' Bea said, 'am very grateful for modern blister plasters. Especially after hearing that!'

And Georgina was really grateful that she had all this material to keep her mind off Colin. Particularly if he was holding interviews with the archaeology team over at the dig today; being busy here would help her resist the temptation to pop over there with tea and cake. Usually he'd talk over a case with her, even though he wasn't supposed to, because he said thinking aloud to her really helped him; she really missed working with him.

'Here's another one for you, Bea,' Sybbie said. 'Their set was clearly keen on the *tableaux vivants*; I think this is Lizzie dressed as Beatrice, and I'm assuming either a friend or a cousin dressed as Hero.'

'Ooh – whoever Benedick was, he was *very* handsome,' Bea said with a smile.

'Wasn't he just? And this is my favourite one,' Sybbie continued. 'Amelia dressed as Lady Macbeth.'

'So they were quite an artsy family,' Georgina said. 'I bet they all loved the idea of the dig, and the possibility of a Roman villa being here centuries ago.'

'They did,' Sybbie said. 'And we have photographs of the dig itself. I can't wait to show Trish these.'

The photographs showed William, Frederick, Robert and another man in front of early excavations. Crucially, Amelia had added a caption: *First stages of the dig. William, Frederick, Robert and Frederick's university friend Timothy Marsden.*

'The hairs have just gone up on my arms, seeing the actual faces of the people we've been talking about,' Bea said. 'Timothy looks like a nice guy. I mean, I know this is a formal photograph, but you can *feel* that they're all comfortable in each other's company.'

'Which brings us back to the question: why was William so curt with Clara on the subject of Timothy's departure?' Georgina asked.

'I'm hoping Amelia's diary will tell us,' Sybbie said. 'But her writing's quite hard to read.'

'We'll figure it out between the three of us,' Bea said. 'Are there any more photographs?'

'There are sketches of the mosaic floor, and the dig in

progress,' Sybbie said. 'But they're signed *EW*, so my guess is that they're Lizzie's rather than Amelia's. That floor really is something, isn't it?'

'I love that peacock. He's practically strutting,' Georgina said. 'It'd be very easy to make that into a cross-stitch pattern. It's very stylised, starting with almost an oval and then graduating lines of colour following round to make the body, then the scallop-shell bit for his back, and finally that glorious tail with the feathers fanned out and the eyes glowing. And it's even more incredible that we've seen that exact floor in real life.' Albeit with a dead body in the middle of it, but she really hoped the cleaning had worked so she'd be able to take proper photographs. And then she felt guilty; Simon Butterfield had *died*, and here she was, more interested in the mosaic floor. What kind of selfish person did that make her? Cross with herself, she took photographs of the sketches and photographs.

But the entries in the commonplace book came almost to a complete halt in September. No photographs, only one recipe for a pudding, and no pasted-in playbills from the theatre or newspaper cuttings.

'There's hardly any correspondence and hardly anything in the commonplace book. Something definitely happened in September 1865,' Georgina said. 'I think we need to look at Amelia's diary.'

'Let's start in the spring,' Sybbie said.

Once Georgina had got used to the handwriting, it was easy to read the diary. Amelia came across as warm, friendly and chatty, enjoying house parties, local performances and visiting local friends. She talked about the finding of the tesserae during ploughing, and Frederick's conviction that they were from a mosaic floor, and there were Roman remains at Little Wenborough Hall.

'I think she was torn between staying here to see the dig happen first hand, and going to London for the Season, meeting up with cousins and old friends,' Georgina said. 'Though she doesn't seem to be in a rush to get Lizzie married off. Lizzie's first Season would've been in 1861. After four years, Lizzie would have been seen as being on the shelf, if she hadn't been betrothed. Isn't that a bit unusual?'

'Thirty years earlier, I would've said yes. But Lizzie was their only daughter,' Bea said. 'And it was the middle of the nineteenth century. Victoria was very happily married to Albert, and I think by then people had started to think about marrying for love rather than for economic status. Maybe Amelia wanted her daughter to choose a man who'd make her happy, rather than marrying her to someone with lots of land.'

'You might be right. I've just seen a name we know – Edwin Rutherford,' Georgina said. 'Amelia's very clear. *He has offered for Lizzie, but she does not wish to marry him. It is my belief he wants to forge closer links between Great Wenborough's lands and ours, and has more of an eye for her dowry than for Lizzie herself.* So it sounds as if you're right, Bea. Amelia's parents weren't going to force her to marry someone she didn't like and who was after her money.'

'Yet we know she *did* marry Edwin, in October of that year,' Sybbie said. 'I have a bad feeling about this. What does Doris say?'

'I asked Timothy when you brought it up, but either he doesn't remember or he really doesn't want to say,' Doris said. 'It feels to me as if he's trying to protect Lizzie, but I'm not sure what from.'

Georgina brought Sybbie and Bea up to speed with Doris's views.

'We'll just have to keep going through the diary,' Bea said.

Among the entries, Georgina found a mention of Timothy. 'It looks as if Amelia and Lizzie went to London for the Season as usual, but they came back early, in June, to see what was happening with the dig. And here Amelia says, *Timothy has taught Lizzie much about the Romans and the buildings he is uncovering. Lizzie is enjoying spending time with her brother and his friend, sketching buildings for them. They think they have found the edge of the mosaic floor Frederick was so sure existed. Frederick says it may be a bath house.'*

'So Timothy and Lizzie spent time together,' Sybbie said.

'Chaperoned by her brothers and possibly her father as well,' Bea added. 'They wouldn't have been left alone.'

'But they definitely like each other,' Georgina said. 'Here's another entry. *I suspect Lizzie is developing a tendresse for Timothy. The way she looks at him, over the dinner table. She shines when he speaks to her. And I think Timothy feels the same way about her. I have noticed him stealing glances at her, and he has a special smile for her. But they are never alone at the dig. Frederick is there all the time, and Robert part of the time, and there are the men from the estate helping with the digging. William and I pay regular visits to see how much more of the villa they uncover. It is all quite fascinating. How strange to think a house stood here fifteen hundred years ago. People who saw the same landscape we do now, who grew their food in these fields and took their water from the same stream.'*

'Bernard would certainly agree with that,' Sybbie said, and slipped a piece of paper between the pages to mark the entry.

A few days later, there was another entry. *'Today they finished uncovering the peacock floor in the bath house,'* Georgina read. *'It is a marvel. To think someone had the patience to set it all out, square by tiny square. Timothy has told us how they made the tesserae, and how the design was marked out. He says the mosaic would have been polished with beeswax to make the tiles glow. The central white circle contains the most beautiful peacock, the symbol of Juno, strutting proudly. The front of his body is made from tiny lines of blue stones, and his feet are planted squarely. The back of his body looks like overlapping scallops, blue on the outside and fawn on the inside, and then the tail flares up, bright orange and red, with three semicircles of eye feathers showing as a rib of white with the blue and turquoise eye at the end. Around the circle is a twisted rope, which turns into a knot at the compass points, and then forms a square outside the circle, with a flower in each corner. Timothy tells us the rope is called a guilloche. Lizzie has made several sketches, and I have pasted one into my commonplace book.'*

'That's the sketch we found earlier,' Sybbie said.

'Frederick advocates for preserving the site and allowing people to visit it. William is inclined to indulge him,' Georgina finished.

'And yet instead it was covered over again and forgotten about,' Bea said. 'This place could've been like Chedworth Villa or Fishbourne.'

'It still could,' Sybbie said. 'Bernard and Giles are thoroughly enjoying it. I think they're planning to talk to Trish about a further excavation, either over the summer or next year.'

'That would be wonderful,' Georgina said.

She continued looking through the diary. 'Here we are again. *Edwin Rutherford has again offered for Lizzie. William and I have discussed the situation. Should she marry Edwin Rutherford, she would live near us. It means I could see my darling girl every day and see her children grow up. Edwin is the elder son and she would live in comfort at Great Wenborough Hall.'*

'I feel a "but" coming,' Sybbie said.

'There is indeed,' Georgina agreed. *'Yet there is something about Edwin I do not like. There is cruelty in his eyebrows. William says I am being foolish, and the poor man cannot help the way he looks. He does however agree that maids never last very long in that house, whereas our maids here stay until they marry their sweethearts and have children.'*

'And we all know why female domestic servants would leave a house after a very short time,' Bea said softly. 'Made pregnant by the master of the house or one of his sons or a younger brother, blamed for the pregnancy and thrown out. It sounds as if Amelia suspects what was happening at Great Wenborough Hall, but she had no power to do anything. The only thing she could do was make sure her daughter was safe by getting William to refuse Edwin's suit.'

'Yet then they allowed Lizzie to marry him, so soon after Timothy disappeared. For the life of me, I cannot understand why,' Sybbie said. 'We know Timothy died – but it sounds as if William didn't know about it.' She bit her lip. 'Unless he was the one who shot Timothy and covered it up, but I can't believe anyone related to Bernard would do that. Well, I don't *want* to believe it,' she finished with a wry smile.

'I don't think William killed Timothy, either,' Georgina said. 'And as for why Lizzie married Edwin – she'd lost the man she loved. Maybe nothing mattered anymore, and she married him to stop him going on at her parents.'

'Hang on. When Dad died, you didn't rush out and get remarried,' Bea pointed out. 'You threw yourself into work. Will and I worried ourselves sick that you were lonely.'

It was true. And she was doing exactly the same thing now that her relationship with Colin was unravelling: keeping herself too busy to think, and too busy to miss being with him and helping out in his investigations. 'Mmm,' she said.

To her relief, Sybbie continued talking. 'Lizzie didn't have to marry anyone. She could've remained a spinster. As her father, William would have provided a dowry; he could have given her that money in her own right.'

'Maybe I'm making connections where they don't exist,' Doris said, joining in, 'but Timothy seems to be determined to protect Lizzie's honour. I think he remembers her, but he doesn't want people to judge her.'

This felt like what Georgina and Sybbie had wondered earlier.

'I've been wondering: what if they'd talked about him approaching her father,' Doris continued, 'and they'd antici- pated William agreeing to let her marry him, but then Timothy died before he could marry her?'

'You think she was pregnant?' Georgina asked. Then, seeing the confusion on Bea's and Sybbie's faces, she told them what Doris had suggested.

'We were thinking along similar lines. And it's a good point, Doris,' Sybbie said. 'Amelia would've known early on, because the maid responsible for the laundry would have told her on the quiet, knowing that Amelia loved her daughter dearly and would protect her. In Amelia's shoes, I would've taken Lizzie away to Scotland or something, before she started showing. The servants here would've been loyal – you heard what she said about their staff staying on. Amelia could've claimed that the baby belonged to a cousin who'd sadly died in childbirth, and they were adopting the baby.'

'Or even claimed that it was her own baby,' Bea said.

'Amelia was born in 1815 – so she would've been fifty,' Sybbie said. 'Perhaps she was a little too old to get away with suggesting that?'

'I've seen plenty of census records showing a mum in her late forties, the youngest daughter being sixteen, and then there's a month-old baby which is also claimed as the mum's youngest child, when with that kind of age gap, it's fairly obvious the baby is actually the daughter's child,' Bea said.

'Amelia is definitely on Timothy's side,' Georgina said. 'Listen to this. *Timothy is the youngest son in his family, with little prospect of inheritance. He is a fellow at the university; should he marry Lizzie, he would no longer be a fellow and could not live in university property. How they would manage to live, I do not know. And London is so very far away. But I know he would be kind to Lizzie. He would not squash her, the way I fear Edwin would. Timothy would encourage her to be who she is. To me, that matters far more than the fact he is not her social equal. I want Lizzie to be as happy in her marriage as I am with William.'*

'You're right about attitudes changing towards marriage, Bea,' Sybbie said.

'Edwin seems to be persistent,' Georgina said. '*Edwin paid yet another visit today. He wished to talk to William about marrying Lizzie. William put him off, saying that Lizzie is not yet ready for marriage. Edwin said at twenty-two she is already losing her bloom and should have a care that she not become an old maid.*'

'That's outrageous,' Bea said, bridling. 'If I'd been Amelia...'

'You wouldn't actually have been able to do very much,' Georgina said. 'But you could have made sure Edwin wasn't on the guest list for any kind of party, and William could have refused him admittance to the house. But listen to this. *I have asked William to make it clear to Edwin Rutherford that he is not an acceptable suitor.*'

'Good for Amelia,' Bea said.

'Here's what we've been waiting for,' Georgina said with a smile. 'The end of August. *Timothy has spoken to William today. Should he leave the university, he has contacts in the Department of Antiquities at the British Museum who may offer him a job to replace his work as a fellow. His spinster great-aunt will allow him to live in her house, should he wish to marry. She intends to leave him the house when she dies. Although he cannot offer Lizzie a title or the wealth she is accustomed to, they will be able to manage. But, more than that, he loves Lizzie for herself. And she has confessed to me that she returns his affections.*'

'So that's all the barriers gone,' Sybbie said in satisfaction. 'They have somewhere to live, Timothy's likely to get another job, and even if the new job pays less, they'd at least have Lizzie's dowry to supplement his salary.'

'*William has told Timothy that he may ask Lizzie for her hand in marriage,*' Georgina continued. '*We will hold a ball to announce her engagement.*'

'And Edwin Rutherford will have to stop pestering her,' Bea said, smiling.

'*The British Almanac says the moon will be full on the 4th day of October, but also that there will be a partial eclipse. Perhaps a day either side would be better for the ball,*' Georgina read. 'It sounds a bit as if Amelia's superstitious, about an eclipse meaning bad luck. And I suppose, back in those days, they usually held balls on the night of a full moon because it meant there would be light for people travelling to a ball.'

'They were the original all-night partiers,' Sybbie said with a grin. 'A ball wouldn't start until about ten in the evening; they had dinner at 1am, then served breakfast to the late stayers. Because the people attending balls didn't have to keep business hours, it meant they could sleep all day.'

Bea laughed. 'Not that much different from being a modern-day student, then.'

Sybbie and Georgina exchanged an amused glance. 'I remember all-night parties,' Sybbie said, 'and the hangover from drinking too much bad red wine – or, worse still, a punch where people tipped bottles of whatever into the punchbowl during the course of the evening to fill it up.'

'Did they get drunk at Victorian balls?' Bea asked. 'What about lemonade? Wasn't that what Regency and Victorian debutantes were offered?'

'It was made from lemons mixed with sugar and water and strained through muslin, I think,' Sybbie said. 'I'm sure I saw a recipe somewhere in the commonplace book.'

'There's bound to be something in Mrs Beeton's.' Bea looked it up on the internet. 'Yes, you're right. The recipe says to rub lumps of sugar over lemons to absorb the oil, add the lemon juice, pour over boiling water, let the mixture cool and strain it through muslin.' She grinned. 'Oh, I love this bit. *The lemonade will be much improved by having the white of an egg beaten up in it; a little sherry mixed with it, makes this beverage much nicer.* So it was a sly way of drinking alcohol while pretending you weren't.'

'I'm not so sure about the egg white,' Sybbie said with a grimace.

'One of my friends is a bartender when she's resting,' Bea said. 'I'll message her to see why you'd add egg whites to a drink.'

Clearly her friend wasn't in the middle of a shift, because the answer came back quickly. 'She says it softens sour drinks and makes them feel lighter. And it adds a foamy top and good mouthfeel to a cocktail,' Bea reported.

'Perhaps it tastes better than it sounds,' Sybbie said, not looking convinced.

'But what happened to the engagement between Lizzie and Timothy?' Bea asked. 'In August, Lizzie told her mum she loved Timothy, and Timothy had William's permission to ask Lizzie to marry him. Amelia was planning an engagement ball for October. Yet, in October, Lizzie marries Edwin – a man she's turned down several times, and a man that her parents don't like, either. It doesn't make sense. Why would she turn down the man she loved?'

'Or did she say yes to his proposal, and then he died?' Georgina asked.

'We know from Doris that he was shot in the back,' Sybbie said. 'But we don't know who fired the shot, or whether it was before or after he'd managed to propose.' She frowned. 'My money's on Edwin Rutherford, because Timothy was his chief rival for Lizzie's affections.'

'But if Edwin had killed Timothy and someone knew about it, Edwin would have ended up on the gallows. Nobody's above the law,' Georgina said. 'William and Amelia were happy for

Timothy to marry Lizzie; but then William was really curt when Timothy's sister wrote to him. That's a complete about-face. What happened to make him change his view of Timothy?'

'And why can't Timothy remember? Or is he still trying to protect Lizzie's honour by not telling us anything?' Bea asked.

ELEVEN

'Again?' Trish asked wearily. 'I've already told you everything I know, Inspector Bradshaw. I can't think of anything else that will help your investigations.'

'I'm sorry if it seems that I'm badgering you,' Colin said. 'I'm trying to get a handle on the nighthawk situation. I believe several of Simon's digs have had problems over the last five years.'

'If you announce your finds early,' Trish said, 'then you tend to get people coming to try their luck on the site.'

But she didn't meet his eye. He decided to ask her directly. 'Was Simon involved with the nighthawks?'

She didn't answer.

'Dr Melton,' he said gently, 'this is a murder investigation. I need answers. If you'd rather talk to me at the station, I can arrange that.' And he hoped that sounded more like an offer than a threat. He had the feeling that trying to pull rank on Trish Melton would make her clam up even more, and that wouldn't be helpful.

She sighed and shook her head. 'I just want to get on with my job. I know that probably sounds heartless, but we only have a limited amount of time. I want my students to get as much experience as they can – and all these questions won't bring Simon back.'

'No, but the answers might stop someone else getting hurt,' he said. 'Was Simon involved with the nighthawks?'

'I don't have any proof,' Trish said. 'But I think he probably was. Not because he needed the money, because he didn't – he had family money.'

'So what would have been his motive for being involved with them?' Colin asked.

Trish considered the question. 'I think he liked taking risks.'

'What would he do with the items taken? Sell them to private collectors?'

'He might have had the contacts to do that,' Trish said, 'but I'm not so sure he sold things. I think he kept the finds for himself. For me, it's the thrill of finding the domestic items, the things that connect us to people who lived here long ago – the hairpins, the little pots of make-up, the glassware, the loom weights and the so rare pieces of fabric; for him, I think it was the treasure. He was never happier than when we found gold or gemstones.'

'So you think he leaked information to the nighthawks and the deal was he kept some of the loot they dug up?'

'It's a theory. I don't have any proof,' she reminded him.

'Did you ever talk to anyone about your suspicions?'

She shook her head. 'I could hardly accuse him without having any evidence.'

'Where might he have kept the things he took?'

'I have no idea. Not in the house, though,' she said quickly. 'My sister had nothing to do with it.'

Her sister, who was a curator at a museum where small and rare things had gone missing – just as small and rare things had presumably gone missing during the nighthawk raids. Was Mei's theory right and Simon was involved in the thefts at the museum, too? What was Joanna's involvement? And was Trish unaware of the issues at the museum, or did she know and she was trying to protect her little sister?

Trish seemed to think Simon had family money. Was that truly the case, or had Simon supplemented his salary with the systematic looting and sale of historical artefacts? Colin had already asked Mo to look into Simon's finances; hopefully his sergeant was gathering answers.

'Thank you for your time, Dr Melton,' he said formally. 'I'm afraid I probably will be back.' Once they'd finished looking at Simon's financial records and phone records.

'Lizzie accepted Timothy's proposal,' Georgina said. 'It's all here. *Our darling Lizzie is betrothed to Timothy! The whole household is delighted. Frederick is very fond of Timothy and says he believes his friend will be a good husband to Lizzie. I wish they could live closer to us, but the great-aunt with whom they will live resides in London. Timothy is travelling back to London for a couple of days on Friday to give his family the good news. He will also talk to the university and his friend at the British Museum. Plans are underway already to hold a ball on October 3rd, to celebrate the engagement. And it is settled that Lizzie shall be a spring bride.'*

'So why did she marry Edwin instead?' Bea asked. 'Can Timothy remember anything about proposing to Lizzie?'

'Doris?' Georgina asked.

'I've already asked. He says it was the happiest day of his life. Lizzie's father gave him permission to propose. He walked with her in the gardens by the herbaceous borders – obviously within view of the house, so it counted as being chaperoned,' Doris said. 'And he asked her to marry him. She said yes. Timothy was going back to London to tell his family about the engagement, and to start sorting out his job and their future home. William allowed him to use the carriage to go the train station. And then it's all a blank, until the moment he was shot.'

Georgina turned back to the diary. 'Oh, my God. Listen to this,' she said. 'This is from the Friday, when Timothy was going back to London. *I cannot,* cannot *believe what has happened. Edwin Rutherford came here in high dudgeon, demanding to speak to William in private. He left, some fifteen minutes later. And what William then came to tell me will break poor Lizzie's heart. Timothy Marsden is already married. To think he would have stood in our parish church, in front of everyone we know and love, to plight his troth to Lizzie when he was not free to do so...'*

'It sounds horribly like *Jane Eyre*,' Bea said.

'I agree. And it's not true,' Doris said. 'Timothy was never married. He loved Lizzie Walters, and she was the only woman he'd ever asked to marry him. The only woman he wanted to marry.'

'It smells incredibly fishy to me,' Sybbie said. 'Timothy was "married"' – she made elaborate speech marks with her fingers – 'and the person who uncovered that fact, suspiciously shortly after Timothy became engaged to Lizzie, was the person Lizzie had repeatedly turned down.'

'It doesn't sound likely to me, either,' Bea agreed. 'Where was Edwin's evidence of Timothy's supposed marriage? Did Amelia and William really take his word for it?'

Georgina turned over the page. 'No – or at least Amelia didn't. *I cannot believe Timothy would be so duplicitous. He* loved *Lizzie. I cannot see him as an Edward Rochester type, locking his mad wife in the attic and pretending that the marriage had never happened, so he could marry again wherever his heart pleased.'*

'It sounds as if Amelia agreed with us,' Sybbie said. 'It was fictional. But Edwin Rutherford must have said something to convince William.'

'*Edwin said he had wanted to marry Lizzie for years, and when Timothy started paying her attention, he was jealous,*' Georgina read.

'You don't say?' Bea drawled.

'If you're going to lie, it's more convincing if you use as much of the truth as possible,' Sybbie said. 'So he's started with the truth.'

'*He was upset that Lizzie had turned him down repeatedly, but he loved her and he wanted to be sure that the man she was choosing to spend her life with was a good man.*'

'And how was that his place?' Bea demanded. 'Surely it was William's?'

'Edwin's obviously trying to paint himself as the noble type,' Georgina said. '*He had heard of Pinkerton's agency in America, and how their detective had safely delivered President Abraham Lincoln from Springfield to Washington, DC. He therefore sought to engage a private detective in London – a man his father knew of who had left Scotland Yard to work on his own. The detective found out what had happened. I begged William for fuller details, but he refused to discuss it with me. He has seen the detective's report and says he is looking into it. I am sure there must be some mistake.*'

'Edwin obviously knew his audience well,' Sybbie said. 'Even if Timothy could prove the report was a lie, Edwin used a third party's name to tell that lie and could weasel out of it by claiming he'd been hoodwinked, too. And he'd focused on William's worries about how Timothy would be able to support Lizzie after the marriage, when he couldn't continue as a fellow at the university. Even if they'd found out the truth, mud tended to stick: there would always be a whiff of scandal attached to Timothy, with people whispering about him.'

'Which means the institutions that might've offered him a job would either retract their offer before he started, or let him go,' Georgina finished. 'You're right. It's all about William's fears again that Timothy wouldn't be able to support Lizzie. And maybe the rumours would make it difficult for the wider family, too – Frederick still needed a wife and an heir, and Robert was unmarried.'

'Surely Frederick would have stood up for Timothy? They were close friends,' Bea said. 'He could've told his father the truth.'

'But, more importantly, how did Timothy end up being shot, and who did it? It can't have been William or Frederick. They would've asked questions, not just shot him – particularly not in the back, because that was dishonourable,' Sybbie said. 'Even if Timothy *had* been guilty of what Edwin accused him of – which we know he wasn't – William would've found a way to make him leave the country, then whisked Lizzie off to live with relations, many miles away from the scandal.'

'Go back to the diary, Mum,' Bea urged.

'*William said we would wait for Timothy to return, and then he could explain himself.*' Georgina shook her head. 'Except obviously Timothy didn't return.'

'I still don't get why they believed Edwin,' Bea said. 'Especially if there wasn't any proof. William would surely have wanted to know the details – who the alleged wife was, when and where the marriage took place, who the witnesses were. There would be records. If it was by licence rather than banns, there would be the three parts – the allegation by the groom that there was no reason they couldn't marry, the bond showing the sum of money he'd pay if that wasn't true, and then the licence itself.'

'Could Edwin have faked the licence?' Sybbie asked.

'Yes – but it would've taken an awful lot of effort, plus he would've had someone else in on the scheme who could potentially blackmail him over it,' Bea said.

'Maybe Edwin thought he could get away with it because he was their neighbour. The families had known each other for decades, so he assumed they'd trust his word over one of Frederick's university friends,' Georgina said.

'Amelia says William is going to look into it. What happened?' Sybbie asked.

Georgina went back to the diary and looked through the next week. '*There are rumours buzzing about Timothy in the village – that he is Norfolk's own Mr Rochester, and he sought to drag Lizzie into his web of lies. Lizzie does not believe it, and neither do I. But the gossips' tongues are spiteful. We are keeping quiet company at home.*'

'And you can guess who started spreading the rumours,' Bea said. 'Edwin. If he knew William was looking into things, he also knew he needed to put some pressure on locally, so Lizzie would give in and marry him.'

'Amelia doesn't write much for the next week,' Georgina said. '*Timothy has not returned from London or sent a single word here. I fear that perhaps we have misjudged Edwin after all, and the horrible rumours are true, else surely Timothy would have come back to refute them? His absence is very telling. Frederick is adamant that his friend would never have betrayed us like that, but what else are we to think, when Timothy continues to be absent?*'

'They've only given him a couple of weeks. And why haven't they sent someone they trusted to look at the church register in the parish where Edwin claimed the wedding took place?' Bea asked.

'Different times, I suppose,' Sybbie said with a sigh.

'Hang on. Here's another entry,' Georgina said. '*Mary, the wife of Perkins, our coachman, came to see me today. She is much concerned about her husband and says he is talking in his sleep, muttering. He will not tell her what is wrong, but she believes he will tell William, if asked.*'

'Did he?' Bea asked.

'*William is visiting the tenants today. I summoned Perkins to find out what he knew,*' Georgina read.

'Go, Amelia,' Sybbie said softly. 'She obviously wasn't going to risk William deciding whatever the coachman said was too shocking for her.'

'*He tells me on the Friday before last, he was taking Timothy Marsden to the train station in Norwich, when our carriage met that of the Rutherfords in the drive. Edwin told Perkins that Timothy Marsden was a bad lot masquerading as a good man. Edwin was going to make sure Timothy went back to London and he would save the good name of Lord Wyatt's family – but the coachman wasn't to breathe a word of what had happened, or it would bring shame upon the family.*'

'Again, Edwin's using a kernel of truth to tell a plausible lie,' Sybbie said. 'Perkins, as the loyal coachman, wouldn't want people to gossip about William or any of the Walters family. Whatever his private thoughts about Edwin or Timothy, he'd put William's honour first.'

'*Horrified that the behaviour of any guest here might threaten our family's good name, Perkins allowed Edwin's men to take Timothy and bundle them into his carriage. He agreed to say nothing to William, and admitted he was only telling me now because I asked directly. He told me he believed that Edwin was taking Timothy to the station to make sure he embarked on the London train and would never return,*' Georgina continued.

'And that's the sad thing. Timothy never did return to Little Wenborough Manor,' Sybbie said. 'Which gave Edwin's lie the "proof" he needed.'

'But Timothy didn't go to London, either – at least, not to his family,' Bea said. 'So where did Edwin take him?'

'Somewhere quiet where he could shoot Timothy without anyone knowing,' Georgina said quietly. 'My guess is that it was somewhere on Rutherford land. But we need physical evidence

– which we're not going to get, more than a century and a half later.'

'I'll double-check the parish and civil registers for a marriage record – not that I think I'll find one – and for a death record,' Bea said, and got to work on Georgina's laptop.

'I'll make us some coffee,' Sybbie said.

'I'll give you a hand,' Georgina offered.

Bea wasn't able to find Timothy's alleged marriage, or any records for his death. 'All I can find is Lizzie's marriage to Edwin,' she said. 'I think your guess is right, Mum – Edwin shot Timothy and then buried him. But I don't understand why William didn't ask more questions. Why he didn't do his own investigations.'

'Maybe he wanted to ask questions, but then they heard nothing more from Timothy until Clara wrote, asking about him,' Georgina said. 'When it was clear that Timothy hadn't returned to his own family, and he hadn't returned to Little Wenborough to clear his name either, then maybe William thought it was proof of Edwin's claim. Worried about being exposed as a potential bigamist, Timothy had abandoned both Lizzie and his alleged secret wife and gone abroad.'

'He could easily have done that. There would've been plenty of work for him at Pompeii or the Valley of the Kings at that time,' Sybbie agreed. 'Is there a clue in Amelia's diary?'

Georgina continued skimming through the diary, and winced. 'Oh, no. There's nothing about Timothy, but there's this entry. *My poor Lizzie tells me today she has missed her monthly courses. She admits that she and Timothy anticipated their wedding night. Just once, and he believed that it would be safe, the first time.*'

'But they were chaperoned, surely?' Bea asked. 'When could they have been alone.'

'There are servants' corridors in the house,' Sybbie said. 'If

Lizzie had told Timothy where the doors were, it would've been easy for him to slip from his room to hers.'

'Lizzie must've been so frightened,' Georgina said. 'She was expecting Timothy's baby, and he had disappeared. Even if she hadn't believed Edwin's story that Timothy was already married, she might've presumed that Edwin had threatened him enough that Timothy had gone abroad and wasn't coming back. Being unmarried with a baby would've meant a huge scandal. People would have shunned Lizzie, and probably her family as well. Frederick wasn't married at that point, and an illegitimate child in the family might be too much for his future wife to stomach.'

'Unless Amelia could get Lizzie away from Norfolk for a while. Somewhere a good week's travel away, to a place where Amelia could trust whoever they stayed with to keep their secret and Lizzie could have the baby,' Sybbie said.

Georgina went back to the diary. '*Timothy's sister wrote to William today, saying that she had not heard from him for a fortnight and was concerned. William wrote back to say that Timothy had returned to his family in London two weeks ago. I think he rather gave her short shrift. We have no idea where Timothy has gone, but neither does his family. It seems that he has abandoned Lizzie, after all. I will talk to William about making an extended visit to my cousins in Yorkshire.*'

'But clearly that didn't happen, because Lizzie married Edwin in October,' Bea said.

'And finally we have this,' Georgina said. '*Edwin again offered for Lizzie, saying that it would scotch the rumours if she married him immediately. He will apply for a special licence.*'

'So he could marry her before anyone found out what he'd done?' Bea suggested. 'Did Timothy know that Lizzie was pregnant?'

'If he did know, he hasn't told me,' Doris said, and Georgina relayed the information to Bea and Sybbie.

'I really wish Amelia had just whisked her away to York-shire,' Sybbie said.

'So do I,' Georgina said. 'The diary entries are quite sparse from here on. *Lizzie has agreed to marry Edwin Rutherford and will not be moved on her decision. She does not want to spoil her brothers' chances of a good match.* And the next thing is the wedding itself.'

'Which, according to the parish register, was at the parish church of Little Wenborough, by special licence,' Bea said from over the laptop's screen.

'Oh, Lizzie. Why didn't you listen to your mother and go to Yorkshire?' Sybbie asked.

'Because it wouldn't have stopped the gossip. And nothing mattered any more, with Timothy gone. Lizzie thought he'd abandoned her,' Doris said.

Georgina relayed the message.

'She knows the truth now, though, right?' Bea asked.

'Yes,' Doris confirmed.

'This is unbearable to read,' Georgina said. '*I wanted to stand up in church and announce, "This man is not fit to be my daughter's husband and I do not trust him." I even braced myself, ready to stand and make the declaration. But William squeezed my hand very tightly, to make me catch his eye, and he shook his head so very slightly. I stayed in our pew and I held my peace. I hope I may not live to regret my actions.*'

'As a mother, I just...' Sybbie shivered. 'I'm so glad Giles chose Cesca.'

'Amelia loses her sparkle for a while,' Georgina said. 'She doesn't write much, and her words are just flat in the few bits that are on the page. And then she worries in the new year. *Lizzie is so delicate in pregnancy. She has headaches and pains in her stomach. Her face, neck and hands are puffy. The doctor has told her to rest.*'

'Headaches and puffy hands,' Sybbie said. 'That sounds horribly like pre-eclampsia.'

'Doesn't it just?' Georgina said. 'That poor girl. But at least Amelia insisted that Lizzie should stay here at Little Wenborough while she was in a delicate condition. She stood her ground. *Edwin was hateful about it, but William spoke to Edwin's father and it is done.*'

'At least we know Lizzie was looked after properly, in her last months,' Bea said quietly.

'Or as much as she could be, where pre-eclampsia was concerned,' Sybbie said.

'I think they lived very quietly here during the pregnancy,' Georgina said. 'Amelia says the mosaic floor and the ruins have been covered over again, because Frederick no longer has the heart to exhibit them to the public. She's still worried about Lizzie, but Lizzie refuses to go to a lying-in hospital because she doesn't want to risk catching puerperal fever. And then it's May 1866. Lizzie has a terrible labour, and her headache gets worse and her face is really puffy.' She swallowed hard. 'The midwife attends Lizzie, along with Amelia. And this is heartbreaking. The baby's born, takes two breaths, and dies. Lizzie says her vision is blurred – and then she has a seizure. The doctor comes and lets blood, but it doesn't work. She has another seizure, and then dies.'

'My poor Lizzie,' Sybbie said softly. 'If you were alive now, they would've sorted this out before you had the baby and you would've been kept safe.'

Bea dabbed at her eyes. 'That's so sad.'

'I can't read any more,' Georgina said. 'I think I need some fresh air.'

'Let's take the dogs into the garden,' Sybbie said. 'I don't think I can face telling Trish about any of this, yet.'

'It's something we definitely need to do over cake,' Georgina agreed. 'Though perhaps not in the f—' She stopped abruptly.

'Not where, Mum?' Bea asked.

'The farm shop café. Between you and me – and I trust you to keep this to yourself, Bea – I don't want Cesca to know anything about this,' Sybbie said quietly.

Bea frowned, and then the penny dropped. 'Ohhh,' she said. 'Congratulations. And I won't breathe a word on either account.'

'Thank you,' Sybbie said.

'I think you need a hug.' Bea stood up and held Sybbie closely. 'That's nightmare stuff to read when someone you love is pregnant. But Cesca's going to be *fine*.'

Sybbie's voice was decidedly croaky when she said, 'I appreciate that, Bea.'

The three of them walked in silence into the garden, the dogs pattering behind them.

'Where do we go from here?' Georgina asked as they reached the lake. 'We suspect what happened to Timothy, but Colin would say our evidence is circumstantial. Or hearsay.'

'Hmm,' Sybbie said. 'Colin might have some good suggestions about what Edwin possibly did with Timothy's body.'

'When I brought up the subject before, it ended up getting very messy,' Georgina reminded her friend. 'He refused to believe me, and I'm not backing down. He'll have to make the first move.'

'Mum, do you not think you're being a tiny bit stubborn?' Bea asked.

'No,' Georgina said. 'Do you not think *he's* being a tiny bit stubborn?'

'He's being very stubborn,' Bea said, 'and I bet he's as miserable about it as you are.'

'Talk to him,' Sybbie urged.

'I'll think about it,' Georgina said, narrowing her eyes. 'But right now, it's more important to think about where we look next to find out what happened to Timothy. Where were they when Edwin shot him – and where did Edwin bury Timothy's body?'

TWELVE

Trish definitely knew more than she was letting on, Colin was sure of it. But how could he get her to open up to him? This was the point in the case where he could really do with talking to Georgina. She'd have some ideas of how he could approach Trish – especially as he knew she'd been talking to Trish about the mystery surrounding Timothy Marsden's disappearance back in 1865.

A murder, which Georgina claimed she'd heard about from a ghost.

He closed his eyes.

Where most things were concerned, Georgina Drake was sensible and rational, funny and wise. But on this one point she was completely flaky.

How could she possibly believe in something that categorically didn't exist?

On the other hand, he really wasn't enjoying his life without her in it. He *missed* her. He missed Bert's plumy tail waving madly and four paws pattering across the floor when he walked into Georgie's kitchen after work. He missed the peace of sitting in the garden with Georgie, holding a mug of coffee and watching the sky darken and the stars come out.

He could be stubborn and wait for her to admit that he was right. Then again, he knew she was just as stubborn; she was probably waiting for him to apologise.

There had to be *some* way they could find a compromise.

Maybe work could be the way to help them bridge the gulf between them. It was worth a try. He pulled his phone from his pocket and texted her.

> Hope you're OK. Can we meet somewhere neutral and talk? C x

She didn't reply for half an hour; he knew she wasn't a game-player, so he assumed she'd left her phone indoors while she was in the garden. She was probably at Sybbie's, he thought, because she'd talked about working in the archives at Little Wenborough Manor.

His phone finally pinged with a message, and he was shocked by how relieved it made him feel.

> Hope you're OK, too. Agree, talking would be good. Where and when? G x

He was glad then that he'd taken a conciliatory tone, because her reply was warm rather than clipped and cool. She clearly wanted to find common ground, too.

> How about the cathedral? We can walk through the Close, down to the river.

And then maybe, when they'd talked a bit, he could take her to dinner at a tiny, romantic restaurant he knew on one of the cobbled back streets.

> Would six work for you? x

> Fine. Meet you by the dragon on the Ethelbert Gate? x

I'll be there x, he replied. And wasn't it funny how the day suddenly felt so much lighter?

The Ethelbert Gate was the southernmost of the two gates leading to the cathedral close from Tombland. Georgina had played tour guide, the previous summer, and told Colin the story about how the citizens had had a huge fight with the monks in the late thirteenth century and the whole city had been excommunicated. Even though investigations had shown that the prior was at fault for the riot and St Ethelbert's church had burned down by accident, Henry III insisted that the citizens build the huge flint-and-stone gateway as reparation.

At the top of the gate, geometric designs cut from ashlar resembling three rose windows were set against the flint; but what had caught Georgina's attention were the carvings on the spandrels just above the arch. On the right-hand side was the dragon, its wings tucked above its body and its face having an almost lion-like mane; on the left-hand side was a man climbing away from the foliage, presumably St George, brandishing a long sword. They'd talked then about going to find all the dragons in Norwich – from the wooden carvings on church pews through to Snap the Dragon, the eighteenth-century costume used on guild days – but they hadn't got round to it yet. Would they get the chance to look for the dragons together, this summer? Or was their relationship damaged beyond repair?

As the cathedral clock chimed and struck six, he saw Georgina walking across the cobbled area of Tombland towards him. He raised one hand in greeting, and almost sagged in relief when she waved back.

'Hello,' she said. Her smile was slightly nervous, and he

longed to wrap his arms round her and tell her he'd fight a hundred dragons for her.

Then again, he knew that Georgina was perfectly capable of fighting the dragons herself.

'Hi,' he said. 'How are you?'

'Fine,' she said, though, to him, it looked as if she'd straightened her spine before she said it. 'How are you?'

'Fine,' he said, even though he wasn't. And then, because he couldn't hold it in any longer, he blurted out, 'I miss you.' He'd missed everything about her – that shrewd green gaze, her smile, the way she laughed.

'I miss you, too,' she admitted.

So she felt as bad as he did? And that in turn made him feel worse. He didn't want to make her feel bad. He wanted her to be happy. 'I'm sorry,' he said. 'I don't want to fight with you, Georgie.'

'I don't want to fight with you, either,' she said. 'But when I told you about Doris, you were so high-handed and closed-minded about it – and that made me furious.'

He blew out a breath. 'We're going to have to find a way of dealing with this, but I have no idea where to start. Shall we walk for a bit?'

'All right,' she said.

They walked through the gateway towards the river, past the cathedral on the left and then between flint-and-brick houses with dormer windows and tall chimneys. The gardens were full of late spring flowers, and a huge magnolia tree was still in bloom. The whole place felt like somewhere out of time, so quiet and peaceful.

His hand brushed against hers deliberately once, twice, and he caught her fingers loosely. She didn't push him away, so he wove his fingers between hers until they were holding hands properly.

'I'm not delusional,' she said quietly.

'I know,' he said.

'And I've told Cesca, Sybbie, Bea – who's staying with me for a couple of days – and Will, on the phone, about Doris. They all believe me.'

Francesca and Bea both had a flair for the dramatic. Sybbie didn't suffer fools gladly, but she could be a bit eccentric; plus she was close to Georgie and would defend her staunchly. But rational, quiet scientist Will... for Georgina's son to believe in the ghost stuff was a little more surprising, Colin thought. 'I don't think you're a liar or a fool, Georgie. I really don't.'

'But you don't believe me.'

'I don't know what to think,' he said. 'Rationally, I know ghosts don't exist. But if I think back over the last year... looking at what you've discovered, your hit rate is better than just guess-work.' He sighed. 'Which I think is because you're good with archives and putting pieces of puzzles together.'

'It's because I know where to start,' Georgina corrected.

'I'm struggling with this. Can we...?' He paused, trying to work out the most tactful way of asking. 'Can we agree to disagree?'

'Sweep it under the carpet, you mean?' She shook her head. 'That isn't helpful.'

'Neither's arguing. We have opposite views on this and there isn't a middle way – at least, not one that I can see right now.' He dragged in a breath. 'But I don't want us to break up. You're too important to me. Can we... I don't know, at least agree to respect each other's point of view?'

'Maybe,' she said. 'As long as you can accept that Doris is and will continue to be a part of my life.'

He gave her a wry smile. 'I'm not a control freak. You make your own choices about who you associate with.' Even if it was something that didn't exist; this felt weirdly like talking about a real person. He shoved the thought away. 'So how's the cold case going?' he asked.

For a moment, her expression still looked constrained and he wondered if she'd refuse to discuss it with him, but then she seemed to soften. 'It's really sad,' she said. 'We've pieced together a lot of what happened from Amelia's diary – that would be Bernard's great-great-great-grandmother. Frederick was the oldest son, and he was at university with Timothy – who was the youngest son in his own family, and worked as a fellow at the University of London. Frederick asked Timothy to come and help with the excavation; and Timothy fell in love with Lizzie, Frederick's sister. Even though he wouldn't have the title and prospects they might have wanted for Lizzie, they liked him and agreed that they could get married.'

'Forgive me,' Colin said, 'but that all sounds pretty good.'

'Oh, it was,' Georgina said. 'Except then we have Edwin Rutherford – he was the heir to Great Wenborough Hall. He wanted to marry Lizzie, but she'd already turned him down, several times. And he claimed he'd hired a private detective to investigate Timothy, and discovered he was already married.'

'That sounds a bit too convenient,' Colin said.

'Doesn't it just?' Georgina agreed. 'Amelia – Lizzie's mum – wrote in her diary that she didn't believe it, either. But Timothy disappeared. He didn't return to his family, nor to Little Wenborough. The family's coachman admitted that Edwin had taken Timothy out of the coach and into his own.'

'That's unusual. Why did he let that happen?' Colin asked.

'Because Edwin lied to him and said that Timothy was about to bring shame on the family, so the coachman needed to keep it quiet. Edwin said he was taking Timothy to the train station and making quite sure he didn't come back.'

'You clearly don't think Edwin took him to the train station.'

'No. But there isn't any proof of that, and obviously, with it being 1865, there's nobody left who was alive at the time.'

Colin was tempted to ask why Doris couldn't ask, but he didn't want to sound snippy. 'No other documents?' he asked.

'No. The Rutherford family died out, the house was demolished years ago, and...' She shook her head. 'I did wonder if maybe Edwin challenged Timothy to a duel, even though duelling had been made illegal years before then.'

'Just because something's against the law, it doesn't stop people doing it,' Colin said.

'That's true,' she said. 'Anyway, that's the point where Timothy disappears.'

She filled him in on the rest of the information she'd uncovered, and it felt so good to be discussing things with Georgina again, the way they'd always discussed her cold cases and the brick walls in his own cases. And if they could work together and solve her cold case together, perhaps their personal relationship would manage to sort itself out, too.

'It definitely raises a lot of questions,' he said. 'Why on earth did Lizzie marry a man she obviously disliked? And why didn't her parents stop her?'

'Maybe Lizzie felt she had to make up for her mistake in anticipating her wedding night with Timothy and falling pregnant,' Georgina said. 'Marrying Edwin would stop him spreading more rumours, because he'd want to protect his own reputation.'

'So Lizzie ended up married to a bully instead of to the man who really loved her.' He shook his head. 'That's such a shame.'

'It gets worse still, unfortunately. She had a difficult pregnancy. Amelia put the symptoms in her diary and it sounds like pre-eclampsia,' Georgina said. 'Though the good thing is that Amelia insisted on Lizzie living back at Little Wenborough for the second half of her pregnancy, so their family doctor could keep an eye on her.'

He didn't need to ask Georgina anything about the medical condition, because he'd lived through that particular nightmare with his wife. Part of him wanted to avoid the subject; then again, what was the point in not being honest?

He didn't want to put yet another barrier between them. 'Marianne had pre-eclampsia, when she was pregnant with Cathy,' he said, as neutrally as he could. 'I read up on it and absolutely terrified myself. She spent the last three weeks of her pregnancy on bed rest in hospital.' He blew out a breath. 'It's why we only had one child. We didn't want to take that risk again.'

Georgina looked horrified and her hand tightened round his. 'I'm so sorry, Colin. If I'd known, I wouldn't have told you any of this.'

Yeah. He knew that. Georgie was all about healing, not hurting. It was one of the things he loved about her. 'I know,' he said, squeezing her hand briefly. 'But Marianne and I were lucky. At least the medics understand pre-eclampsia and how to treat it, now. I'm assuming that back when Lizzie had it, there was a lot less knowledge.'

'Sadly, you're right,' she said softly. 'The baby died almost as soon as she was born. Then Lizzie had a seizure and died.'

The cathedral clock tolled its melancholy quarter-chimes, and Colin shivered. 'Her family must've been devastated.'

'They were. Sybbie and Bea are telling Bernard tonight, and I'm going to tell Trish as much as I know, tomorrow.' She sighed. 'Though I have no proof that Edwin killed Timothy, and still no idea where the body might be buried.'

'Bert can't find it?' Colin wrinkled his nose. 'Well. I guess you can't exactly let him dig at the excavations.'

'I don't think that's where Timothy was buried. Otherwise D—' She stopped. 'Let's just say the team's drawn a blank.'

He could guess what she wasn't saying – that Doris had told her before where the bodies were buried – and he appreciated it. He wasn't going to make an issue out of it. Not when they had a chance to patch things up between them. 'Let's assume Edwin bundled Timothy into his carriage. Why didn't Timothy struggle or fight back?'

* * *

Georgina was glad that Colin hadn't made a snippy comment about Doris. He could've done, but he hadn't, which gave her hope that they could maybe work their way through this sticky patch. Together.

Plus she was enjoying talking to him about the cold case. He paid attention and his comments were always thoughtful and measured. He might see something she'd missed – just as when he thought aloud to her about his own cases, she sometimes had insights that he'd missed. They were a good team.

'Maybe Timothy did try to fight back, but I'm certain Edwin had a pistol, if you remember?' Georgina suggested, trying to remind him of what she'd told him about Timothy's death but without making things awkward again.

'Timothy was a university fellow, so he would've been bright enough to realise that he'd need to go along with Edwin until he found out what the other man was planning to do, and then he could work out how to escape,' Colin said. 'I think we can also assume that, despite what Edwin told the coachman, he didn't take Timothy to the train station. Edwin lived at Great Wenborough Hall, you said?'

Georgina nodded. 'Apparently the hall once stood where the football and cricket pitches are, now. The War Office used it as a training school, and it was demolished a few years after the end of the Second World War.'

'So the lands probably adjoined Bernard and Sybbie's,' Colin said.

'Which is probably the reason why Edwin was so keen to marry Lizzie. She wouldn't ever have the Little Wenborough lands herself, being a woman and having two older brothers, but it still meant there would be a dynastic link between Edwin's family's lands and her,' Georgina said. 'Plus Edwin would be able to get his hands on Lizzie's dowry.'

'The chances are, Edwin killed Timothy on his own family's lands,' Colin said. 'But then he would've had to dispose of the body. I'm assuming his henchmen were loyal, either because he paid them enough or because they had a similar character to his.' Colin had a tiny pleat between his eyebrows when he was thinking about something, which Georgina found cute. 'My best guess is that he would have buried Timothy where people were unlikely to find the body, even accidentally,' he said. 'Possibly in woodland – he might even have shot Timothy in the woods, too, and anyone hearing a gunshot would've thought it was from a gamekeeper's gun or a shooting party. It might be worth checking if there's been any housing development on the site of former woodland nearby, and if any skeletons were found when the foundations were dug.' He looked at Georgina, wrinkling his nose. 'Though I'm sorry, I don't have the resources to mount a search of a large area of woodland, especially for a body we can't be absolutely sure is buried there.'

'I wouldn't expect that,' Georgina said. 'I know if Timothy's remains had been found in the last fifty or so years, the skeleton would've been treated as "bones of antiquity". It's not going to be a high priority. But it would be nice to find him and give him a proper burial – and give some closure to Trish's family.'

'Yes, I can see that,' Colin agreed.

'I know I'm not supposed to ask, but how's your case going?' she asked.

He glanced around; she guessed he was checking whether it was private enough for him to discuss things with her. The riverside walk was almost deserted at this time on a weeknight, apart from a few joggers with headphones, and hopefully he still realised that she would never pass on anything he told her. She'd missed his usual custom of thinking aloud to her about his cases over the last few days.

'It's not. At the moment, the most likely situation is that Simon was killed by nighthawks – heritage thieves,' he said.

'You think he disturbed them while they were looting the site?'

'Either that, or he was involved with them and they fell out about something. We're doing background checks, but we keep coming up against brick walls,' Colin admitted. 'There was definitely tension between him and Trish. Not only because of their working relationship; he was married to her younger sister. I don't think Trish killed him, but I also think she knows – or suspects – more than she's telling me.' He shook his head in frustration. 'Though I can't get her to tell me about it.'

This was the point in a case where Georgina had helped him, in the past. She'd persuaded people to open up to her, and then to tell Colin.

But.

Were things different now? Could they still work together? Or had her revelation about Doris made him question her reliability and destroyed his faith in her?

'I would offer to help,' she said quietly, 'given that I'm talking to Trish tomorrow, but I'm not sure you trust my judgement anymore.'

He flinched. 'Actually, I do. You're good at getting people to talk to you – much better than I am.'

Even though part of her knew she ought to drop the subject, because there was a good chance that raising it again would lead to another row, she also knew that if they didn't keep everything out in the open, it would just fester and get worse in the long run. 'Even though I talk to a ghost?'

He sighed heavily. 'Even though you do something I believe is impossible. Georgie, I don't want to fight with you. I miss your company. I miss Bert. And I could really do with your help. Please can we reach some kind of... I don't know, understanding?'

'Bea says I'm being a bit stubborn,' Georgina said. 'Then again, she says you're being *very* stubborn.'

'And I'm the one who walked out on you,' Colin said. 'Mainly because I didn't know what to say, and I didn't want to fight with you and end up saying something unforgivable that I didn't actually mean. I've learned the hard way that it's easy to say the wrong thing.'

'Scorched earth. That's what I thought it would be if I told anyone else about what I could hear. But Bea, Will, Sybbie and Cesca have all accepted it. They believe me,' Georgina said.

Colin looked torn. 'If it makes any difference, I believe that you believe you can hear Doris.'

'But you still don't think she exists. Because you can't hear or see her.'

He shook his head. 'And if that makes me narrow-minded, I'm sorry,' he said.

'I'm sorry, too,' Georgina said. Because they were still going round in circles. Maybe there wasn't a way to compromise, after all. 'I'd better get back to Bea.'

'Of course,' he said. 'Give her my best.'

'I will,' Georgina said. And then – even though it felt as if she was giving in and seeing the end of their relationship as inevitable, now, and her heart felt heavier than lead – she released his hand, turned and walked away.

THIRTEEN

On Thursday morning, Georgina went to find Trish at the excavations.

'Sybbie, Bea and I have been going through the paperwork and we've found out quite a bit of Timothy's story,' she said. 'I've got printouts of various bits we thought you'd find interesting, including a sketch that Bernard's great-aunt did of the peacock mosaic. Have you got a quarter of an hour to grab a coffee and go through it with me?'

'I'd love to,' Trish said. 'Hang on. I'll just let Helena know where I'm going, and she can ring my mobile if I'm needed for anything.' A couple of minutes later, she returned and went with Georgina to the farm shop café.

'I should warn you, it's a sad story,' Georgina said. 'But, on the bright side, you'll get to see a picture of Timothy.'

Once they were settled at one of the quieter tables with their coffee, Georgina showed her the photographs of the dig in 1865 and the sketch Lizzie had made of the peacock floor.

'That's amazing, to see Timothy at the dig,' Trish said. 'I've seen a couple of photos of Clara, over the years, but never one of Timothy.'

'I'll email them over to you,' Georgina promised.

'Thank you so much.' Trish smiled. 'I think I can see my mum in him. She'll be pleased to see these, too. And I hope somehow Timothy knows that his great-great-great-great niece is carrying on with his work.'

'Oh, he does,' Doris said.

'I'm sure he does, and he'd be really proud of you,' Georgina said.

'So did you actually find out what happened to him?' Trish asked.

'Not quite,' Georgina said. She told Trish what they'd found out about Timothy and Lizzie, showing her the diary entries.

'Edwin sounds a thoroughly nasty piece of work,' Trish said. 'Do you think he killed Timothy, rather than putting him on the train?'

'That's our theory,' Georgina said, 'though we have no proof, and there's no way of getting any. And also we don't know where the body's buried.'

Trish shook her head in obvious disappointment. 'So Edwin got away with it.'

'In terms of the law, maybe,' Georgina said. 'But you could look at it another way: he ended up a lonely widower, and then his family died out. Nobody remembers him.'

'Which is what he deserves. But poor Timothy. He and Lizzie could've been so happy together,' Trish said. 'And maybe, if they'd lived in London, the doctors there might've heard of new treatments for pre-eclampsia – something better and more effective than bloodletting.'

'There's no way of knowing,' Georgina said. 'Though at least Lizzie had her mum with her.'

'There is that,' Trish agreed. 'There's a lot to be said for having a supportive mum. I would've been lost without mine.'

Georgina took a strategic sip of coffee, giving Trish the space to talk.

'I kind of followed in Lizzie's footsteps,' Trish said. 'I fell pregnant when I was a student. It wasn't planned, and the baby's dad wanted nothing to do with us, but I didn't want a termination. I had a bit of a row with my supervisor, who wanted me to take a year out while I had the baby – but I was really well during my pregnancy, and I could work on a dig just as well as I had when I wasn't pregnant. The hardest bit was sitting at a desk, trying to write my exam papers over the bump when I was eight months.' She smiled. 'But I don't regret keeping Laura, not for a single minute. My daughter's amazing.' She took a sip of coffee. 'I have to admit, I'm not looking forward to her going to university in October – and I'm pretty sure it's a when, not an if, because she's worked hard enough to get her grades. I'm going to miss her horribly. She's applied to Durham – which feels like a very long way away.'

'I missed my children, as well, when they were students – though you do eventually get used to them being away, and it's always lovely to see them when they come here,' Georgina said. 'And I'm eternally grateful to whoever invented video calls. I'm old enough that I had to make sure I had enough coins and queue up to use a phone box, as a student, if I wanted to call home.'

'I had a mobile phone,' Trish said, 'but back then it was calls and texts only, and if your text was too long, it'd split into two and cost you twice as much.'

'What's your daughter going to study?' Georgina asked.

'She's half following in my footsteps, and totally in her dad's – she's going to study history,' Trish said. 'And I admit, I'm hoping I get a chance to go up north on a dig and see her.'

'Bea half followed in my footsteps, too, and totally in her dad's – I did English, and she went to RADA,' Georgina said. 'She's between rehearsals at the moment, so she came and helped with the research; in return, I'm testing her on her lines.' She smiled. 'She's finally playing Beatrice.'

'I love *Much Ado*,' Trish said. 'Do I assume you named her after Beatrice?'

'I did,' Georgina said. 'Her dad was an actor-director. Beatrice was his favourite Shakespeare heroine, too.' She smiled. 'And our son surprised both of us by becoming a scientist.'

'Funny how things work out,' Trish said. 'I never expected to be a mum just before I turned twenty-one. I would've been really stuck without my mum helping me.'

Georgina waited, and Trish went back to her tale. 'I moved back home after university. I took a couple of years out, doing temporary office jobs just until Laura was old enough to go to nursery, and then I went back to university to do my master's. Mum was the most brilliant support. But Joanna – my younger sister – was really jealous. She felt our parents favoured me above her, and she also thought I shouldn't have kept Laura because it held me back in my career.'

Which sounded as if they'd clashed badly; yet Trish had identified Simon's body to save her sister from the pain of having to do that. So had they made up their argument, or were they still partly estranged?

'That sounds tough,' Georgina said. 'I'm an only child, so I have no real experience of what it's like in a larger family. But I imagine sibling rivalry must be hard to deal with.'

'It is. Or was, when we were younger – we didn't get on that well as teenagers. Jojo's three years younger than me,' Trish said. 'She was horribly competitive and definitely didn't have patience with children, back then, and I think having a squalling baby around cramped her style a bit. When I moved out, we didn't speak for a while. I was upset about her looking down on me and saying I should've had a termination or put Laura up for adoption, and I said some fairly unforgivable stuff to her, too.' She shrugged. 'But when she was at uni, she grew up a bit. She did a master's in Heritage Studies, and got a really good job in a museum. I was pleased for her; I had my job at St Edmund's College by then, and Laura was settled in nursery. I hoped maybe Jojo and I could manage to be polite to each other if we were both at our parents' for Christmas and what have you, but then she reached out to me and said she wanted to see me. I agreed to meet her, not really knowing what to expect – but she was so sweet. She apologised about what she'd said and actually seemed interested in Laura.' She shrugged again. 'I decided to give her the benefit of the doubt. I apologised for what I'd said, too, and we got closer again.'

'That's good,' Georgina said.

'It is. I'm glad I have my sister back,' Trish said. 'Thankfully, she got on OK with my partner.'

'Laura's dad?'

'Adopted dad. Her biological father didn't change his mind after she was born and still didn't want to be part of her life,' Trish said. 'But Drew adores Laura, and it's very much mutual. Although she knows he's not her biological father, she says he's her real dad.' She sighed. 'I wish Jojo had ended up with someone like him, instead of Simon Butterfield. Someone who mucks in with everyone else and makes an effort to be part of the family.'

'I know exactly what you mean,' Georgina sympathised. 'I know I can't choose Bea's or Will's partner for them, but I hope they find someone who loves them for who they are, doesn't want to change them and will at least try to rub along with their family.'

'That's what I want for Laura, too,' Trish said. 'Someone who cares.'

'How did your sister meet Simon?' Georgina asked.

'Sadly, through me. And I've never stopped regretting it.' Trish wrinkled her nose. 'It was my thirtieth birthday, and I'd invited everyone in the department to my party. I didn't know Simon very well, because he'd only just joined the department.

If I'd known what he was like, back then, I would never have invited him – or at the very least I would've warned her off him.'

'He was difficult?' Georgina asked.

'You can say that again.' Trish rolled her eyes. 'I know you shouldn't speak ill of the dead, but Simon really wasn't great to work with. He always managed to muscle in and take the credit for other people's ideas. Though that wasn't what I really loa—' She grimaced. 'Never mind.'

'I often find it helps to say something out loud,' Georgina said mildly. 'Then it gets the words out of your head and stops them weighing on your mind.'

'That's a good point.' Trish sighed. 'Jojo got together with Simon and it was a real whirlwind romance. They were married within six months. I thought it was way too quick, but she said I was just jealous because Drew and I weren't married – even in the early days, Simon changed her and brought out that horrible competitive streak again.' She bit her lip. 'Simon had family money, so they had a nice house and everything Jojo could possibly have wanted. They didn't want kids, so they spent their money on nice holidays, new cars and weekends in posh hotels.' She flapped a hand. 'I'm not saying that's a *bad* thing – if that's what you want, great. Just don't insist that everyone else has to want exactly the same things that you do.' She sighed. 'Drew, Laura and I were fine with our little two-bed terrace and a week in a cottage by the seaside. I wasn't jealous of my sister at all – but Simon made her think I was. He was all about money and status, and he brought that side of Jojo out, too.'

'I'm sorry. That must've been hard,' Georgina said.

'It was. I thought Jojo and I were finally past all the scratchiness of when we were younger. All the nonsense about her having to get better grades than I did, go to a more prestigious university, that sort of thing.' She pulled a face. 'Nobody *cares* which uni you went to, after you've got your first job. But Simon encouraged her competitive side, with the swanky holidays and the new car she changed every eighteen months – I mean, you don't even need a car when you live in London.' Trish pushed her coffee cup round on its saucer. 'I tried to rise above it, because I didn't want him to push us apart. I didn't want him to win. But then Jojo hit thirty and her biological clock started ticking. She was so desperate to have a baby, but it just didn't happen for them. There she was, desperate to conceive and couldn't, while I fell accidentally pregnant at the age of twenty – I'd got the one thing she really wanted and couldn't have.'

'That must've been hard for both of you,' Georgina said.

Trish nodded. 'I tried to cut her some slack. I had other friends who had trouble conceiving, so I know how much the disappointment can eat away at you, and the way you can end up hyper-focused. So I used to ignore it whenever she took it out on me. She always apologised whenever she went too far, a few days later. I tried suggesting they went on the list for adoption or fostering – but she said Simon wouldn't do it, because he didn't want a child who wasn't biologically his. The way I see it, you don't have to be related by blood to be a parent – you just love the child you're bringing up, just like Drew loves Laura.'

'Absolutely,' Georgina agreed.

'I asked if she'd consider trying IVF, but according to Jojo, Simon said it was too expensive.' She scowled. 'I hated the way he reduced everything to money. If he'd been worried about how it was going to affect Jojo, about the mental and physical toll IVF treatment can take on your health and how she'd cope if it didn't work, then I would've understood him not wanting to do it, because it meant he was trying to put her first. But because of *money*? For pity's sake, they weren't anywhere near struggling.'

Georgina gave her a sympathetic smile.

'Then our gran died and left us both money, so I said to Jojo she could have my share to pay for the IVF. I knew how much she wanted a baby and I wanted to do something to help her. I would even have offered to be her surrogate, if that's what it took. But bloody Simon refused to do any of the medical procedures. I'm pretty sure he was the one with the problem and he knew it, because he threatened to leave her if she used a sperm donor.' Trish shook her head. 'She wouldn't discuss it with me, after that. It's a total no-go area between us, so I'm glad she wasn't here when you told me about Lizzie's baby. I think that would've broken her, and I'm really going to have to think about how I tell her.' She closed her eyes briefly. '*If* I tell her. She wants to come to Norfolk, and I've been trying to put her off because – well, it won't bring Simon back, and she's fragile as it is because of the way he's behaved towards her.'

And to tell her about a baby who'd died after the first couple of breaths... 'It's going to be tricky,' Georgina said.

'Every time I see my little sister, she looks sadder and sadder, and it's all because of that slimy, smarmy git she married.' Trish looked at Georgina. 'I didn't kill Simon. I know this is going to sound bad, but I'm glad he's dead – because now Jojo might have a chance of getting on with her life. I think she'll be a lot happier without him.'

'From what you've told me, he sounds like the kind of guy I'm glad I didn't get to meet,' Georgina said.

'Actually, he would've been totally charming to you at first,' Trish said. 'But he wouldn't have been able to resist telling you how to take the photographs.'

'I've met a few people like that. I just smile sweetly and say I know it's all very easy – just point and snap,' Georgina said with a grin. 'Which is what I'll be doing tomorrow, with any luck.'

Trish nodded. 'We've been able to clean up the mosaic floor, thankfully. And I know that sounds horrible – someone died, and I should be more concerned about that than about the preservation of the floor. But Simon really wasn't a nice man, and I hated the way he changed my sister. She was all bright and confident, and he took that from her.'

'What do you think happened to him?' Georgina asked.

'I really don't know,' Trish said. 'The police have been asking questions about the nighthawks, so I assume that's what they think. Nobody heard anything, and nobody saw any lights or anything. Which is pretty much the way it's gone whenever we've been raided by nighthawks – like we were, earlier in the dig here. So either he saw the nighthawks and got in their way... or he was part of them.'

Georgina raised her eyebrows. 'Do you really think he was one of the nighthawks?'

'It's the only thing that really makes sense. If he was part of them, he'd know about us having the security lights up and he'd know how and where to switch them off. Maybe that's why the lights didn't go on, the night he was killed. And perhaps he fell out with the gang he was working with.' Trish wrinkled her nose. 'He tends to fall out with everyone, eventually.'

Georgina frowned. 'I don't quite understand. Why would an archaeologist work with people who dig randomly and mess up all the archaeology layers – people who destroy everything you take such pains to record when you work on a site?'

'Because that way Simon could keep whatever he found; there wouldn't be any records,' Trish said. 'There's a black market for antiquities without a proper provenance. They can't ever be exhibited anywhere, but the people who own them don't care – because *they* know they own the artefacts and can gloat over them whenever they like.'

'But if he took things illegally,' Georgina said, 'surely your sister would've known about it?'

Trish spread her hands. 'Not if he kept his treasures somewhere outside the house. Though don't ask me where that could be. I don't have the faintest idea.'

'I think you should tell Colin Bradshaw what you've told

me,' Georgina said. 'It might tie up with some evidence, and help him find the killer.'

'Maybe,' Trish said, sounding dubious.

'Think about it,' Georgina urged. 'Colin's one of the good guys.'

'He's your partner, isn't he?' Trish asked.

'Mmm,' Georgina said, not quite sure how to answer that honestly. She and Colin were still at odds. But that didn't change the way she knew he worked. Where his job was concerned, she'd trust him with her life. 'He's not perfect,' she said eventually, 'but he's honest, and he'll do his best to help you and your sister. And we might think that something isn't relevant, whereas it could turn out to be the thing that breaks the case open and helps him solve it. Tell him.'

'I'll think about it,' Trish promised.

FOURTEEN

After Trish had left to go back to the dig, Georgina rang Colin. 'I think Trish needs to talk to you.'

'She opened up to you?' Colin asked.

'Sort of.' Georgina sighed. 'I don't want to break a confidence. What I will say is that she's had a tricky relationship with Joanna over the years, and Simon's behaviour made things worse.'

'Trish said her sister was fragile,' Colin mused.

'Mmm,' Georgina said. After what Trish had told her, she completely understood what the other woman meant. 'You need to talk to her about that. Let's just say that Trish has personal reasons to dislike the man, and in her shoes, I'd feel the same.' She paused. 'I've suggested she talks to you. Because you're honest and you'll do your best to help her.'

'Thank you,' Colin said. 'Speaking of her sister – and I know you'll keep this to herself – the museum she works at has had a problem with little things going missing over the years, because the cataloguing of past items hasn't always been accurate.'

'Do you think it's linked to Simon's death?' Georgina asked.

'At the moment, I can't say,' Colin said.

That old chestnut. Then again, she might not be Colin's partner anymore, in which case of course he wouldn't confide in her. And that felt like scraping a scab off a wound. It *stung*. 'Simon had family money, according to Trish. He and Joanna were well-off, and lived the lifestyle to match. Why would she need to steal anything?'

'Maybe they weren't as well-off as they liked to tell people,' Colin said.

Trish *had* said that Joanna was competitive... Georgina pushed it aside. 'Trish would've known.'

'Or maybe it wasn't for the monetary value of the items,' Colin said. 'Trish said that Simon liked rare things.'

'And she told me there's a black market for antiquities. Private collectors who don't care that they can never show off their treasures, because they just like to possess things for their own sake. Maybe he was one of those people and had a private collection.' She paused. 'Do you think Joanna might have been stealing things for him?'

'It's a potential line of enquiry,' Colin said.

'Trish told me she thinks he either disturbed a group of nighthawks, or he was involved with them and they fell out,' Georgina said.

'If Simon did have a private collection of artefacts, it would explain the nighthawks and it could tie up with the thefts from the museum. The problem is, I don't have enough evidence to get a warrant to search his house,' Colin said. 'You're right. I need to talk to Trish. Does she know where he might have kept his collection?'

'No, but she thinks it wasn't in his house. Ask her about her sister. Ask her *why* her sister's fragile. But be sensitive about it,' she warned.

'I will.' He paused. 'Thank you, Georgie. I appreciate what

you've done.' His voice sounded slightly rusty when he added, 'I appreciate *you*.'

And that was balm to her misery. Maybe they could work out this thing between them. 'You're welcome,' she said softly. 'Talk to you soon.'

Georgina had left Sybbie and Bea working through more of the estate archives; wanting to treat them to something nice, she went to the counter to pick up some cake.

Jodie was serving. 'Are you all right?' she asked. 'I heard about what happened at the dig.'

Jodie had had a similar experience of finding a dead body, a few months ago, and it had really shaken her. 'I'm fine, thanks,' Georgina reassured her with a smile. 'It's not something I think I'd ever get used to, but Colin's dealing with everything.'

'I like your Colin. He was really kind to me when... you know. When it all happened.' Jodie wrinkled her nose.

'He's a good man,' Georgina agreed. Even if they were a bit at odds right now. 'How are Bethany and her mum?'

'They're doing all right. They have good days and bad days.'

Like Jodie, Georgina guessed, but her friend was good at putting on a brave face and getting on with things.

'There was something I was going to ask you.' Jodie lowered her voice. 'As you've been here with Sybbie all week, and I don't really want to bother Sybbie.'

In other words, Jodie was still a tiny bit in awe of Sybbie, and Georgina knew the younger woman would rather ask her than Sybbie because Jodie knew her a lot better and was comfortable with her.

'Is Cesca all right? Only she's not been herself, this last couple of days. She's a bit tired and snappy, and she practically went green when I offered to make her a coffee this morning. I don't want to ask her, in case something's really wrong – I don't want to put my foot in it and upset her even more.'

Georgina did actually know what was up, but this wasn't

her secret to tell. 'She might be going down with that bug that's doing the rounds,' she said instead. 'When that happens to me, I go off coffee and all I want is chicken soup, or a mug of honey and lemon.'

'The stuff my mum used to give me if I was poorly,' Jodie said. 'She won't let anyone fuss over her, but I'll make her a mug of honey and lemon and try to get her to rest a bit.' She rolled her eyes. 'You know Cesca. She's only got one speed.'

Georgina smiled and paid for the cake. 'If I don't catch you before, see you tomorrow for changeover at the barn,' she said. Jodie cleaned the holiday cottage for her, though Georgina saw the younger woman more as a friend than as an employee. 'I'm dropping Bea at the train station first thing, but I should be back in time.'

'Don't rush. I've got my keys,' Jodie said. 'School's not back until next week, so is it all right if Robbie's with me?'

'Of course it is,' Georgina said. 'If it's not pouring, I'm sure Bert will enjoy fetching endless tennis balls in the garden.' She made a mental note to pick up a packet of the biscuits that Jodie's son loved, too.

Back at the manor house, she rapped on the kitchen door and walked in. 'Hey, guys,' she called. 'I come bearing cake.'

Jet and Max came bounding across to greet her, their tails a blur; Sybbie and Bea followed.

'Excellent,' Sybbie said. 'I'll put the kettle on. And we have news for you.'

'You've found out what happened to Timothy?' Georgina asked.

'No – but we have big suspicions,' Bea said. 'I've been going through the local newspaper reports. There was a fire in September 1865, a couple of days after Timothy allegedly caught the train back to London. It was in a barn belonging to one of the tenant farmers on the Great Wenborough estate; somehow the hay in the loft caught alight. Luckily the animals were still out at pasture, and the only loss was the hay and the barn itself, because it started raining and that stopped the fire spreading to the farmhouse and the other buildings nearby. Police investigating the cause of the fire found the body of a vagrant, and apparently nobody realised the man had been sheltering in the barn so they hadn't tried to rescue him.'

'A vagrant,' Georgina said. 'Or could it have been a body that was already dead and someone wanted to get rid of the evidence?'

'If that's what happened, it definitely worked. He was badly burned about the face, and nobody could identify him,' Sybbie said. 'The remains were buried in a pauper's grave at Great Wenborough church.'

Which, Georgina remembered, was the first building you came to when you left Little Wenborough Manor and headed in the direction of Great Wenborough.

'The farmer wasn't insured,' Sybbie continued, 'and the Rutherfords were moved by his plight to pledge to build him a new barn.'

'Or was it a guilt payment because Edwin had ordered the old barn to be burned down in the first place?' Georgina asked.

'That's what we suspect,' Bea agreed.

'And there weren't any other barns burned down in the area – it wasn't part of a wider protest?' Georgina asked.

'No,' Bea said. 'I checked. Can Doris ask Timothy?'

'Of course I will,' Doris said. 'But if there's a grave, would the bones still be there? Could we do DNA sampling to identify him, like you've done before?'

'I don't know,' Georgina said, and told Sybbie and Bea what Doris had suggested. 'But I know two people who can help us find out.'

She went to find Trish, who was working in a trench with a couple of the students she recognised, Helena and Adam.

'I know you're busy, so I'm not going to ask you to leave the trench, but can I interrupt for two minutes, please?' she asked.

Trish smiled. 'Sure. What can I do for you, Georgie?'

'It's a possible lead on what we were discussing earlier – and I think you're the most likely person to know the answer to my question,' Georgina said. 'If someone was burned in a fire – badly enough for him not to be recognisable, but there were some remains that were then buried – could we still do DNA testing?'

Trish blanched. 'You think someone was burned alive?'

'No, no,' Georgina hastened to explain. 'Sorry, that didn't come out right and I really didn't mean to make you think that. I'm talking about your ancestor. We still believe Timothy was killed, but our theory is that afterwards his body might have been hidden in a barn, and then the barn was burned down to cover up the murder.' Georgina told Trish what Bea had found in the newspaper report.

'I agree. That's a bit too much of a coincidence,' Trish said. She looked thoughtful. 'Bones are often damaged in a fire but not destroyed. Teeth tend to survive, and you can get DNA from them. But that's assuming you can find the grave in the first place – a pauper's grave often wasn't marked. Plus you'd need to get permission to exhume the remains.'

'I know someone who might be able to help me with that – Rowena Langham, the county's finds liaison officer, who happens to be a friend of mine,' Georgina said. 'And I was going to ask you if she could perhaps join me here tomorrow afternoon, when I take the photographs of the mosaic floor. She really loves ancient history, and she'd be so excited to see what you've been doing here.' She'd meant to ask about this earlier, but the upset of finding a dead body at the mosaic followed by her row with Colin had pushed it out of her head.

'Of course she can,' Trish said. 'If you think she'd be interested in what we've found, I'd be happy to take her through the small finds personally.'

'Small finds?' Georgina asked.

'A bit of a misnomer, because they can be quite big – but they're the unique things we find in the dig,' Trish said. 'It could be something expensive, like a brooch or a ring, or it might be a large chunk of pottery. We mark them on the plan to help us build up a picture of the site. Then they go to the finds tent to be recorded; they're dried out so we don't get any moisture degradation while they're in storage, and then they're bagged and processed. So the tesserae are small, but they're not counted as "small finds" because we have a lot of them.'

'Got you,' Georgina said. 'Thanks, Trish. That'd be great. I'll keep you posted.'

'What you said earlier,' Trish said. 'I think you're right. I need to talk to Inspector Bradshaw.'

'He'll give you a fair hearing,' Georgina said. 'And, just so you know, I didn't tell him what you told me.'

'Thank you.' Trish gave her a wry smile. 'Jojo texted me just now. She's on her way out here. So I'm going to have to work out how I tell her what you told me about Timothy and Lizzie.'

'Let me know if I can do anything to help,' Georgina said.

On her way back to the manor house, she called Rowena.

'What can I do for you, Georgie?' Rowena asked.

'I'm at the dig at Little Wenborough Hall – I'm taking pictures of the mosaic floor tomorrow afternoon,' Georgina said. 'I know it's short notice, and I apologise because I meant to ask earlier this week, but would you like to come? Trish Melton, the lead archaeologist, says she's happy to show you the small finds, too.'

'I'm supposed to be deskbound tomorrow,' Rowena said, 'but I can always finish my reports at home over the weekend. I'd love to come. What time do you want me to meet you?'

'Two?' Georgina asked.

'Perfect,' Rowena said. 'I would have suggested grabbing a bite to eat afterwards, except I'm already going out to the theatre.'

'We'll definitely have dinner together another night,' Georgina said. 'Before you go, there was another thing. Where would I find a pauper's grave?'

'Usually there would be a cemetery by the poor law union's workhouse,' Rowena said.

'I don't think a workhouse would've been involved in this case. And I don't mean a pauper, exactly, because I don't even have a name. What about a vagrant found in a village?' Georgina asked.

'You've found another skeleton?' Rowena had helped at both Hartington Hall and the lighthouse, when Bert had discovered buried skeletons.

'No. This one's tricky.' Georgina explained about the newspaper article and their suspicions about Timothy's death.

'If you're quite sure the workhouse isn't involved, I'd try the parish records,' Rowena said. 'There's a good chance the vicar would have buried him in the parish churchyard out of charity, but at the boundary rather than in one of the plots that people paid a lot of money for. If it's a pauper's grave, it probably won't be marked as such, but some vicars were very chatty in the parish records and noted all kinds of things down. There might be some clues there.'

'Does a pauper burial mean someone was buried in a coffin?' Georgina asked.

'Sometimes,' Rowena said. 'Sometimes there was a parish coffin, which looked like a normal coffin but had a hinged bottom. The body would be wrapped in a winding sheet; when the coffin was placed over the grave, the hinge would be released and the body in its winding sheet would go into the grave.'

'A sheet obviously wouldn't protect the remains as well as a coffin would,' Georgina mused.

'The sheet would probably have disintegrated by now, but there should still be bones,' Rowena said. 'A bit degraded, possibly, but there.'

'What about a death certificate?' Georgina asked. 'Where would I find a certificate for someone whose name isn't known?'

'There might be something in the coroner's files,' Rowena said. 'You couldn't bury someone without a death certificate. If they didn't know who the deceased was, the case would've gone to the coroner, and the coroner would've given permission for burial once the inquest had been held. If you found the report of the death in the newspapers, there might be an inquest report a week or so later.'

'Thank you, Rowena – that's really helpful,' Georgina said. 'If I do find a grave, we'd be looking at DNA testing with Timothy's great-niece – and, if our theories are correct, reburial with a proper headstone.'

'Let me know if you find a grave, and I can help organise the exhumation,' Rowena said.

'I appreciate it,' Georgina said. 'I'll see you tomorrow. If you drive up to the manor house, you'll see the paddock with the dig.'

'Lovely,' Rowena said. 'I'll look forward to seeing you – and Bert.'

Back at the manor house, Georgina relayed the information to Sybbie and Bea.

'Has Timothy remembered any more about what happened?' Sybbie asked.

'I told him we knew about the baby and he didn't need to protect Lizzie's reputation anymore. And that we were on her side anyway,' Doris said. 'He didn't know about the baby, but he loved Lizzie very much and he'd planned to marry her. He was horrified that she'd married Edwin, but I told him we didn't think Edwin had harmed her – Amelia insisted that Lizzie should stay here and be looked after. And obviously he was devastated to learn of Lizzie's death – and the baby's. He went quiet on me for a while; I think he needed to come to terms with it. He says Edwin drove him to Great Wenborough, somewhere on the estate, and railed at him like a madman, saying he'd seen Lizzie first and he wasn't going to let Timothy drag her into a life of squalor. Which is ridiculous, because Timothy was a university fellow. Even if he'd got the job at the museum, Lizzie wouldn't have had to work.'

Georgina duly relayed the information to Bea and Sybbie.

'Timothy was in one corner of the coach, and luckily the door catch was nearest to him. He managed to open the door, and when Edwin was mid-rant, he pushed the door open and tried to escape into the woods,' Doris said. 'Except Edwin must've been in the habit of travelling with a loaded pistol, and he was a good shot. That's when he shot Timothy in the back.'

'So it was murder,' Georgina said, and told the others what Doris had said.

'And it sounds as if Edwin covered it up by the fire, to make sure Timothy wasn't recognisable and the death could be seen as an accident,' Bea said.

Georgina shivered. 'That's horrible. Let's check the newspaper.'

The inquest report came a week after the fire, in the *Norwich Mercury.* 'Here it is,' Bea said. 'There's a whole column of inquests, including ones in London. *Held Saturday last at the Feathers public house in Great Wenborough, Norfolk, before S. H. Asker, Esquire, deputy coroner.*'

'The inquest was held in the pub?' Sybbie asked.

'A lot of inquests were – there's one here at the Adelaide public house in Adelaide Street, and another at Blofield Workhouse,' Bea said.

'What happened at the inquest?' Georgina asked.

'*On the body of a vagrant killed in a fire at Hopgood's Barn, Great Wenborough, the particulars of which appeared in the Norwich Mercury of Monday last. John Hopgood, on being sworn, said: "The Monday before last, I was working in the field when one of my men saw flames in the direction of the barn. I knew the cows were out in the pasture, but there was hay in the barn and it must have caught light. We brought buckets of water from the stream, but it was hopeless. I feared my house would be next, but there was a squall and the rain put the fire out."*'

'John Hopgood being the tenant farmer?' Sybbie asked.

'I think so,' Bea said. '*On investigation, police constable William Watson found the charred body of a man in the barn, presumed to be a vagrant as all Hopgood's men were accounted for. The features had been burned and nobody could tell who he was. There was a stone bottle of gin by the body and a meerschaum pipe. He believes that the vagrant had become intoxicated and fallen asleep before dropping his pipe. The tobacco still being on fire, it set light to the barn. James Pollard, surgeon, said the man had died from suffocation in the smoke. The Coroner having summed up, the Jury, after a short deliberation, returned a verdict of Accidental Death by Suffocation.*'

'Nobody thought to check for other wounds?' Georgina asked.

'This was 1865,' Sybbie reminded her. 'This was a logical cause of death. And it's still possible that there really was a vagrant who accidentally set the barn on fire and burned to death. Edwin's men might still have buried Timothy's body somewhere in the woods.'

'It feels too convenient for the man in the barn to have been a vagrant,' Georgina said. 'We need to see if that body was buried in the churchyard – and if the vicar had anything to say about it in the records. And if we can find the body and match the DNA with Trish's, we'll know what really happened.'

FIFTEEN

Colin picked up the phone. 'Bradshaw.'

'Inspector Bradshaw, it's Trish Melton from the dig. I wondered if we could have a chat about what's been happening here.'

Colin silently punched the air. Whatever Georgina had said to Trish had worked. 'Of course. Would you like to come here?'

'I know it's a bit of a cheek,' Trish said, 'but it would be really useful if we could meet here. I don't want to leave the students on their own for too long.'

'That's fine,' Colin said.

'The only thing is, my sister's on her way to Norwich. I'd like to get this over with before she arrives,' Trish said.

'I'll be on my way as soon as I put this phone down,' Colin said. 'Would you mind if my colleague Larissa Foulkes joins us?'

'I guess it's fine,' Trish said, sounding slightly dubious.

'Whatever you tell us is confidential,' Colin reassured her. 'We'll see you soon.'

When they got to Little Wenborough, he and Larissa went to find Trish.

'Could we talk in your car, perhaps?' Trish asked. 'It's more private.'

'Sure,' Colin said, surprised and intrigued. Was this something to do with Simon's death? Had she discovered something about the nighthawks and didn't want to risk the information behind overheard, in case it was leaked?

Once they were sitting in the car and he'd introduced her to Larissa, Trish started talking. 'The nighthawks,' she said. 'I've been thinking about it, and there's a pattern to the digs I've been on with Simon. The raids always seem to happen just after something's been found, but before the press prints the details of what happens. Not all the other digs I've been on have been targeted by nighthawks, but usually a raid would happen after the press had talked about finds and given away the location.'

'So you think someone leaked the information to the nighthawks?' Larissa asked.

'Either a reporter from the newspaper – or, given that it's happened in several different places, more likely somebody from the dig,' Trish said. 'I was thinking about what all the digs I've been on with Simon had in common... and it's Simon, a couple of the students and me,' she said. 'I can assure you, I'm not the leak. I don't want my dig site trashed. I want to excavate the site properly and find as much information about the settlement as I can. And I really couldn't care less about treasure. I like the human interest stories – things that don't have so much of a monetary value.'

'Now Simon's dead, do you think that means the raids will stop?' Colin asked.

'If he was the leak, yes. But, as I said, a couple of the students have been on all of the recent digs that were affected by the nighthawks. I don't want to make any accusations without proof,' Trish said, 'but what if Simon somehow dragged them into it?'

'If Simon was involved,' Colin said carefully, 'then surely he wouldn't want extra people in on it, because then it would dilute his share of the proceeds.'

'On the other hand, if anyone started getting suspicious, it would give him someone to blame,' Trish said.

'So who are the students?'

'At the moment, I'd rather not say,' Trish said with a grimace. 'Because it's only a suspicion – as I said, I don't have evidence, and I'm really hoping it isn't either of them.'

Colin would rather have known the names, but he wanted to keep Trish onside for now. He'd ask her again, a bit later. 'Supposing he did drag these students into it: do you think they could still be involved?' Colin asked.

'Maybe,' Trish said. 'We'll see at the next dig, I guess.'

'Unless we set a trap – which would catch the nighthawks and maybe lead us to Simon's killer,' Colin said. 'When do you leave?'

'Sunday,' Trish said.

'What are you thinking?' Larissa asked.

'The nighthawks came before when treasure had been found. Supposing they thought more treasure had been found?' Colin asked. 'If you tell the two students you suspect – privately and separately – that you've found something, they might pass the information on.'

Trish was silent for a while, clearly thinking about it. 'Actually, that's a good idea. We could say I'd found some Roman silver,' she said at last. 'Nothing as big as the Mildenhall treasure – I don't think I'd get away with claiming I'd found a huge bowl without anyone else at the dig knowing about it. But a couple of spoons or a small drinking cup would be plausible and they'd be worth enough to tempt the nighthawks. Or a silver seal ring, with hints there might be more jewellery buried nearby.'

'Won't they want to see what you found?' Larissa asked.

'I can fudge it. Say I'm keeping it quiet for now while I do a bit of work on it, because I don't want the papers to know.' She paused. 'Or I could talk to the finds liaison officer to see if one of the museums can lend us something – even better if they have something that hasn't been cleaned properly yet.'

The finds liaison officer, who seemed to be cropping up at a lot of his cases nowadays. 'You know Rowena Langham?' Colin asked.

'I haven't met her yet, but she's coming to see the dig tomorrow,' Trish said. 'I think Saturday night's the most likely night for the nighthawks to turn up – it's just before we have to close everything up on Sunday. If my suspicions are right, the students will contact the nighthawks and I reckon we'll be raided on Saturday night. If you can sort out the surveillance side of things, hopefully we can catch them in the act.'

'Will you tell me their names?' Colin tried again.

Trish shook her head. 'I'd rather not.'

'I'm not going to rush in and collar them,' Colin said gently. 'It won't be going any further than my team.'

She sighed. 'All right. Helena and Adam.'

Helena was the student Trish had high hopes for, Colin remembered, and Adam was the one who was lazy and a bit too sure of himself. 'Thank you. You don't think it's worth doing surveillance tonight or tomorrow night?'

'Not tonight,' Trish said, 'because I won't have enough time to "find" the things to lure them with. But maybe tomorrow, because Rowena will be looking round the dig in the afternoon and I can make sure people overhear me telling her about a special find.'

'It's worth a try,' Larissa said.

'All right,' Colin said. 'You're absolutely sure you don't want to do this tonight?'

'Not tonight. My sister's arriving in an hour or so,' Trish said. 'She's going to need my support.'

'You said she was fragile,' Colin prompted, hoping that

whatever Georgina had said would persuade Trish to open up to him, too.

She looked awkward, then sighed. 'I trust Georgina, and she said you can be trusted, too. I hope she's right.' Then she told Colin about the IVF treatment and Simon's behaviour towards Joanna.

'Thank you for telling us,' Colin said. 'Obviously you're aware that gives you more of a motive for killing him.'

'It does,' Trish agreed. 'And I admit, I've had times when I've really wished he'd just vanish off the face of the earth and we never had to deal with him again. But I swear I didn't kill him.'

'Has Joanna confided in you about any problems at work?' he asked.

Trish looked surprised. 'No. Should she have done?'

'Just a line of enquiry,' Colin said. If Joanna was involved with the thefts from the museum, she clearly hadn't told Trish about them.

'I hope what I told you will be useful,' she said. 'I'd better get back to my students now.'

'Thank you for your help, Dr Melton,' Colin said, meaning it. 'I'll be in touch about the surveillance. I'll put the finds liaison officer in touch with you and you can discuss what you need from her.'

'Thank you, Inspector,' she said with a smile, and left the car.

'We need to check the parish death register for 1865,' Georgina said. 'Rowena Langham said even if there wasn't a name, there would have been a death certificate written by the coroner, and the vicar might have written extra notes in the records.'

Bea logged into the system she used at work and got the parish registers up on her screen. '1865 – we're looking at late

September or early October,' she said. 'Yes, here it is. *Burials in the Parish of Great Wenborough in the county of Norfolk, in the year 1865. Number 432. Name: vagrant suffocated by smoke. Abode...*' She winced. 'I think it's a continuation of the previous box. *In the fire at Hopgood's Barn. When buried: October 11th. Age: unknown. By whom the ceremony was performed: G Saunders, curate.*'

'The body could be Timothy's,' Georgina said. 'Did the curate write anything in?'

'Yes. We're in luck. *Buried in unmarked grave by the north churchyard wall, at the corner. Burial paid for by Edw.* – presumably Edwin – *Rutherford.*'

'We know Edwin paid for the barn to be rebuilt, and he paid for the burial of the so-called vagrant. That definitely sounds like a guilty conscience to me,' Sybbie said.

'If Edwin actually had a conscience,' Bea said. 'It sounds like a cover-up, at the very least. But this means that as long as the boundaries haven't changed, and the curate really did mean the corner of the church grounds by the wall, we should be able to find the grave.'

'I'll ring Rowena,' Georgina said, 'and ask her for her help in sorting out an exhumation.'

Later that afternoon, Georgina went to the dig in search of Trish.

'Ah – sorry, you're obviously busy,' she said, seeing Trish at the side of the trench with a woman she didn't recognise.

'No, no, it's fine,' Trish said. 'Georgie, this is my sister, Joanna. Jojo, this is Georgina Drake, the photographer I was telling you about. She's part of the team who's been researching our great-uncle Timothy.'

'Pleased to meet you.' Joanna gave her a wobbly smile.

Joanna looked like a younger, rather more polished version

of Trish, Georgina thought, with expensively highlighted hair and designer clothes. Though even her perfect make-up couldn't hide the purple smudges under her eyes, and Georgina's heart went out to her.

'I'm so sorry about your husband,' Georgina said.

'Thank you.' Joanna swallowed hard. 'I still can't believe Simon's gone. It just doesn't seem possible. He was only supposed to be away for three weeks. We were going to book a holiday when he got back – he doesn't have lectures on Fridays, so we were going to have a romantic weekend in Venice. For my birthday, just before the place gets really crowded with tourists. He was going to book a hotel on the Grand Canal, so we'd have breakfast overlooking the gondolas, and we were going to dance in St Mark's Square.' She closed her eyes, clearly willing the tears to stay back.

'I lost my husband nearly three years ago,' Georgina said quietly. 'That first week, I remember feeling that I was never going to cope. But you just take it day by day, putting one foot in front of the other. And eventually...' She wrinkled her nose. 'It's not so much time being a great healer, but you learn to cope with the tough days; the more you do it, the easier it becomes. So my advice is don't beat yourself up about having a wobbly day. You'll get through it, and tomorrow will probably be a little bit better.'

'Thank you. That's kind,' Joanna said.

'What can I do for you, Georgie?' Trish asked.

'I wanted to give you an update on the parish record situation,' Georgina said, unsure how much Joanna knew and not wanting to make things awkward for Trish.

'If you've got a few minutes,' Trish said, 'I haven't had time yet to tell Jojo about what you've found out about Timothy. Could we perhaps go through it together?'

'That'd be fine,' Georgina said. 'Shall we go to the farm shop café?'

'Brilliant idea,' Trish said. 'I'm buying.'

Once they were settled in the café – and Georgina had recommended the lemon drizzle cake to Joanna – Trish brought her phone out. 'So this is our great-great-great-great-uncle Timothy Marsden, with his friend Frederick Walters and some of his family, when they first discovered the bath house,' she said, showing Joanna the photograph of the dig. 'Can you see Mum in his face?'

'Definitely,' Joanna said, peering at the photograph and seeming to brighten up a bit. 'He's got the same nose. Has Mum seen it yet?'

'No. I was going to send it to her tonight,' Trish said.

'And that's what, the 1860s? How amazing there's actually a photo of him.'

'That photograph was in the commonplace book belonging to Frederick's mother,' Georgina said. 'There were sketches, too, of some of the Roman remains.' She stopped herself mentioning the peacock floor, knowing that it would be upsetting for Joanna to be reminded of where her husband had died.

'You know I always wondered why he'd gone missing, Jojo? Our theory now is that he fell in love with Frederick's sister, Lizzie,' Trish continued.

'According to Frederick's mother's diary, Timothy asked Lizzie's parents for permission to marry her, then proposed to her. They were going to hold a ball to celebrate the engagement,' Georgina said.

'Except the eldest son from the stately home in the next village wanted Lizzie for himself,' Trish said. 'He spread rumours that Timothy was already married – even though he wasn't – and people assumed that was why Timothy left and didn't come back.'

'So what actually happened to him?' Joanna asked. 'Clara's correspondence with William Walters suggested that Timothy came back to London – but we know he didn't.'

Georgina winced. 'I'm sorry, Joanna, there isn't a tactful way of saying this.'

Trish took Joanna's hand and squeezed it. 'We think Edwin made sure Timothy wouldn't return – either to London or to Norfolk,' she said quietly, 'and it looks to us as if he covered up the murder when a barn belonging to one of his tenants burned down.'

'We've found newspaper reports of the fire and the inquest, and we've been looking in the parish records today,' Georgina said. 'That's why I came to find Trish. We think we know where Timothy is buried, and my friend Rowena – the county's finds liaisons officer – is sorting out permission for us to exhume the bones. If we can do a DNA test, maybe with your mum, and it proves there's a familial link, then you'll be able to rebury him properly.'

'Well, that would definitely clear up the family mystery,' Joanna said. She shivered. 'How horrible to think there have been two murders in our family. First Timothy.' She swallowed hard. 'And now Simon.'

'I'm sorry,' Georgina said gently. 'There wasn't a tactful way of putting it.'

'No.' Joanna bit her lip. 'So this Lizzie sketched the ruins?' She swallowed hard. 'Including the mosaic floor?'

'Yes,' Georgina confirmed, as gently as she could.

'The spot where Simon died.' Joanna dragged in a breath. 'Did Timothy die there, too? Is the place unlucky?'

'We don't know.' Trish squeezed her sister's hand again. 'I'm sorry. I know I didn't get on with Simon, but I would never have wished that on him.'

'No,' Joanna said dully.

Trish's mobile shrilled. She grimaced. 'Sorry, Jojo. I need to get this.' She answered the phone. 'Helena. Uh-huh. Yes. You need me there now? All right. I'll be there in a couple of minutes.' She ended the call. 'Sorry. Something else they've found at the dig. She wants me to see it in situ.'

Georgina noticed Joanna had only drunk half her coffee. 'If you want me to stay with you while you drink that, I can walk you back to the dig afterwards,' she offered.

'Thank you,' Trish mouthed, and downed the rest of her coffee. 'Tin throat,' she said wryly. 'You learn how to do that on your first dig. See you in a bit.'

Joanna turned her mug round in her hands, and Georgina wasn't sure what to say to her. Eventually, she said, 'Trish said you work at a museum.'

Joanna nodded. 'It means I get to catalogue and exhibit the stuff people like Trish and Simon find – *found*,' she corrected herself.

'Being a curator must be such a fascinating job.'

'It has its moments,' Joanna said. 'I enjoy the school trips coming in; half the kids expect to be bored out of their skulls, but then they get to touch things that are thousands of years old, or dress up and learn what life would've been like for them a couple of hundred years ago, and you can see the moment it sparks something in their imagination.'

'That must be very rewarding,' Georgina said. And something in Joanna's expression made her take a risk. If she could get Joanna to talk about her struggles, it might help Joanna deal with it – and it also might help Colin's case. Even though she already knew the answer, she asked, 'Do you have children?'

'No.' Joanna's eyes shone with unshed tears. 'But now Simon's dead, maybe I can. Isn't that funny to think? Maybe I can foster, or adopt, to make life a bit better for a kid who's had a tough time.'

'Parenting is hard work, but for me, it's been well worth it,' Georgina said. Feeling slightly guilty for asking, she added, 'Did Simon not want children?'

'We tried, and it just didn't happen.' Joanna sighed. 'He was ten years older than me. I knew he'd been married before, and it didn't work out; his wife went off with someone else. He didn't like talking about it, but when we'd been trying for a baby for two years and were getting nowhere, and he refused to see a fertility clinic, it made me wonder if that was the real reason why his ex left him. Maybe she wanted a baby and they couldn't have one. He was so adamant about not having a child who wasn't related to him. I didn't get why he made such a big deal out of it – the way I see it, being a parent is more than just biology.'

'You're absolutely right,' Georgina said. 'Being a parent means being there for your child.'

'Trish suggested fostering or adoption.' Joanna bit her lip. 'He told her to keep her nose out of our marriage or he'd make sure she did.'

Which definitely sounded like a man who didn't want to face his own infertility, Georgina thought.

'He didn't mean it like *that*. He wasn't threatening her, or anything.' Though Joanna's voice suggested she wasn't so sure about it, and to Georgina, the words sounded aggressive and threatening.

'You didn't try IVF?' Georgina asked.

'I wanted to. Trish even said she'd give me her share of the money we inherited from our gran, because Simon was making a fuss about how expensive IVF treatment was. He was furious with her about that, too.'

'That's a shame,' Georgina said. 'I have a couple of friends who went through IVF – it didn't work first time for either of them, but when they tried again, they were lucky.'

'That's all I wanted,' Joanna said. 'I would've done *anything* to be able to try.'

Georgina waited, giving Joanna space to talk. Would she tell a kind stranger something she couldn't bear to share with her sister?

Joanna stared into her coffee mug, as if she dearly wanted to say something, but at the same time she thought she ought to keep her mouth shut. And then she looked at Georgina, weighing up the older woman and the fact that her sister clearly liked her and got on well with her.

'He knew how desperate I was,' Joanna said, her voice cracking.

And at that moment it was as if a dam had broken: as if now that Joanna was free of Simon keeping her silent, the words were coming out and not stopping. 'We came to a deal. If I'd give him something he wanted, he'd give me what I wanted.'

What had Simon wanted? Georgina wondered. And was it connected to the nighthawks Colin had mentioned?

'The thing is... our museum was founded a really long time ago. In the early days, when they took donations, they didn't record things the way we do now. There are things in storage that were never properly catalogued, and there was never enough time to work on them – other things had higher priorities, so the cataloguing was just left and left. Nobody even really knew what we had,' Joanna said. 'Simon said if I got him access to the stores, so he could look at what we had, then he'd agree to do the IVF.' She dragged in a breath. 'I was going to sort out a proper visit for him, but he said he didn't want anything official. He just wanted a look at the things that weren't on show. I mean, he's – he *was*,' she corrected herself, 'an archaeologist. His job was finding things that haven't been seen for decades, if not thousands of years, and he loved it. I thought he liked the thrill of seeing things that were out of bounds to the general public, things that might've been found years ago and kept in storage ever since. So on nights when I was working late, I'd let him in to look at the stores.'

Georgina was pretty sure this wasn't going to have a happy ending, but she wasn't going to stop the flow of words. Joanna obviously needed to talk.

'How stupid am I?' Joanna asked, shaking her head in apparent disbelief. 'It never even occurred to me that he might be doing more than just looking. Not until an art student was doing a project on intaglios – they're the carved gems you get in seal rings and the like – and wanted to take some photographs. It was my job to show her the stuff behind the scenes, and I could see that things were missing from the drawers. Some of the gemstones had been rearranged. I definitely remembered seeing a carved lapis lazuli in one of the drawers – the colour was unmistakeable and I'd wanted to display it properly in the museum. But it wasn't where it should've been, or in any of the drawers around it. And there didn't seem to be as many intaglios as there should've been in the drawers.'

'You think Simon took them?' Georgina asked.

Joanna looked miserable. 'God help me, yes. I'm not even sure how many. It's so easy to slip little things into your pocket. If they're not set into a ring, there's no metal; the gemstones wouldn't set off a detector when you walk through a door. I confronted him about it, and he just laughed at me. He said I didn't have any proof – and if I told anyone what I suspected, as soon as they investigated, they'd see CCTV showing me letting him through without my pass and without signing him in properly. I'd be prosecuted as an accessory. I'd lose my job.' She dragged in a breath. 'He said if I didn't bring him more, then he'd tell the museum everything he knew.'

'So he blackmailed you into taking things for him?'

Joanna nodded. 'I didn't know where he was storing the intaglios, or if he'd sold them on,' she said. 'And I think he would've made sure that he got rid of any evidence. I was stuck. I've been taking one gemstone a fortnight for him for almost the last two years.'

Fifty gemstones.

No wonder Joanna had made the subject of her infertility a

no-go subject with her sister, Georgina thought. In case what was really going on accidentally slipped out.

'He kept promising he'd do the IVF – and then something always cropped up at the last minute and we'd have to reschedule,' Joanna finished.

'Couldn't you have confided in Trish?' Georgina asked. 'She would've supported you.'

'I was too ashamed,' Joanna said. 'Firstly, I'd been so stupid, listening to Simon – I mean, yes, he was my husband, and you don't expect your husband to be on the wrong side of the law, especially when he's an eminent archaeologist. And, secondly, I'd stolen things that belong to everyone, which is the last thing a historian should do. I didn't want her to judge me, and I definitely didn't want her to get dragged into it. We didn't get on very well when we were teens, and I resented her when she fell pregnant with Laura; I thought she was an attention-seeking cow.' Joanna gave a wry smile. 'Which is pretty much what she thought of me. We went for quite a while without speaking to each other.'

'But you made up?'

Joanna nodded. 'When I got my first job, there were a couple of older women who job-shared and nanny-shared. Listening to them made me realise how hard it must've been for Trish to work as an archaeologist when she was a single mum to a toddler. I felt a bit guilty about the way I'd treated her, and I reached out to her. She could've told me to get lost, but she made an effort, too. And it's good to have my sister back.'

'Maybe you could talk to her about this,' Georgina said gently. 'I'm sure she'd help you.' She paused. 'I should tell you, my partner's a detective.'

Joanna's eyes went wide with fear. 'Are you going to tell him what I just told you?'

'No,' Georgina said. 'What you told me is in confidence. But he's one of the good guys. If you talk to him and tell him what you've told me, he'll help you.'

'How can I?' Joanna went pale with panic. 'I'll be facing prison. I stole things and I helped my husband steal things. At the very least, I'll lose my job and I'll never be able to work in another museum again. And I've let Trish down. She can't ever know about this.'

'Think about it,' Georgina advised. 'As for letting Trish down, I don't think she'll blame you. If anything, I think she'll blame herself for introducing you to Simon in the first place.'

A tear rolled down Joanna's cheek. 'This is all such a mess. And I know Simon wasn't a good man, but I did love him. That probably makes me a bad person, too.' She bit her lip. 'He could be so lovely, sometimes.'

And so horrible at others, from what both Joanna and Trish had said. 'I think all humans are complicated,' Georgina said, 'and it's not my job to judge you. If I've never been in your situation, how do I know what I would've done in your shoes?'

Joanna dragged in a breath. 'I don't know what to do now.'

'Sleep on it,' Georgina said. 'But if you go to the police voluntarily and tell them what you've done, the judge will look more favourably on your case. You won't be completely exonerated, but the penalties you face will be less severe. If you warn Trish before you talk to the police, it'll be less of a shock to your family.' She reached over to squeeze Joanna's hand. 'And, more importantly, it'll give you your integrity back. You'll be the woman you were before you met Simon.'

Later that evening, Georgina messaged Colin.

> You definitely need to talk to Joanna. I'm trying to persuade her to talk to you. But it's complicated – you'll need to be tactful.

SIXTEEN

On Friday morning, Georgina dropped Bea back at the train station. 'Text me when you get home,' she said. 'It's been so lovely seeing you.'

'And you, Mum.' Bea hugged her. 'And please talk to Colin. I completely understand why you're fed up with him, but I can also see why he's struggling with the idea of Doris. I mean, I'm not saying he has no imagination, but his life is built on finding solutions to puzzles. He's all about logic. If he's never really experienced anything he couldn't explain, then it must be difficult for him to accept what you're saying. I'm sure you can reach some sort of compromise. I bet he misses you as much as you miss him. And I've noticed Bert looking for him.'

Georgina gave a wry chuckle. 'We're both old enough to be sensible. It's just…' She sighed and shook her head.

'You're both stubborn,' Bea said. 'I think you're going to have to agree to disagree. I know it upsets you that he doesn't accept that Doris exists, but at the same time he's finding it hard that you expect him to believe something he's never experienced.'

'I guess,' Georgina said.

Back at Little Wenborough, she finished getting Rookery Barn ready with Jodie, then headed to the manor with Bert to meet up with Sybbie and Trish to photograph the mosaic floor.

Rowena was already there. 'I needed to talk to Trish about something else, so I came a bit early. Good to see you again, Georgie,' she said, shaking Georgina's hand. 'And lovely Bert.' She crouched down and made a fuss of the spaniel. 'Such a beautiful boy.'

'You really could have brought him to the dig earlier, you know,' Trish said, making a fuss of him, too. 'He's gorgeous.'

'Last time I saw him, he'd just found a—' Rowena spotted Georgina's frantically widened eyes and tiny shakes of the head, and stopped.

'Found what?' Joanna asked.

Georgina winced. 'I'm sorry, Joanna. I probably shouldn't have brought him with me. He's, um, found *remains*, before now.'

Joanna gave a brave smile. 'Ah. So you wouldn't want him in the middle of a dig, because he wouldn't quite know how to respect the archaeology.'

Georgina took her hand and squeezed it briefly. 'Sorry.'

'It's all right,' Joanna said. 'I know you're all trying to be careful with me. It's going to be hard, seeing this floor and knowing that's where Simon died, but I need to face it. Besides, Trish says the mosaic is gorgeous. We can't let it be lost again, just because...' Her voice wobbled, and Trish gave her a hug.

'You've got this. And I've got you,' she told her sister. 'Now, we need to go and find Adam. He was supposed to be here to help me with the tarpaulin.' She shook her head in annoyance. 'He's late, as usual.'

'He's young. He'll learn,' Sybbie said. 'I'll give you a hand.'

'Bert, *sit*,' Georgina said. 'And stay.'

'I'll hold him, if you like,' Joanna said.

And it would give the younger woman something to focus

on other than the fact that the last time the tarpaulin had been removed, it had also uncovered her husband's dead body, Georgina thought.

And then a nasty thought struck her. Simon had been late, which was why Colin had had to help with the tarpaulin. This time, Adam was late. Did that mean...?

No, of course not. This couldn't be history repeating itself. She shook herself and focused on Joanna's question. 'Thank you. That's kind. He's fairly well-behaved, and he loves having a fuss made of him.'

Georgina was just about to take the first photographs of the mosaic when Rowena came over to her. 'When you see Colin,' she said, keeping her voice very low, 'let him know that I sorted out the loan of the spoons.'

'Loan of what spoons?' Georgina asked, keeping her voice equally low.

'Ah – that might be something I shouldn't have said,' Rowena said. 'Not to worry. I'll email him.'

Why did Colin want spoons? And what sort of spoons would the county's finds liaisons officer be lending him?

She didn't have a chance to ask, but the fact that Rowena had practically whispered to her – a whisper Georgina had only just managed to pick up, despite her hearing aids – meant that it might have something to do with Simon's murder. Which meant she needed to keep it quiet for the meantime.

Somehow the archaeology team had managed to clean the blood off the floor, and if Georgina hadn't seen it with her own eyes, she would never have known that blood had seeped from Simon's head onto the tesserae.

Georgina had just finished taking the photographs and taken Bert's lead back, and Trish and Sybbie had replaced the tarpaulin when Adam strolled up.

'You were supposed to be here half an hour ago,' Trish said, glaring at him.

'Well, I'm here now,' he said. 'What do you need me to do?'

'Nothing. It's all done, now,' she said.

'Soz.' He shrugged. 'Look, I'll go and do the coffee run to make up for it. What does everyone want?'

'Nothing for me, thanks,' Rowena said. 'I'm afraid I need to get back. I'll be in touch about that issue we discussed, Trish – and I'll give you a ring to sort out dinner, Georgie.'

'Lovely,' Georgina said, smiling at her.

'The coffees are on me,' Sybbie said. 'I'll message Cesca and tell her I'll settle up with her later. Bring some cake, too.'

'Cheers,' Adam said. 'I'll be back in a bit.' He bent down towards Bert. 'Nice dog.'

Bert responded by backing away, surprising Georgina; Bert usually wanted to be everyone's best friend. Yet he'd seemed wary of one of Trish's other students, too; when Helena had tried to pet him, earlier, Bert had pressed very hard against Georgina's legs, as if seeking reassurance. She couldn't quite work out why Bert would be worried about them.

'Suit yourself,' Adam said, shrugging. Although his subsequent mutter was too low for anyone to interpret, Georgina was able to lip-read what he said. Knowing that Trish didn't like the young man very much, she decided not to stir up more bad feeling by repeating it, but her sympathies were most definitely with Trish and Bert.

When Adam came back – having taken rather longer than any of them had expected – and broke off a bit of the sausage roll Francesca had sent for Bert, the dog refused it.

'Oh, well. Your loss, dog. I'll eat it myself, later,' Adam said, wrapping the remainder of the sausage roll in a paper napkin and stuffing it into his pocket. 'Better get back to work before Trish starts cracking the whip.'

'I really hope he doesn't put me down as a referee for his first job,' Trish said when he'd sauntered off. 'Because I don't think

my conscience would let me recommend him to anyone. He's
not that popular with the rest of the students, anymore – they've
gone from seeing him as a good laugh who's always the life and
soul of the party to realising that he never stands a round in the
pub and he tends to leave everyone else to clear up after him.'

'He'll get a wake-up call eventually,' Sybbie said. 'Perhaps
he'll come good by the time he graduates.'

'Perhaps. I normally like to think the best of everyone,' Trish
said, 'but there's something about Adam that really grates on my
nerves.'

Georgina lingered just long enough to finish her coffee, then
said her goodbyes and clipped Bert's harness into the back of
her car. Even though she only lived a couple of minutes' drive
away, she was feeling weary by the time she pulled up outside
her farmhouse, and she couldn't summon up the energy to sort
out her photographs.

'Maybe I need a nap,' she said to Bert as she let him out of
the car and unlocked her kitchen door. She hadn't slept properly since her row with Colin, and clearly her sleep debt had
built up. That, or perhaps this was the bone-deep menopause
tiredness her friends had been grumbling about and she'd been
lucky to avoid so far.

Bert galloped around the garden, cocked his leg against a
shrub, then trotted into the kitchen behind her. Georgina
locked the back door, put her camera bag on the kitchen table
and hung her handbag over the back of one of the mismatched
chairs, then put her shoes into the rack in the hall. Bert whined
as she pressed the thumb-latch in the oak plank door leading to
the narrow staircase.

He had a point. Mindful of what had happened to Doris on
this very staircase, fifty-odd years ago, and feeling a bit woozy,
Georgina decided not to risk the stairs and to lie on the sofa
instead.

'Georgie? Georgie? Don't go to sleep,' Doris said, sounding worried.

'Just five minutes,' Georgina mumbled. She just about managed to take out her hearing aids and put them on the coffee table; she felt Bert leap onto the sofa and settle at her feet, and then she drifted into oblivion.

'You just missed Georgie,' Trish said to Colin when he arrived at the dig site with Larissa. 'She's already done the photographs and gone home. Rowena was here, earlier. Everything's all set.'

The finds liaison officer had sent him an email to let him know that she'd arranged for the loan of two Roman spoons to Trish, to bait their trap, and she'd sent photographs as well as copying the email to someone senior at the museum that had loaned the spoons. 'It's a shame I missed them both,' he said. 'But, actually, I wanted a chat with your sister.'

'You have news about Simon?' Trish asked.

'Not exactly,' he said.

'Then can I ask what's it about?' she asked. 'I know you'll tell me it's not my business, but I've already told you that Jojo's fragile.'

'I'm asking her to help us with some enquiries,' Colin said.

Trish folded her arms. 'Then I'll sit in with her.'

'Unless you're a solicitor as well as an archaeologist,' Colin said, 'that isn't appropriate.'

'Oh, for pity's sake, have some compassion! Her husband has just been killed. She's upset; she's my sister and I want to support her,' Trish said.

'That needs to be her decision,' Colin said.

'What aren't you telling me?' Trish demanded.

Colin rubbed a hand across his forehead. This was giving him a headache. 'Dr Melton, I appreciate you want to be there for your sister, but she might prefer to talk to me on her own about this particular matter. I'd prefer not to have to charge you with obstruction, but if I have to, then I will.'

Trish's eyes widened. 'Oh, my God. Are you saying she's in trouble? Is this something to do with Simon?'

'Dr Melton, I'm sure you appreciate that I can't discuss current investigations with people who aren't directly involved in them,' he said quietly. 'Could you please just tell me where I can find Joanna Butterfield?'

For a moment, he thought she was going to refuse. But then the fight went out of her. 'All right. She's helping to catalogue stuff in the finds tent. I thought it might help to give her something to concentrate on, so she doesn't keep thinking about Simon having his head bashed in.'

'Good idea,' Colin said. Though, given what he knew and he was pretty sure Trish didn't, he really hoped that Trish hadn't left her sister alone with the more valuable finds. 'We could do with somewhere quiet to talk.'

'If it's not for long, you can use the finds tent,' Trish said. 'I'll take you over there.'

'Thank you,' Colin said.

In the finds tent, Trish asked the students working there to go and help some of the others. When they'd gone, she said to Joanna, 'Inspector Bradshaw wants to interview you.' Throwing a challenging glance at Colin, she added, 'Do you want me to stay with you?'

Joanna looked like a rabbit in headlights, caught in a difficult situation and not sure where to turn. 'I...' She bit her lip, and a tear trickled down her cheek. 'Did Georgina tell you what I told her?' she asked Colin.

'No. She said that she thought you needed to talk to me about something,' he said gently.

'And if I don't have anything to say?'

'Then,' Colin said, 'I'm afraid I'll have to take you to the station for a formal interview.'

She swallowed hard. 'You're going to arrest me if I talk to you.'

Yeah. There was that possibility, Colin thought, depending on what she told him.

'And I don't want Trish thinking any the less of me,' Joanna said looking miserable. 'I'm so sorry.'

'You're my sister. I'm not going to think less of you.' Trish frowned. 'What have you done, Jojo?'

Haltingly, Joanna stumbled through her story – how she'd thought Simon just wanted to look at all the rare things that weren't on view to the public, how she realised eventually that he'd been taking things, and how he'd told her that if she didn't keep up the supply, he'd send an anonymous tip to the police which would see her arrested and lose her job. 'I'm so ashamed,' she said. 'I knew it was wrong, but I couldn't see a way out.'

'That's coercion,' Trish said. 'He made you take things. And he lied to you. He promised you he'd sort out the IVF, and he didn't.' She narrowed her eyes. 'If he wasn't already dead, I'd be tempted to smack him over the head with a spade myself.'

'That sort of comment can be very unhelpful,' Colin said warningly. 'Particularly when you don't have an alibi for the time when he was killed.'

Trish sighed wearily. 'How many more times do I have to tell you? I didn't kill him.'

Until they found out who *had* killed Simon, Colin wasn't crossing her off the list.

'What's going to happen now?' Joanna asked.

'We'll read you your rights, arrest you on suspicion of theft and ask you to accompany us to the station, where we'll need to go through everything you've just told me,' Colin said.

Joanna's eyes widened. 'Am I going to jail?'

'If you mean are we going to hold you in custody overnight, we might be able to let you out on bail,' Colin said. 'As for your sentence: that rather depends on the magistrate who hears your case. They'll assess your role in the thefts and look at aggravating and mitigating factors – things that would increase or decrease the severity of the sentence.'

'This is all so wrong,' Trish said. 'For pity's sake. You know what's happened here.'

'There may be a link between what your sister's just told us and Simon's death,' Colin pointed out.

'There's got to be a way I can help Jojo,' Trish said.

'I'd suggest remaining calm and finding a solicitor,' Colin said. He turned to Joanna. 'You have a right to have a solicitor present at your interview, Joanna, and I'd recommend that you do. You can instruct your own, or you can use the duty solicitor.'

'I'm so sorry, Trish,' Joanna said.

'I just...' Trish shook her head in frustration. 'This is all such a mess.'

'And we're going to sort it out,' Colin said.

'I'll find a solicitor,' Trish said.

Colin gave her his card. 'That has all the details you need, including my work mobile. We'll look after your sister,' he promised. 'Joanna Butterfield, I'm arresting you on suspicion of the aiding and abetting theft, and of carrying out thefts over the period of the last two years, because we have evidence that shows you may have been involved and your arrest is necessary to question you about your involvement. Do you understand this?'

'Yes,' she whispered.

'You do not have to say anything. But it may harm your defence if you do not mention when questioned something which you later rely on in court. Anything you do say may be given in evidence,' Colin said. 'Again, is that clear, Joanna?'

'Yes.'

'Do you have any illnesses or take any medication that we need to know about?' he asked. 'Because we have a duty of care to you while you're with us.'

'No,' Joanna confirmed.

Colin glanced at Trish, who gave a brief nod to signal that her sister was telling the truth.

'OK. We'll take you to the station now. You don't have to talk to us until your solicitor arrives, but in the meantime, we'll make sure you've got something to eat and drink,' Colin said. He looked at Trish. 'I trust this doesn't change the other issue we talked about?'

'I...' She sighed. 'No.'

'Good. I'll be in touch later about that,' he said briskly.

He and Larissa took Joanna to his car.

As he sat behind the wheel, it felt as if there was a voice in the back of his head, saying, 'You need to get to Georgie.'

He didn't have time right now. He needed to get Joanna back to the station and deal with that before the surveillance started this evening.

All the same, the feeling wouldn't go away. Unease. Worry. It was like a constant voice in his ear.

'I just need to check something,' he muttered, and stepped out from the car. A quick check of his private phone – thankfully, Georgina hadn't deleted him from the app that showed him her location – told him that she was at home. Feeling a bit sheepish, he rang her. As soon as she picked up, he'd know she was fine, he'd make some ridiculous excuse for calling her and he could just get on with his job.

Except she didn't pick up.

He knew her phone was connected to her fitness watch, so if her phone was on silent, she'd feel the vibration of the watch on her wrist. Even though things weren't quite back to normal between them, he didn't think she'd just ignore his call. Georgina wasn't petty.

His uneasy feeling got a lot worse.

'Copper's hunch,' he said to Larissa. 'We need to stop at Georgina's on the way to the station.'

'Got it, guv,' she said.

SEVENTEEN

It was only a couple of minutes' drive from Little Wenborough Manor to Rookery Farm. Georgina's car was parked on the gravel next to the farmhouse, but everywhere was quiet. Even the birds didn't seem to be singing. And Bert wasn't barking his usual welcome when Colin crunched across the gravel.

Something's wrong. Something's wrong. The words kept echoing in his head.

He tried the kitchen door. Locked.

Maybe Georgina had taken Bert for a walk – but somehow he didn't think so. Especially when the spaniel ran into the kitchen and jumped up at the door, whining.

Colin hadn't given Georgina her key back, yet. She might be furious with him for using it, but he couldn't shake the conviction that something was wrong. Better to feel foolish now than to regret it later, he told himself.

Bert was still whining instead of barking, and that was worrying, too.

He unlocked the door. Bert circled him twice and rushed out of the kitchen.

Remembering that the poor girl in the house who'd died fifty years ago had fallen down the stairs, Colin made his way into the hallway, a sick feeling of dread in his stomach. *Please don't let history have repeated itself.* To his relief, Georgina wasn't lying unconscious on the floorboards. There was also no scent of chemicals, so he was pretty sure she wasn't in her dark room, either.

'Georgie?' he called.

Still there was no answer, but Bert circled him and whined anxiously.

'Find Georgie, Bert,' he said. 'Find her.'

Bert gave a soft wuff and rushed to the living room door, then turned to check where Colin was before going back into the room and barking loudly.

'Georgie?' Colin called again.

Still there was no answer. It might be that her hearing aids were switched off, but his hunch or whatever it was said otherwise. Something was really wrong.

Panic flooding through him now, he went to the living room and knocked on the open door before going inside.

Georgina lay on the sofa, perfectly still. Bert whined anxiously and jumped onto the sofa by her feet.

If her hearing aids were in, she'd hear him; if they were out, Colin knew she wouldn't even be able to hear the dog, but he also knew that she was woken by light and movement. It was still light outside, and she must've felt Bert jumping on the sofa. And yet she just lay there. Was she really deeply asleep, or was she unconscious?

It brought back memories of last year, when he'd found Georgina at the farmhouse after she'd been poisoned. Had the same thing happened again? He wasn't taking any risks; he crouched down next to her and shook her shoulder. 'Georgie, wake up,' he said – and then brushed her hair away from her ear. No hearing aid. Of course she wouldn't hear him. But she should've been aware of her shaking him, and the movement would normally have woken her.

He tried to push the fear away and think logically. Had she been taken ill and collapsed? Or was there a more sinister reason for her unresponsiveness?

He put a hand just in front of her face and could feel her breathing, but it was slow. When he checked her pulse, that was slow, too.

He rang Larissa, who was waiting with Joanna in the car. 'Georgie's here – but she seems unconscious. I can't wake her.'

'Do you want me to call an ambulance?' Larissa asked.

'Yes, please. And I'll call Sybbie. Hopefully she can take Bert, so Georgie doesn't have to worry about him.'

'OK, guv. I'll bring Joanna into the kitchen, and I'll patch the paramedics through to you if I need to,' Larissa said. 'Bert knows me, so it should be OK.'

'Thank you.' Colin continued trying to wake Georgina while he called Sybbie on speakerphone.

'Colin? What's the matter?' Sybbie asked.

'Georgie's unconscious and I can't wake her,' Colin said. 'Larissa's calling the ambulance. Would you be able to look after Bert, please?'

'Of course. I'm on my way now,' Sybbie said crisply.

Georgina still didn't wake, but she was at least breathing and her airways were clear. Colin moved her into the recovery position and used the throw from the back of the sofa to keep her warm but not overheated. In his head, he went through the causes of unconsciousness. She didn't appear to have been in any kind of accident and there was no bruising to suggest a blow to her head. It most probably wasn't carbon monoxide poisoning, because her face didn't have that telltale redness he'd seen in cases when someone had been affected by a faulty boiler. Could it be low blood sugar or a heart condition she didn't know about, perhaps? All the while, panic slithered up his spine, mingled with guilt. What if she didn't regain consciousness? What if she died, when they hadn't made up their fight? He couldn't even remember his last words to her.

'Wake up, Georgie,' he begged quietly, knowing that she couldn't hear him or the desperation in his voice, but needing to say the words anyway. 'Wake up. We'll sort everything out between us later. But please, please wake up.'

'Guv, the emergency services want to talk to you,' Larissa called; he guessed that she was probably standing in the kitchen. 'Where are you?'

'The living room, just across the hall,' he called back. 'What about Joanna?'

'She's with me,' Larissa said as she walked into the room, followed by Joanna.

'Don't worry. I'm not some reckless teenager who's going to make a run for it,' Joanna said wryly.

'Thank you,' Colin said, meaning it, and took the phone from Larissa to talk to the emergency team.

By the time Sybbie and Bernard arrived, a few minutes later, Georgina had finally woken but looked woozy and not at all with it.

'What are you all doing here?' she asked drowsily, scanning the room.

Colin knew she wouldn't be able to hear him. He held up one finger in a signal to wait because he'd explain in a moment, and looked for her hearing aids. When he spotted them on the coffee table, he scooped them into her hand and waited while she put them in.

'Sorry for alarming you. I, um...' How could he explain it? 'I had a funny feeling and you didn't answer your phone. Your car was here but you didn't answer the door, and I could hear Bert whining. He seemed distressed.' He coughed. 'I used your key to come and find you. Bert showed me where you were – but then I couldn't wake you.'

'I...' She peered at him as if trying to make sense of his words. 'What time is it?'

He glanced at his watch. 'Half past four in the afternoon.' Relief that she'd woken made him snappy. 'And you never nap in the afternoon, so don't try to tell me you're OK.'

'I'm fine,' she shot back, and struggled to get to a sitting position.

He knelt down next to her. 'Don't try to get up, Georgie. I'm sorry. I didn't mean to be stroppy with you. I was just so worried when you didn't wake. There's an ambulance on its way.'

Shock registered on her face. 'But I don't need an ambulance.'

'You most definitely need checking over, dear girl,' Sybbie said. 'What happened?'

'I don't know.' Georgina struggled to rise again and this time Colin helped her to a sitting position, sliding an arm round her shoulder to brace her – but keeping his arm there because he needed to be close to her even more than he wanted to help her.

'You don't remember how you got here?' he asked gently.

'I was taking photographs at the dig. Then I came home to put the shots on my computer and work on them, except...' Her eyes widened. 'I don't remember doing that.'

'Your camera bag's safely on the kitchen table,' Colin said. 'And you'd locked the kitchen door.'

'I don't remember locking the door or coming in here for a nap,' she said, 'but obviously I did. And I must've taken my hearing aids out. But I don't remember doing that, either.' She bit her lip, clearly worried. 'I don't remember anything.'

'I'm glad you had the sense to come in here rather than trying to go upstairs to bed and ending up falling down the stairs,' Sybbie said.

Colin's feelings precisely, but he wouldn't have dared say so.

'I'm a first aider at work,' Joanna said. 'Are you diabetic, Georgie? Or on any medication that might have affected you?'

'No,' Georgina said.

Still unable to shake off the memories of last year, Colin asked, 'Have you eaten or drunk anything today that you didn't prepare yourself?'

'I had a coffee after the shoot at the dig, yes.' She frowned, clearly remembering the same thing. 'But don't you dare accuse my friends, this time. They haven't poisoned me.'

'I'm not accusing anyone,' Colin said, as neutrally as he could. Though he rather thought *someone* might have tried to poison Georgina. Particularly as she'd been asking questions... 'I'm just looking at what might have made you flake out. Would the coffee cup you drank from still be around?' he asked, trying to sound casual.

'No. One of the students took a tray with all the mugs back to the farm shop café, just after Georgina left,' Joanna said.

'Cesca would've put everything straight in the dishwasher,' Bernard said. 'That cup would've been washed, dried, used and washed again, by now.'

So the evidence had vanished. That was a little too convenient for Colin's liking. And it was also frustrating, because there was only one other way to check whether Georgina had been poisoned.

The paramedics arrived, and Colin had to ask the difficult question. 'I think someone may have put something in Georgina's drink to incapacitate her. Georgie, will you consent to a blood or urine sample being taken so we can get it tested, please?'

'I agree,' Sybbie said, supporting him. 'At least then we'll know if someone did give you something and you can be treated properly. And if it's not that, then you'll need a whole barrage of tests anyway to see why you flaked out like that.'

'All right. Take a sample, if you must,' Georgina said with a sigh. 'But, even if your theory's right and something does show up, how are you going to know who spiked my drink?'

'I'll investigate,' Colin said grimly.

'I really don't need to go to hospital,' Georgina said.

'Can you stand up?' Bernard asked.

Georgina lifted her chin. 'Of course.'

'Prove it,' Sybbie challenged.

Georgina stood up, wobbled and sat down again. 'All right. Point made. Maybe I do need to be checked out.'

It was common sense, but the fact she'd agreed so quickly worried Colin even more.

But then she added something that made him feel a lot better, as if she was coming back to her normal self. 'But I'm absolutely *not* going anywhere in a wheelchair.'

'I'll walk you to the ambulance,' Colin said. He wanted to go with her to the hospital, too, but he was meant to be taking Joanna Butterfield to the station for an interview. He'd already made the mistake of putting his job before his family too many times; his divorce was proof of that. Georgina wasn't quite his family... but he wanted her to be. She needed to come first. But how could he do his job properly and look out for her at the same time?

As if sensing how torn he was, and why, Sybbie said quietly, 'I'll go with Georgie to the hospital, Colin. Bernard will take Bert back to our place, and then he'll come to the hospital. I'll keep you posted. If they let her out, we'll bring her back to the Manor so we can keep an eye on her.'

'Thank you, Sybbie,' he said gratefully. 'I appreciate this more than you know.'

'There's no point in worrying Bea and Will just yet,' Sybbie said. 'We'll see what's going on; then either you can call them or I will.'

'Good plan,' Colin said. 'I owe you.'

'Dear boy, it's the least I can do. Georgie's one of our own,' she said, patting his arm.

EIGHTEEN

Back at the station, Colin organised a phone call for Joanna to talk to her lawyer, then made sure she had something to eat and drink before talking to Mei Zhang about the case. They agreed that Colin would do the preliminary interviews in Norwich, and worked out their initial questions, but the bulk of the investigation would be based in London, where the alleged offences had taken place.

When the solicitor arrived, they moved into the interview room; Colin made sure that Joanna and the solicitor both had a drink and there were biscuits. Then he went through all the housekeeping procedures, and re-cautioned Joanna before interviewing her again.

Thankfully Joanna didn't change her story during the formal interview; she was clear about when she'd first allowed Simon access to the museum's stores, when she'd first realised something was missing, what she'd taken for him over the next couple years, and how she'd changed some of the records at the museum to hide the thefts.

'I don't know if Simon sold any of the gems, or where he

stored them,' she said. 'I didn't dare ask him in case it made him angry and he went back on his agreement to do the IVF. Looking back, I know how stupid that was.' She grimaced. 'I'm pretty sure it's not at our house. And there was no sign of any money going into our joint account.'

'We'll need to search your house, I'm afraid,' Colin said. 'Obviously we'll have a warrant, and we'll try to be as least intrusive as possible.'

'You're going to search it without me there?' she asked, looking worried. 'Does that mean you're going to break down my door?'

'Hopefully not.' He'd already set the wheels in motion for the warrant, not wanting to give her time to have the evidence removed by a friend. At the same time, he wanted her to help their investigation, and smashing her front door unnecessarily would make her cooperation less likely. 'Does a neighbour keep your key for emergencies when you're away?' he asked.

'Yes,' she said, and gave him the details, along with the code for the burglar alarm.

'Thank you. I'm going to pass these to my colleague in London. If you know anything about any of Simon's bank accounts, that would be helpful,' Colin said.

'We have a joint account for paying bills,' she said, 'and our accounts are separate for everything else. I don't have access to his internet banking or his investments, but I know which bank he uses, if that's any use.'

'It will be,' Colin said, taking down the information. 'Do you happen to know the passcode for his phone?' Even though all the mobile phone companies recommended not sharing your passcode with anyone, in practice he knew a lot of people shared their phone code with their partners.

'Yes,' she said. 'It's the same as mine.' When Colin had written it down, she asked, 'What happens now?'

'We'll put you on bail,' he said, and explained to her how it worked. 'You're technically still under arrest, and I'll ask you to report to my colleagues in London – that's your bail return date. If you don't turn up when you're supposed to, it's a criminal offence.'

'I'm hardly going to flee the country,' she said dryly. 'Not when I need to organise my husband's funeral.'

'Which I'm afraid you won't be able to do until we've finished our investigations,' he said gently. 'We're doing our best to find out what happened and who was responsible.'

'Does it change things? That Simon took the gems, I mean?' Joanna asked.

'It widens the investigation,' Colin said. If Simon had sold the gems, and then fallen out with some of the people he'd sold them to, those people would become potential suspects in the murder case. There might even be a connection with the nighthawks, though in Colin's experience, things rarely tied up that neatly.

When the interview was over, he sent the recordings to Mei, then called her to give her a quick debrief and check that her team would get the warrant to search Simon Butterfield's house and his bank accounts.

Then he checked his phone and was relieved to see a message from Sybbie.

> Doctor gave Georgie the all-clear to come home. She and Bert are staying with us tonight.

Whatever had made Georgina pass out like that clearly hadn't had any knock-on effects, and he knew she'd be safe with Sybbie and Bernard. Though he still wanted to know what had actually happened; if someone had deliberately tried to hurt her, he wanted to bring them to justice and make sure they didn't do it to anyone else.

'I'm going back to Little Wenborough,' he said to Joanna, 'if you'd like a lift.'

'Thank you,' she said. 'I was going to get a taxi. I mean, I don't want to cause Trish any more hassle by dragging her out here to pick me up. I know she's up against it, with everything at the dig finishing this weekend.'

Joanna didn't chat much in the car, and Colin wasn't in the mood for making small talk. Once he'd dropped her off at the dig, he headed to the supermarket at Great Wenborough – it was about the only shop still open to sell flowers, at this time of the evening – and bought flowers for both Sybbie and Georgina.

'Just to say thank you for looking after Georgie – and for keeping me in the loop,' he said, when Sybbie answered the front door and he presented her with one of the bouquets.

'Dear boy, you really didn't need to,' Sybbie said. Then he realised what an idiot he was, bringing a bunch of flowers to someone who not only had an enormous garden, she opened it to the public every Sunday during spring and summer. But she gave him one of her trademark wide smiles and accepted the flowers gracefully. 'Though it's very sweet of you and it's very much appreciated. I take it you want to see Georgie?'

'Yes, please.'

'Come with me.' She ushered him through the hallway and into one of the sitting rooms, where Georgina was talking to Bernard, with Sybbie's dogs and Bert sprawled on the rug between them. The dogs leaped up and wound round Colin's legs, their tails wagging, and he made a fuss of the three of them.

'Bernard, you couldn't give me a hand, could you?' Sybbie asked.

Bernard looked slightly nonplussed, but clearly his wife's expression told him that she thought Georgina and Colin needed some time alone. 'Of course,' he said, and followed her out of the room, clicking his fingers so the three dogs followed, too.

'How are you feeling, Georgie?' Colin asked.

'Still a bit spaced-out, but there's no real harm done,' she said.

'I, um, brought you these.' Awkwardly, he handed her the flowers.

'That's kind,' she said.

'A cheap bunch of flowers – even if they were the best I could do at this time of day – is nowhere near enough,' he said. 'I'm sorry we had a fight. Seeing you lying there on the sofa, and not being able to wake you, was one of the worst moments of my life. All I could think of was what if you didn't wake up again, and I didn't get the chance to say sorry?'

'I'm sorry, too,' she said. 'Bea says I'm being as stubborn as you are.' She rolled her eyes. 'Oh, come *here*.'

He sat down beside her, gingerly took the flowers from her and placed them on the newspaper on the coffee table so they wouldn't drip water everywhere, and wrapped his arms round her, closing his eyes with relief at being close to her again. They stayed like that for a while, not speaking; when he finally drew back, he took her hand. 'I'm just glad you're all right,' he said. 'Did the doctor find anything in your blood tests?'

Of course that was one of the reasons why he was here, Georgina thought. She was part of the case now and he needed to investigate what had happened to her and who was involved. Though that hug hadn't been professional; it had felt distinctly personal. As were the flowers. Colin had clearly been worried about her.

'He said it was diazepam. I haven't taken anything like that for a couple of years,' she said, 'and I have absolutely no idea how it ended up in my system.'

'I'm pretty sure it was put in something you ate or drank,' he said. 'Though thankfully we won't be able to test that theory.'

She knew what he meant: she was still alive and the pathologist wouldn't have to test the contents of her stomach. She had no idea how many tablets she'd unknowingly taken, but if she'd fallen asleep at the wheel while she was driving, she could've killed or seriously injured someone coming in the opposite direction.

She shivered. 'How did you know something was wrong?'

'Copper's hunch,' he said, sounding slightly embarrassed.

'No, it wasn't,' Doris said. 'Ask him why he went to the house.'

That was an odd question, and Georgina wasn't quite sure what point Doris was trying to make. But she asked anyway. 'Why did you go to the farmhouse?'

He didn't meet her eyes. 'As I said, it was a copper's hunch. Just a feeling that something wasn't right.'

Doris sighed. 'Ask him if he felt he needed to talk to you. Did he have words echoing in his head – like "something's wrong"?'

'This is a weird question,' Georgina said, 'but did you feel you needed to talk to me? Did it feel as if the words "something's wrong" were echoing in your head?'

'Well, yes – that's what I mean about a copper's instinct,' Colin said. 'I rang you and you didn't pick up.'

'I might have been busy in my dark room,' she pointed out.

'Or you might not have wanted to speak to me right then, considering how things are between us,' he said, disarming her. 'I get that. But it felt...'

'As if someone was sitting beside you, saying, "Something's wrong,"?' she finished, finally twigging what Doris had been trying to tell her.

He raked one hand through his hair. 'Yes, I suppose so. But don't try to tell me that was Doris. You said you were the only one who could hear her.'

Was that true?

'Can you hear me now, Colin?' Doris asked.

Georgina waited, almost holding her breath; if Colin could actually hear Doris, that would make all the difference in the world.

Colin frowned. 'What?'

'No. Obviously he can't hear me now,' Doris said, answering her own question. 'But I sat in his car and I kept saying it, over and over again. I wasn't going to give up until he listened.'

'You had a hunch,' Georgina said gently. 'Maybe it was' – she paused – 'prompted.'

'I don't beli–' he began, then stopped and closed his eyes. 'Maybe it *was* prompted. I don't know. I just felt very strongly that I needed to see you. And if that was...' He frowned, as if trying to work out how to say it. 'Look, if it was... someone... trying to tell me something...' he said haltingly, 'then I'm truly grateful.'

'That's good enough for me,' Doris said. 'I'll leave you together in peace. But don't push him any harder, Georgie. He looked terrified when he saw you lying there unconscious.'

And at least Colin finally seemed to be entertaining the possibility that Doris existed, instead of flatly denying it. That was a move in the right direction.

'Thank you for rescuing me and making sure I woke up,' Georgina said. She refrained from saying that the doctor at the hospital had said she probably would've woken anyway in a few hours, because she appreciated the effort he'd made.

'This is only a flying visit,' he warned. 'I'm at work.'

'Is this to do with...?' She stopped, frowning. 'Rowena said something to me. I was meant to tell you something. And I can't remember.'

'That's probably because of the diazepam,' he said. 'She arranged for me to borrow something.'

'What did...?' She shook her head. 'Of course you're not going to tell me. It's to do with work, which means a case, which means asking you counts as interfering and you can't answer me.'

'Yes,' he confirmed, but he was smiling.

'What you're doing isn't dangerous, is it?' she checked.

'No,' he said.

'That isn't true. You just rubbed your nose,' she said.

He grinned. 'Are you calling me Pinocchio? I'm not sure if I like that any better than Fitzwilliam Darcy, to be honest with you.'

'Yes.' And she liked the fact that he was lightening up a bit.

'I'm not taking any big risks,' he said. 'But I do have to be somewhere. I just needed to see you, first.'

'Don't worry about me,' Georgina said. 'Sybbie won't let me move a muscle. And Bert, Max and Jet seem to be taking their guard dog duties very seriously.'

'Good.' He drew her hand up to his lips, dropped a kiss in her palm and folded her fingers over it. 'I'll see you tomorrow.'

On his way out, he had a quiet word with Sybbie. 'Georgie drank something at the dig. Who gave her the drink?'

'The student Trish doesn't like. Adam,' Sybbie said. 'Though that doesn't necessarily mean he was the one who put the diazepam in Georgie's coffee.'

'It makes him a suspect. Did anyone else have a cappuccino?' Georgina might not necessarily have been the target; Adam might have been careless.

'I think so, but Georgie's was the only one without a sprinkle of chocolate on the top, because Cesca knows how Georgie likes her coffee.' Sybbie frowned at him. 'I hope you're not accusing my daughter-in-law.'

'No, I'm not accusing Cesca.' Though it did clarify one thing: Georgina's coffee had been distinctive, so she hadn't been accidentally given a mug of adulterated coffee intended for someone else. 'But I will check with her, in case Adam was acting oddly in the café,' Colin said.

'Actually, there was something else strange, now I think of it. Cesca sent a sausage roll for Bert, and Bert turned his nose up at it,' Sybbie said. 'I assumed it was because he didn't like Adam, and dogs won't generally take a treat from people they dislike.'

'Considering Bert thinks everyone is his best friend,' Colin said, 'that's really suspicious.' Or had he smelled something that shouldn't have been in the food?

'Adam broke a bit off the sausage roll for him; when Bert refused it, Adam said he'd eat it himself.'

Which could have been a bluff; though Adam had had more than enough time to get rid of the evidence. Pulling the student in for questioning now could affect the surveillance tonight; it might make whoever was in touch with the nighthawks decide that the risk of digging where the Roman silver spoons had been 'found' was too great and cancel any possible meeting. 'Thank you, Sybbie. That's helpful,' Colin said.

Colin, Bernard and Trish had already gone through how the surveillance would pan out. Bernard had given permission for the cameras to be used on his land. Trish, having the Roman silver spoons on loan via Rowena, would 'find' them in one of the trenches that afternoon, and make sure all the students knew about the find. Trish, Joanna and the students would all go to the Red Lion for dinner, leaving nobody at the site; meanwhile Colin's team would put the infra-red cameras unobtrusively in place, focusing on the trenches and particularly where Trish had claimed she'd found the spoons, and then move into surveillance position to wait for the nighthawks to arrive.

Trish seemed to think that Saturday night was the more likely night for the raid, because it would give the suspects more time to contact the nighthawks after the 'find', but Colin wasn't taking any chances. He'd rather do two nights of surveillance than take a guess – even if it was an educated one – and miss the raid.

Once the cameras were in place, Colin settled down to wait. It was going to be a long, long night; and if tonight was fruitless, then he'd have to do it all over again tomorrow. And then there would be reckoning with Adam for what he'd done to Georgina.

NINETEEN

By six o'clock the following morning, Colin had to admit that Trish was right. The raid hadn't happened on Friday night. If it happened at all, it would be on Saturday night. He and his team removed the cameras and left the site, so that none of the students would be aware of the overnight surveillance, and he sent Trish a message to let her know they'd be back later that evening.

He sent Mei a message to say that nothing had happened, then headed back to his flat to get some sleep. On waking, he found a message from Mei that they'd got the warrant to search the Butterfields' house; they'd searched thoroughly, and found no sign of any of the gemstones. But then, when he walked into the office, Larissa waved a hand at him. 'I was just about to ring you, guv! I've found something in Simon Butterfield's financials.'

He went over to her desk and looked at the screen.

'It's a regular monthly payment – £25 a month, for "services", she said. 'From the bank. I rang them to ask what that would actually mean on a statement, and I had to go through about three people before one said it sounded like the price someone would pay for a medium-sized safety deposit box.'

'Good work,' he said. 'We haven't returned Simon's personal possessions to Joanna yet, have we?'

'No,' Larissa said.

'Let's see what's on his keyring. Because I'm guessing he'd want to keep a safety deposit box key with him rather than leave it hidden in a desk drawer,' Colin said.

The car key and house key on Simon's keyring were obvious; there was also a small silver-coloured key with several horizontal notches in the blade. The bow of the key was plain, apart from a five-digit number.

Colin took a quick photograph and sent it to Mei, along with a message.

> Larissa found a regular payment in Simon Butterfield's financials which we suspect is for a SDB. This was on his keyring and looks like a SDB key to me. Let me know if you need me to courier it to you.

If the gemstones were there, Simon had broken the standard terms of deposit boxes by using them to store stolen goods, but Colin knew that the bank would insist upon Mei having a warrant before they allowed her access to the box.

He checked in with Georgina, who was still staying with Sybbie.

> Am fine. S also fussing. Are you all right? x

That felt as if things between them were starting to get back to normal, and he was surprised by how relieved it made him feel.

> Am fine. Doing the same thing this evening. See you tomorrow, perhaps? x

> Might have some news about Timothy Marsden
> by then. Exhumed remains from churchyard
> with Rowena, Sybbie, Trish and Joanna this
> morning x

He wasn't sure what news Georgina would be able to give him, because it would take a while to get the DNA results. But it was one step closer to possible closure for Trish and her family. He only hoped he'd be able to get the same kind of closure on Simon Butterfield's case.

'So this might or might not be our great-great-great-great-uncle, Timothy Marsden,' Trish said, looking at the bones that had been exhumed that morning and Rowena had laid out on the table.

'I can't confirm anything until we've done the DNA testing,' Rowena said. 'But these bones look consistent with the remains of a male.' She indicated the skull. 'Georgie and Joanna, you'll see the supra-orbital ridges and the glabella – that's the brow bone and the bit between the brows – are quite pronounced.'

'The nuchal crest at the back of the skull looks more pronounced to me, too,' Trish added.

'There's a narrow pelvis, and no ventral arc,' Rowena continued. 'So it definitely suggests the remains are male. From the wear on the teeth, I'd say the man was in his late twenties when he died.' She paused. 'But there's something a bit odd, here. You said the body had been in a barn fire, Georgie?'

'According to the newspaper report, the body was found among the ruins after a barn had burned down,' Georgina said.

Rowena nodded. 'There are u-shaped fractures on the bones, which suggest the body was burned before any decomposition took place. But there's also what looks like trauma to the spine. There's no sign of the bones healing, which means the trauma would've happened around the time of death. It was caused by a high-velocity projectile – and the bevelling shows the entrance wounds here and the exit wounds there.' She pointed to the evidence.

'As if he'd been shot in the back?' Trish asked.

'As if he'd been shot in the back, probably with a pistol,' Rowena said. 'Is that what you think happened?'

'We don't have proof,' Georgina said, and filled Rowena in on what they'd pieced together from Amelia's diary, the newspaper articles and the coroner's report.

'So is your hypothesis that the body found in the barn was Timothy,' Rowena checked, 'and the fire was set deliberately to cover up a murder?'

'Yes,' Trish said. 'It all fits.'

'The evidence fits the hypothesis, too. These wounds definitely suggest this person was shot in the back, and then the body was burned,' Rowena said. 'If the DNA matches, I'd say that's your proof. Poor man. What did he do to upset Edwin Rutherford enough to kill him?'

'He fell in love with Frederick Walters' sister, Lizzie,' Sybbie said. 'Bernard's great-great-great-aunt, who'd already refused to marry Edwin but accepted Timothy's proposal.'

'Edwin told Amelia's father that Timothy was already married, so if he married Lizzie, the marriage would be bigamous and a huge scandal,' Trish explained.

'Though we haven't found a scrap of documentary evidence for any marriage,' Georgina added. 'We think Edwin made it up. A clandestine marriage and a hidden wife: it sounds too much like *Jane Eyre*.'

'Edwin wanted Lizzie, but Lizzie wanted Timothy. Jealousy's a pretty strong motive for murder. And if you're the kind of man who's not used to anyone saying no to you, especially a woman...' Rebecca spread her hands. 'Your hypothesis definitely works for me. What happened to Lizzie after Timothy disappeared?'

'She was pregnant – and she married Edwin. We think she did it so Edwin wouldn't spread gossip and the baby wouldn't be illegitimate,' Sybbie said. 'But unfortunately Lizzie had pre-eclampsia, and the condition wasn't well managed back in those days. Neither she nor the baby survived.'

'That's so sad,' Rowena said. 'And it makes you realise how lucky we are to be living now, when medical care is so much better.'

'Doesn't it just?' Georgina said.

'What happens now?' Trish asked.

'I'll take a sample of the DNA from these remains to match with the one your mum's giving in London, Trish and Joanna. If our theory's right and this is Timothy, you'll be able to lay him to rest properly, instead of in an unmarked grave – either with your family in London, or maybe here with Lizzie?'

'I think here with Lizzie would be nice, so at least they're united in death,' Joanna said. 'If that's all right with Bernard, Sybbie?'

'Oh, I rather think it will be,' Sybbie said softly.

Colin caught up with Trish later in the afternoon. 'I have a difficult question for you,' he said. 'I know you have a duty of confidentiality to your students, but there's been a case of bodily harm and I need to make sure it isn't repeated. Do any of your students take medication for anxiety, or for sleep problems?'

'Sedatives, you mean? My students are under no obligation to tell me if they're on medication,' Trish said. 'Though they might confide in their personal tutor.' She frowned. 'Sybbie said Georgie wasn't well, yesterday. Is that what happened – someone gave her sedatives?'

He chose not to answer that one. 'Do you take anti-anxiety medication?' he asked instead.

'No,' she said, and gave him a weary smile. 'When I get

anxious, I eat a ton of chocolate and listen to music – and I sing along very loudly and very badly until I feel better.'

He believed her. 'Are you the personal tutor for any of the students on the dig?'

She winced. 'Yes, but there are data protection rules.'

'And this is a murder investigation,' he reminded her. 'I'll repeat my question. Are you aware of any of your students taking medication for anxiety or sleep problems?'

She rubbed a hand across her face. 'Yes. Helena. My bright student. I told you earlier, she's gone off the boil a bit, recently. I suggested she talk to her GP – I was hoping they'd offer her some kind of talking treatment – but they put her on medication.'

'Do you know what the medication is, and the dose?' he asked.

'No.' She bit her lip. 'I'm pretty sure she'd never give her medication to anyone else, though.'

'But maybe someone else knew she was taking it. That "someone" could have stolen some of the tablets,' Colin said.

'I don't think any of my students would do that – for their own use or to knock someone else out,' Trish said.

'Unfortunately, it seems that someone did. Maybe in the normal scheme of things, they wouldn't dream about doing that, but something definitely isn't normal around here. I'll need to talk to your students tomorrow, because I don't want to jeopardise this evening's surveillance,' Colin said. 'What time are you planning to leave?'

'About four,' Trish said.

He nodded. 'In the meantime, in your shoes, I'd keep an eye on the students, in case any of them suddenly flake out. I'd advise you to be a bit careful about what you eat or drink, too. Don't leave your food or drink unwatched.'

'Surely nobody would want to hurt me?' Trish asked, frowning.

'I don't want to scare you, but someone killed Simon Butterfield,' Colin said. 'And possibly that same someone drugged Georgie. If they realise the net's closing in, they might panic and get careless, so I'd advise you to be on your guard.'

Colin was prepared for another evening of failure. The hours dragged by; once the students had all come back from the pub and settled in their tents, the site was silent. Not even a mouse or a rat seemed to be stirring. But, at half past one in the morning, his phone pinged with information that there was movement on the camera screen. The night vision of the camera was good enough that he could see four figures, three of them wearing balaclavas and one with a scarf round his face.

The nighthawks.

He felt his pulse start to race. Timing would be everything. His team needed to wait long enough to catch the nighthawks in the act of breaking the law, but at the same time they also needed to be quick enough to stop the nighthawks fleeing the scene.

When they started digging in the area where Trish had told the students she'd found the spoons, the scarf fell off. Colin recognised the young man immediately.

'Four suspects at the trench,' Colin said quietly into his radio, knowing it would go straight to his colleagues' earpieces and not disturb the four treasure-hunters. 'Obviously they're going to run. We need to focus on the ones in balaclavas, because we already have the video evidence to arrest the fourth. Go, go, go!'

As one, they opened the doors of the vehicles, and ran across the site.

'Stop! Police! You're under arrest!' Colin yelled.

As he expected, the nighthawks ran. But his team were prepared for it and gave chase. Colin rugby-tackled one of the four himself, and although the man wriggled and kicked, and landed a blow to Colin's face that felt as if it would bruise badly, Colin was able to bring the suspect's arms behind his back before handcuffing him.

Twenty minutes later, it was all over, with the four suspects arrested and handcuffed and a police van on the way. Colin made sure he read all four of them their rights.

Trish, who was fully dressed and Colin suspected she'd stayed awake to see for herself if the bait she'd dangled had worked, came over from her tent to see what was happening. Her jaw dropped as she recognised the student. 'Oh, my God. *You.*'

'Don't say any more,' Colin warned her. 'He's under arrest and we're taking him to the station. I'd rather you went back to the camp and asked the rest of your students and your sister to stay exactly where they are, please. We'll talk to them later.'

Back at the station, the custody sergeant processed the four suspects. The three nighthawks opted to have their own solicitors; Adam, looking suddenly a lot younger and having lost his devil-may-care attitude, asked for the duty solicitor.

'Guv, you can't ask him about spiking Georgina's drink,' Larissa reminded him. 'She's your girlfriend.'

Colin wasn't completely sure that Georgina was still his girlfriend, given that they hadn't finished sorting out the issues dividing them; but he didn't want anyone in the station speculating about the situation, even though he liked and respected Larissa and Mo. 'I guess,' he said.

'Mo and I will do that bit,' she said. 'I know we've been here before and you hate not being in charge, but you really can't interview someone about whether or not they drugged your girlfriend.'

'Yeah. I know. You're right,' he said. And he was glad his team had his back.

Once the duty solicitor had come to the station, been

briefed and spoken to Adam, Colin was able to go through all the legal necessities for the tape – introducing himself and Larissa, making sure everyone's phone was switched off, stating Adam's name and that of the duty solicitor, then re-cautioning Adam that he was there for questioning under suspicion of heritage crimes and his involvement in the death of Simon Butterfield. He checked that Adam understood the nature of the charges, and that anything he said could be used in evidence – and anything he didn't say which he later relied on in court might harm his defence – and then began the interview.

'We have video evidence which shows your face, when you and three people wearing balaclavas were digging in a trench on land belonging to Bernard Walters which contains the remains of a Roman villa,' Colin said. 'Which you were excavating under the supervision of your tutors, Simon Butterfield and Trish Melton. You showed the three other detectorists where to dig.'

Adam obviously realised he couldn't get away with trying to charm his way out of this, and this time he didn't flash an insincere smile at anyone. He just hunched his shoulders very slightly and kept quiet.

'Tell me in your own words how you came to be acquainted with the three people I arrested with you this morning,' Colin invited.

Adam shook his head. 'I'm not. I never met them before this week. They're part of a network.'

'How did you contact them?'

'I have a phone. I only use it to contact the network if I'm at a dig where we find something. I give them the coordinates and tell them what we've found.'

'When did you get in touch with the network initially?' Colin asked.

'Halfway through my first year.'

'Why? What led you to getting in touch with them?' Colin asked.

Adam grimaced. 'I got a bit behind on my rent and my parents wouldn't help me out.'

Colin tried not to think how entitled Adam sounded. If he'd spent his rent money elsewhere, why on earth did he expect his parents to pick up the shortfall? 'So what did you do about it?'

'I didn't have any other choice, did I? I had to borrow some cash to pay the arrears.' He looked sulky about it. 'Someone in the pub introduced me to someone they knew who could lend me the money I needed. I thought I'd be able to get a job in the summer holidays and pay it back – except I didn't earn enough, and the debt kept growing faster than I thought it would.' Then he dropped his aggrieved stance and looked slightly scared, as if remembering how much he'd underestimated his lenders. 'They called me in for what they said was "a little chat". It was...' He shuddered. 'I thought they were going to beat me up and break my arms or something, but I was just told that they'd clear the debt if I helped their friends. They knew I was an archaeology student and I went on digs. They gave me a phone. All I had to do was text them the coordinates of our dig if we found something.'

'What if you'd found something and didn't tell them?' Colin asked.

Adam shook his head. 'It was made very clear to me that wasn't an option.'

'Why didn't you tell anyone?'

Adam scoffed. 'Because I would've been kicked off the course if anyone knew what I was doing.'

'So nobody at the university knew?'

Adam winced. 'Simon did. The nighthawks went to every dig I was on. And he'd worked out I was the one telling them. He confronted me.'

Simon Butterfield – who'd insisted that his wife should steal gemstones for him, from the museum where she worked. How would he have reacted when he realised that his undergraduate was involved with the nighthawks and helping them steal treasure? 'What did he say?'

'He told me that if I didn't cut him in on the deal, he'd report me to the university – and to the police.'

That explained why Simon had wanted Adam to be on every dig, even though Trish didn't feel the student pulled his weight properly, Colin thought. And perhaps Adam would've been the fall guy if Simon had ever been caught. 'What happened then?'

'He made me give him my phone. And he texted them. I have no idea what he said – he deleted everything – but they texted me and said I should take my instructions from him.'

And clearly Adam had resented it; it showed very clearly on his face. Had it been enough to make him want to kill Simon? Or were the nighthawks the ones behind the murder? 'What happened on the night Simon died?' Colin asked, keeping his tone neutral so the solicitor wouldn't jump in and stop Adam talking.

'We had an argument. He was going to try cutting the nighthawks out.' Adam's eyes widened, and Colin could see the fear flooding through the younger man. 'I knew if that happened, they'd come after me, because I still hadn't finished paying back the loan – it was just the interest that had stopped. He laughed and said it was hard luck for me. He *laughed*.' Adam looked shocked that someone would be so callous – clearly not recognising his own capacity for that very same characteristic. 'And I just snapped. I've spent a year and a half trying to pay everything back, and he didn't care. Everything was like... I dunno, a red mist. I was so angry, I couldn't think straight. Obviously I must've hit him with the shovel I was carrying – and then he was lying on the floor. I rolled him onto his back, and he wasn't breathing. And blood was pooling round his head. There was no way he was still alive. And I... I didn't know what to do.' He dragged in a breath. 'And then it occurred to me, if I didn't say anything, I could get the nighthawks to back off. I could threaten to tell the police they killed Simon when he disturbed them trying to dig up stuff from the drain under the mosaic floor.'

'Yet they were here tonight,' Colin pointed out.

Adam nodded. 'I was going to tell them tonight that this was the last time I'd do this – I'd tell the police everything I knew if they didn't cancel my debt and back off. When Trish found those silver spoons, I knew they'd want to know where she found them – there might even be something like the Milden-hall hoard, with a huge silver platter or something, or at the very least some silver bowls. I took a photograph of the spoons and sent it to them. They said we'd dig here tonight – it's the day before we have to cover everything up, so it was a good time to do it. Everyone would've had a few beers to celebrate the end of the dig and wouldn't hear them.'

'There were three of them against one of you,' Colin said. 'You're young – but they're far from being old and decrepit. Didn't you worry that they would hurt you when you said you wouldn't help them anymore?'

'I had insurance. I posted myself a letter yesterday morning telling everything,' he said. 'I sent it to my parents' house. I know my mum wouldn't open a letter addressed to me – not unless something happened to me. It's got names and dates, all the details.'

'And you were going to tell them that?' Colin asked. 'What if they'd decided to retrieve the letter from your parents and hurt your parents?'

Adam's jaw went slack as the implications sank in. 'I... I didn't think of that,' he whispered. 'I just wanted it all to stop. I was way out of my depth.'

He still was, Colin thought. And even though Adam's

earlier arrogance had annoyed him, as a parent to a teen part of him felt sorry for the boy. It was harder to find your way in the world than it had been when Colin was Adam's age. And it was all too easy to make a mistake, follow with another, and end up in a mess where you had no idea where to even start trying to fix things. 'Anything you can tell us about the nighthawks will help your case,' he said, his voice slightly gentler. 'And the loan sharks. But you'll still be facing a murder charge.'

Adam covered his face with his hands. 'Oh, God. My life's over.'

'No. But Simon's is,' Colin said quietly. 'Because of you.' Adam wasn't really taking responsibility for his own actions or showing real remorse about what he'd done. The word 'sorry' hadn't even passed his lips. He'd taken a life, for pity's sake. And then he'd seen it as a chance to get himself off the hook for the debt he'd got himself into. Would he carry on blaming others for his choices? Wanting to make the boy think a bit more about his actions now and maybe do things differently in future, he said, 'If you'd called for help after you'd hit him, there might have been a chance of saving him.'

'No.' Adam shook his head vehemently. 'He was *dead*. There was blood coming out of his ears. I've seen that sort of thing on the telly – my girlfriend likes watching those programmes about the emergency department in hospitals. When there's blood coming out of their ears, they always die.'

Clueless as well as callous, Colin thought. He summarised what Adam had told him. 'Is there anything I need to correct, or anything else you want to say?'

'No.'

'We'll keep you here in custody until later in the morning,' Colin said, 'and then speak to the Crown Prosecution Service to see how they want to proceed. In the meantime, you need to speak to my colleagues about another matter.'

Adam frowned. 'Another matter?'

'I can't investigate,' Colin said, 'because it concerns someone close to me.' And he wasn't going to wait and watch on a screen, feeling helpless; he'd rather throw himself into the next lot of interviews and keep himself too busy to think about what *might* have happened to Georgina. 'But I'd strongly advise you to be honest. Forensics nowadays is very, very good.'

He borrowed one of the uniformed team to come and do the other interviews with him. The three nighthawks answered everything with, 'No comment.'

'It's your prerogative,' Colin said. 'But I'm sure your solicitor will advise you that you could be harming your defence. The courts often draw an adverse inference from refusal to answer questions. You'll need to give them an extremely good reason for not answering my questions now.'

Frustratingly, he didn't get through to any of them.

But Larissa and Mo reported back to salve one of his worries.

'Adam admitted drugging Georgie,' Mo said. 'He knew Helena was on diazepam. He took some of her tablets and dropped a couple in Georgina's coffee after he left the farm shop café. He'd put one in the sausage roll, too, but Bert refused to eat it.'

'Maybe he could smell the sedative,' Colin said. 'Did Adam give a reason why he picked on Georgie?'

'She was asking too many questions and getting too many people to talk to her. He was worried she'd find out his role in Simon's death, and about the nighthawks,' Larissa said. 'He didn't intend to kill her – just warn her off.'

'If she'd fallen asleep while she was driving, it could've been a very different story,' Colin said. The possibilities made his guts twist.

'Luckily for us all, she's fine,' Larissa said, patting his shoulder. 'And you need to get some sleep. We all do.'

'Yeah,' he admitted.

TWENTY

THREE WEEKS LATER

Colin stared at the kitchen door on his way to collect Georgina for Timothy Marsden's burial. Only a few weeks ago, he would have walked straight into the house without knocking, because he spent more nights at Rookery Farm than he did at his flat. But, since his fight with Georgina over Doris, things had been strained between them and he'd gone back to his own flat every night. Although things were better now than they had been the night of the row, he still felt too awkward to pretend everything was completely back to normal. Because it wasn't.

He knocked.

A few moments later, Georgina opened the door, Bert at her heels; dressed formally in black trousers and a black silky top, she looked gorgeous. The spaniel wagged his tail in welcome.

'Come in,' she said. 'We've got time for a cup of tea before the service.'

'Thank you,' he said, knowing that he sounded buttoned-up and stuffy, and not knowing how to fix this.

She gestured to the kitchen table. 'Take a seat.'

She busied herself making tea, and Colin tried and failed to start a conversation at least three times.

Eventually, he said, 'Obviously the DNA results show there's a familial match between the body from the churchyard and Trish's mum, or we wouldn't be going to the Manor for the reburial. But did you ever find out what actually happened to Timothy Marsden?'

'Remember I told you – in this very room – that he was shot in the back?' Georgina said. 'Except at the time I didn't have the physical evidence.'

Colin felt a muscle twitch in his jaw. That conversation had come very close to fracturing his relationship with Georgina beyond repair. According to Doris, Timothy remembered a terrific pain in his back, and then there was nothing. Timothy's ghost had told Doris, who in turn had told Georgina, who in turn had told Colin – who'd found the whole thing way too far-fetched and handled it badly.

'And now?' he asked, as neutrally as he could.

'Now we have physical evidence. The body. As you say, DNA shows it's Timothy. Rowena says the skeleton bears the marks of high-velocity impact,' Georgina informed him. 'From a pistol, she thinks. The entry wound was at the back, and the exit wounds at the front.'

'You said Edwin had kidnapped him. It sounds as if Timothy managed somehow to escape from Edwin's carriage, but Edwin had a pistol on him, was a good marksman and shot him in the back,' Colin said.

'Then his corpse was hidden under the hay in a barn belonging to one of the tenant farmers, and the barn was set on fire. When the body was found, his clothes would've been burned away, and the burned flesh would also have destroyed the evidence of the gunshot wound,' Georgina said. 'The coroner said the "vagrant" had a pipe in his pocket and had fallen asleep, drunk – which explains how the fire started – and the smoke from the fire overcame the drunk man so he didn't wake up.'

'Either the coroner was a friend of the Rutherfords and went along with their story,' Colin said, 'or he wanted an easy life and didn't do a thorough investigation. Even back then, and even with the burns, there should've been a post-mortem. There would've been evidence of gunshot wounds in the organs or the skeleton itself, and if he was dead before the fire started, there would've been no signs of smoke inhalation in the lungs. The coroner should've had a proper post-mortem done.'

'The Rutherfords paid for the body to be buried in the churchyard. Which you could see as benevolence on the part of the Lord of the Manor, so the parish didn't have to pay for it; or you could see it as guilt on the part of his son, who knew what had really happened,' Georgina said. 'I know you're going to say the evidence is all circumstantial, and he's never going to face justice anyway, but I think Edwin murdered Timothy out of spite and jealousy – Amelia's diary is very clear that Lizzie refused several proposals from Edwin, and she fell in love with Timothy.' She sighed. 'Though at least we can disprove the story that Edwin spread about Timothy being already married. His alleged "proof" from a private detective was completely fabricated. Why didn't Lizzie's family check?'

'Because it would've been much harder to check, in those days,' Colin said. 'There wouldn't have been centralised records. Plus, even if they'd proved it wasn't true, gossip would still have spread and there would've been repercussions.' He spread his hands. 'The Walters family is still here. The Rutherfords died out and are forgotten. It's a kind of justice.'

'I suppose,' she agreed. 'And we can reunite Timothy and Lizzie in the grave.'

'I'm glad Bernard agreed he could be buried with Lizzie,' Colin said.

'Bernard's a good man.' Georgina brought the tea over. 'I know, strictly speaking, I can't ask about your cases.'

How he missed talking to her about things. He missed her clear sight. 'I'll tell you anyway – with the usual caveat.'

'Obviously it goes no further than me,' she said. 'And I know some things anyway, through Trish.'

'Adam's awaiting trial for the murder of Simon Butterfield. He's also admitted to drugging you, because you were asking questions and he was afraid you'd work out what he was doing.' He paused. 'Apparently there was also diazepam in the sausage roll he offered Bert.'

'I can forgive him for what he did to me,' Georgina said, 'but *not* for intending to hurt Bert.'

Colin couldn't forgive him on either count. 'It's all a bit murky. The police in London are looking into the moneylender, and the nighthawks will also be facing trial for a number of heritage crimes they're linked to – Adam's told us about the ones he knows about, but it's possible they're linked to more. Mei's team is investigating Simon, too. Thankfully he hadn't sold any of the intaglios or jewellery he'd stolen from the museum or coerced Joanna into stealing for him; he'd kept them all in a safe deposit box at the bank, and it seems he just used to go and look at them from time to time. The things he'd looted from digs and blamed on the nighthawks were there as well.'

'What's going to happen to Joanna?' Georgina asked.

'She'll face charges of theft, unless the museum decides not to press charges,' Colin said. 'There are some mitigating factors – but also some aggravating ones, because the thefts took place over a couple of years and they added up.'

'I still don't understand why Simon stole things. He wasn't poor,' Georgina said. 'He could've afforded to build his own collection.'

'Maybe it was greed; maybe it was arrogance. Or maybe it was the challenge of being able to take things without leaving any traces,' Colin said. 'We can't exactly ask him.'

'I guess not,' Georgina said.

Finally, leaving Bert to look after the house, Colin drove Georgina to Little Wenborough Manor. Sybbie, Bernard, Francesca and Giles were all already there, with Trish, Joanna, their mum, Trish's partner and Trish's daughter. The vicar from Great Wenborough also looked after the parish of Little Wenborough, and came to read the service in the tiny chapel in the Manor's grounds.

Sybbie had arranged for them each to have a rose to place in the grave when Timothy's remains were interred with Lizzie, and Bernard read Elizabeth Barrett Browning's Sonnet 43, ending with, '*And, if God choose, /I shall but love thee better after death.*'

Francesca had prepared a buffet; afterwards, Trish and her family left for London, and Georgina and Sybbie made Francesca sit down in the kitchen while they cleared up.

'I need to tell you,' Francesca said quietly. 'I saw Lizzie again this morning, while I was setting up the buffet. She told me I'm definitely having a little girl, and she also asked me to thank you both – and Bea and Doris, too – for helping Tim. She's glad his name is cleared and you've found the truth of what happened to him. He's with her properly now.'

'That's good to know,' Georgina said. Not that she could ever discuss it with Colin. He'd steadfastly avoided the subject of Doris. 'I'll tell Bea when I see her.'

'Talking of Bea, it's the opening night of *Much Ado* in a couple of weeks, isn't it?' Sybbie asked. 'I'm looking forward to us all being there to give her a standing ovation. She'll be wonderful.'

'She will indeed,' Georgina agreed.

Colin came into the kitchen. 'I need to head back to the station,' he said. 'Can I give you a lift back to the farmhouse, Georgie?'

She almost said not to worry, because she could do with a walk; but there was something in his manner that gave her the feeling he wanted to talk to her. 'All right,' she said.

On their way back to Rookery Farm, she gave him space until he was ready to bring up whatever he wanted to talk about. It wasn't until he'd parked his car next to hers that he spoke.

'I've been thinking,' he said.

'Oh?'

'Well – I talked to Bernard,' he admitted. 'Who told me that Sybbie had taught him there was much more to life than met the eye. And that the women in his family... Well, there's that story about the Grey Lady.'

'Who turned out to be Lizzie, as in the woman Timothy Marsden wanted to marry,' Georgina couldn't help saying.

Colin sighed. 'I find it very, very hard to get my head around this ghost stuff. A copper's hunch sounds as if it's instinct without reasoning, but it's not – it comes with experience, and it's really that your subconscious recognises the patterns.'

'So every time in the future that I don't answer my phone, because it's happened twice so far, you're immediately going to assume I've been poisoned or drugged?' Georgina asked.

He winced. 'No.'

She shook her head. 'I don't want to fight with you. But I hate that you won't believe me. When we hadn't even found his remains, how could I possibly have known that Timothy had been shot in the back? And yet, when Rowena looked at the bones, she could see what had happened.'

'That's true,' he admitted. 'But you've solved other cold cases by looking at the evidence and interpreting it correctly.'

'By finding the evidence to prove what I already knew from Doris,' she said. 'Bea and Will believe me. Sybbie and Cesca believe me. Why can't you?'

'What about Jodie?'

'I haven't discussed it with her,' Georgina admitted. 'But I think she'll believe me, because she trusts me.'

'*I* trust you,' Colin said. His clear grey eyes were sincere as he looked at her. 'I'd trust you with my life.'

'But this is always going to come between us,' she said, realising with a stab of misery that there would never be a way they could resolve the issue.

'It doesn't have to. I don't want to be without you,' Colin said. 'You're important to me. I know I'm your typical middle-aged man, rubbish at emotional stuff and preferring to do practical things to show how I feel, but I love you, Georgie. I hate the distance that's opened up between us, and I want to fix it.'

'I hate the distance between us, too, and I want to fix it,' she said. 'But how can we compromise? I know Doris exists – and you can't believe me. And don't,' she added, 'say that you believe I believe she exists. That's a cop-out.'

The corner of his mouth quirked. 'Did you hear what you just said?'

She groaned. 'That wasn't an intentional pun.'

'I believe in your sincerity – and that isn't me trying to squirm out of anything. I trust your judgement,' he said. 'But I've never experienced anything remotely supernatural. I've only seen the fallout from people who've been conned by so-called mediums, and I hate that unscrupulous people prey on the emotions of vulnerable people who've lost someone they loved.'

'I'm not claiming to be a medium, and neither is Doris. What about your feeling that something was wrong here, when you had no proof?' she asked.

Colin wrinkled his nose. 'I'd say that was my subconscious.'

'Doris was sitting in your car, yelling at you that something was wrong and you needed to find me,' Georgina said. 'I can't give you any proof of that, but it's true.'

'I think,' Colin said, 'we're going to have to agree to disagree.

And I know it's a huge issue. I don't think you're a liar and I don't think you're crazy. But it's like... I don't know. The only way I can describe it is like those pictures where a left-brained person sees one thing and a right-brained person sees something completely different.'

'So what now? We sweep it under the carpet and pretend nothing ever happened?'

'No. We respect that this is one area where we see things very differently,' Colin said. 'You're right. We can't compromise. But we don't have to do the scorched earth thing, either. We can...' He paused, as if searching for the right phrase. 'Co-exist. That's the best I can offer. I understand that you believe in ghosts – and, even though I don't believe in them, I'm not going to mock you, or criticise you, or belittle you. Just as I know you'll treat me the same way.'

'That,' Georgina said, 'sounds like a workable compromise. All right.'

'Good.' He kissed her lightly. 'And now I really do have to go to the station.'

'See you tonight?' she asked. 'I'll cook.'

'I'll bring pudding. And a sausage for Bert.'

'It's a deal.' And Georgina was smiling as she climbed out of the car.

A LETTER FROM THE AUTHOR

Huge thanks for reading *The Body at the Roman Baths*; I hope you enjoyed Georgina, Doris and Colin's journey. If you want to join other readers in hearing all about my new releases and bonus content, you can sign up for my newsletter!

www.stormpublishing.co/kate-hardy

If you enjoyed this book and could spare a few moments to leave a review, that would be hugely appreciated. Even a short review can make all the difference in encouraging a reader to discover my books for the first time. Thank you so much!

This series was hugely influenced by three things. Firstly, I grew up in a haunted house in a small market town in Norfolk, so I've always been drawn to slightly spooky stories. (I did research it when I wrote a book on researching house history, but I couldn't find any documentary evidence for the tale of the jealous miller who murdered his wife. However, I also don't have explanations for various spooky things that happened at the house – including the anecdote about Sybbie's dogs in *The Body at Rookery Barn*, which happened in real life with our Labradors and a tennis ball.) Secondly, I read Daphne du Maurier's short story 'The Blue Lenses' while I was a student, and... I can't explain this properly without giving spoilers, so I'll say it's to do with how you see people. Thirdly, I'm deaf; after I had my first hearing aid fitted, once I'd got over the thrill of hearing birdsong for the first time in years, my author brain started ticking. The du Maurier story gave me a 'what if' moment: what if you heard something through your hearing aids that wasn't what you were supposed to hear? (The obvious one would be someone's thoughts; but that's where my childhood home came in.) It took a few years for the idea to come to the top of my head and refuse to go away, but what if you could hear what my heroine Georgina ends up hearing?

And so Georgina Drake ends up living in a haunted house in a small market town in Norfolk...

The Body at the Roman Baths comes from one of my early passions – when I was about six, I went to the British Museum for the first time (to see the Tutankhamun exhibition) and we looked round the Roman Britain section as well. From then on until my teens, I desperately wanted to be an archaeologist and I loved helping my dad dig the garden because I'd always find odd little bits of pottery and china. (Sadly they were never Roman, but it didn't stop me trying!)

My Roman baths in Little Wenborough are fictional, but there is some real-life inspiration behind them. One of the three Roman towns in England that was never built over – Venta Icenorum, at Caistor St Edmund – is about ten miles from my house, and I've been privileged to have a tour of the annual dig there. There is a mosaic floor with the remains of a bath house at Gayton Thorpe in Norfolk, but they're not open to the public. There's also the bath house complex at Letocetum (Wall, Watling Street – or, as my husband puts it, 'Is this another one of your piles of stones in a field?' – um, sort of, but imagine what it was like...). And of course the one at the Jewry Wall in Leicester (where I went to university); the peacock owes a lot to Leicester and also to the mosaic under the Duomo in Florence. The Crownthorpe and Mildenhall hoards mentioned in the book are both real and part of them can be seen at Norwich Castle Museum and the British Museum respectively.

There are some other real-life snippets in here. The Victorian lemonade recipe is from Mrs Beeton; the quote about Pepper's Ghost is from a real newspaper, about an event in Norwich at the Assembly House (which is one of my favourite places in Norwich – and Pepper's Ghost had a lot to do with the set-up of *The Body Under the Stage*). The inquest report is all my imagination, but the newspaper and the coroner are both real.

Little Wenborough isn't a real place, but the name is a mashup of the town where I grew up and the river where I walk my dogs in the morning. Norfolk is an amazing place to live. Huge skies (incredible sunrises and sunsets), wide beaches (aka my best place to think, and the Editpawial Assistants are always up for a trip there), and more ancient churches than anywhere else in the country (watch this space!).

Thanks again for being part of this amazing journey with me and I hope you'll stay in touch – I have so many more stories and ideas to entertain you with!

All best,
Kate Hardy

facebook.com/katehardyromanceauthor

x.com/katehardyauthor

instagram.com/katehardyauthor

ACKNOWLEDGEMENTS

I'd like to thank Oliver Rhodes and Kathryn Taussig for taking a chance on my slightly unusual take on a crime series; Emily Gowers for being an absolute dream of an editor – incisive, thoughtful and a wonderful collaborator as well as being great fun; and Shirley Khan and Maddy Newquist for picking up the bits I missed! I've loved every second of working on this book with you.

Gerard, Chris and Chloë have been particular stars with location research (aka beach walks, 'stones in fields', and a very treasured trip to Pompeii a few years ago).

Special thanks to my family and friends who cheer-led the first Georgina Drake book, made useful suggestions about Roman archaeology/cake/ghosts, and are there through the highs and lows of publishing: in particular Nicki Brooks, Jackie Chubb, Siobhàn Coward, Sheila Crighton, Liz Fielding, Philippa Gell, Rosie Hendry, Rachel Hore, Jenni Keer, Lizzie Lamb, Clare Marchant, Jo Rendell-Dodd, Fiona Robertson, Michelle Styles, Heidi-Jo Swain, Katy Watson, Ian Wilfred, Susan Wilson, Jan Wooller and Caroline Woolnough. (And apologies if I've missed anyone!)

Extra-special thanks to Gerard, Chris and Chloë Brooks, who've always been my greatest supporters; to Chrissy and Rich Camp, for always believing in me and being the best uncle and aunt ever; and to Archie and Dexter, my beloved Editpawial Assistants, for keeping my feet warm, reminding me when it's time for walkies and lunch, and putting up with me photographing them to keep my social media ticking over while I'm on deadline.

And, last but very much not least, thank you, dear reader, for choosing my book. I hope you enjoy reading it as much as I enjoyed writing it.

Printed in Great Britain
by Amazon

61779366R10139